# PRIZZI'S
# FAMILY

*Also by Richard Condon
in Thorndike Large Print:*

**PRIZZI'S HONOR**

# PRIZZI'S FAMILY

## RICHARD CONDON

Thorndike Press • Thorndike, Maine

**Library of Congress Cataloging in Publication Data:**

Condon, Richard.
  Prizzi's family.

  "Thorndike large print."
  1. Large type books. I. Title.
[PS3553.0487P68 1987]    813'.54     86-23168
ISBN 0-89621-768-X (lg. print : alk. paper)

This is a work of fiction. The events described are imaginary,
the characters fictitious.

Large Print edition available in North America by arrangement
with G. P. Putnam's Sons, New York.

Large Print edition available in the British Commonwealth by
arrangement with Abner Stein, London.

Cover design by Ralph Lizotte.

*For my darling
Evelyn*

"Life is so difficult God gave everybody a family to make sure that he had somebody who would always help him."

CORRADO PRIZZI
*1897-*

# 1

The St. Joseph's Laundry, business headquarters for the Prizzi family, was a large, low,
triangular building that occupied a pie-cut
block in central Flatbush. In October 1969 Vincent Prizzi had been Boss of the family for five
months, since the day his father retired; for his
father, this had meant transferring the title to
Vincent and not going into the Laundry anymore. It didn't change anything else. Vincent
was Boss, but Don Corrado was his boss.

Vincent was a serious man with a face like a
clenched fist and an attitude of barely controlled violence, as if one of Señor Wences'
hand puppets had developed antisocial tenden-
cies. He had gout, high blood pressure, ulcers,
and psoriasis because he was a resenter. He had
been his father's *sottocapo* and *vindicatore* for
twenty-four years; now he was the Boss. He
resented that. Vincent conspired with his own
ignorance. He was a perpetually baffled man
who chewed on pieces of himself and then

spat them out at the world.

Vincent had a two-window office with a big desk, clear of everything except two telephones and a neat bronze sign facing outward that said, THANK YOU FOR NOT SMOKING. A large table against the left wall held a collection of nine-inch-high religious statues surrounding a picture of the Sacred Heart of Jesus framed in bronze. His own saint, the saint with whom he shared a birthday, was St. Nympha, the virgin of Palermo, who underwent martyrdom in Sicily and whose relics are united with those of St. Respicius and St. Tryphon in Rome; their statues were assembled with those of St. Anthony and St. Gennaro on the tabletop. On the wall facing Vincent's desk there was a framed IBM slogan in Italian saying CREDERE in large black letters on silver appliquéd on an orange background. Three chairs, a blond leather sofa, and a blond carpet completed the decor.

He took a blood pressure pill, a diuretic, a gout pill, and the 325 grams of aspirin to cut down on the blood clots, then he waited for some kind of change in the way he was feeling. Nothing happened.

He yelled at the open door. "Get Charley Partanna in here." Each word came out sounding like a stroke of a crosscut saw. He had been practicing the way he spoke for forty-five years.

10

It was the diction of all the young men in the environment when he was coming up, cultivated so that anyone would know instantly that they were hard guys.

Charley Partanna's office was two doors down the hall. It was the same size as Vincent's without the decoration: no signs, no carpet, no statues, no sofa. Charley was Vincent's underboss and enforcer. He was thirty years old. He had a quality of tentative detachment, as if he were not a part of whatever had been going on. When Charley was thirteen, Corrado Prizzi said he would grow up to be a contractor because nobody noticed when he was there; he could make a hit in Macy's window and no one would know he had done it.

Charley Partanna was a heavy-boned, lithe man with a face like a carousel horse: expressionless; long and narrow; with large chrome eyes pasted on either side of his nose. His eyebrows were like awnings. His voice worked at making sounds like a heavy steel sledge being pulled over ashes. He contracted his thoughts slowly but with earnest precision. He sat behind a desk whose drawers were empty except for the one that held a Swiss Army knife with small scissors that Charley used to cut his fingernails. He was a tidy man.

Seated in three chairs around the desk were

the three *capiregime* of the Prizzi family, each in command of a cohort of about six hundred men; specialists or muscle; active or in reserve.

Tarquin "Little Abe" Garrone, the labor *capo*, was talking about new developments in the mayor's office. Garrone got his nickname thirty years ago from the chin whiskers he wore when he was first trying not to shave every day. He was short and meaty, like double. He spoke as if he had taught diction to Louis Armetta. He ran the construction unions in the city and just now he wanted to pull the plumbers, plasterers, and electrical workers from the Garden Grove development, a gigantic luxury condo going up on the site of a lot of low-cost housing that had been razed and from which the mayor's people had taken a bundle without sharing.

"The little fuck is walkin' wit' like a million nine, fahcrissake," Little Abe said.

The two other *capi*, Rocco Sestero and Sal Prizzi, the latter Vincent's son by his first mar-riage — Vincent was now a widower for the second time — both started to talk at the same time, outraged by the amount the mayor was stealing without sharing when the Plumber burst into the room, interrupting everybody. "The Boss wants you, Charley," he said.

"Tell him ten minutes."

"Not me. His gout is killing him."

Charley turned slowly in his chair to look at the Plumber. He hosed such fear all over him that the Plumber flinched. Rocco Sestero, the Plumber's *capo*, felt sorry for him.

"Keep your hat off when you're in the building," Charley said. The Plumber backed out of the doorway, closing the door carefully.

When he finished the meeting, Charley went to Vincent's office.

"You took your own fuckin' time," Vincent said.

"Elections are like six weeks away. They gotta be organized."

"So how does it look?"

"The mayor is a shoo-in."

"What about Mallon?"

"Not a chance."

"Good. Lissena me, Charley. Gennaro Fustino and Farts Esposito come into town yesterday. They wanna go to the Latino tonight. I work all day here and they expect me to stay up all night like some fuckin' Good Time Charley. My gout is killin' me. So you take them, okay? They're at the Palace."

"What about school?"

The reference to Charley's night school made Vincent's ulcers grind against each other, but Don Corrado was proud of Charley deciding to get a high school diploma after dropping

13

out of school at fifteen, so Vincent couldn't do anything about it.

"The Latino is a *night*club, fahcrissake. It starts after. Anyway, the other people never miss a night at your school?"

"That's okay, Vincent. I'll handle it. Just so I don't miss school."

# 2

The Casino Latino was a big nightclub in New York owned by the Prizzis. It was in the straightest part of the East Sixties near Central Park, a neighborhood so unlike Brooklyn that Charley could only recognize the building at night.

Although it made a solid profit, the place existed primarily for the entertainment of out-of-town people who had come to New York to close various arrangements with the Prizzis. There was a bar and cocktail lounge on the ground floor. The nightclub was in the basement of the building. In the flowered centerpieces on each table were tiny microphones that could be switched on selectively to feed to the master tape machines in the subbasement.

The Latino featured the top cabaret talent in the country, the biggest names, performers who had gotten themselves so deep into hock by gambling when they were playing Prizzi hotels and clubs in Vegas, Atlantic City, Kentucky, and Miami that they had to appear wherever the Prizzis sent them to work off what they owed. For three or four of them it had become their life's work.

The Casino Latino also had a great line of chorines and an absolutely sensational-looking sextet of showgirls. Angelo Partanna said, forget the headline acts and the movie stars in from L.A. for a couple of days to dress up the ringside; the place was all gorgeous flesh, the original draw.

There was no pressure on the girls to deliver for Prizzi customers. That would have been against family policy, and the girls knew it. From time to time, if people were important enough, Smadja, the headwaiter, would invite one or two of the girls to sit at a table with people between shows, but only the chorines; the showgirls were reserved for people who were being entertained by Prizzi executives. Even to get the chorines to a table took a lot of clout but, if the customers were heavy enough to be able to tell Smadja to bring out some girls, they had plenty of clout in the first place.

The girls knew — they were sure, there was no problem about it — that they didn't have to leave the joint with a customer, no matter who it was, even if they were at a table with Vincent Prizzi's party. But, on the other hand, if they were at a table with Vincent Prizzi, they usually thought it over and delivered.

Gennaro Fustino was the Boss of the New Orleans outfit. He was married to Don Corrado's baby sister, Birdie, and ran a territory from Louisiana, across Texas and Oklahoma, then westward across the southern rim of the country to the California border. His fleet of small planes out of Mexico delivered smack and watches into three dozen small American airports and dried-up lake basins. He was in partnership with the Prizzis in the international counterfeit watch operation and in *sbuffo* and boo, and was beginning to organize his part of the country on Corrado Prizzi's latest innovation: the recycled postage stamp franchise by which the cancellation marks were removed by a chemical the Prizzis provided from New York and the stamps could be resold at a forty-five percent discount of their face value. The two families collaborated on importing racehorses from England and Ireland for Gennaro's tracks in Louisiana and Arkansas.

Gennaro Fustino had industrialized the counterfeit watch dodge. The Prizzis had the watch movements made in Hong Kong and the cases and faces done in Italy, where they were assembled. They faked every great Swiss watch in the business and Gennaro merchandised them for between ten and thirty percent of what the real watches would cost, and still rolled up a $17,000,000-a-year business. "It proves the public are thieves in their heart," he said to Angelo Partanna after the first year with the watches.

"So what else is new?" Angelo said.

Natale "Farts" Esposito was Gennaro's *caporegime*. Natale had the ability to fart at any time: loud, medium, or soft. This talent made him a popular entertainer at Fustino parties. He and Gennaro were so close, Angelo Partanna said, that when Gennaro ate too much — which he always did even when he was on one of his diets — that it gave Natale Esposito gas.

Tonight Charley, Gennaro, and Natale met for dinner at the Latino. Gennaro decided he wanted to eat Chinese so the club had to send out to a Prizzi-owned Cantonese joint at 127th Street off Broadway. When the food arrived, it was reheated expertly and served elegantly. While they were waiting, Gennaro ate a baked Alaska.

After dinner Charley gave Smadja the nod and three showgirls were brought to the table. They were dressed in evening gowns, not show costumes, so as not to attract attention. Moving across the room to the table, they could not have called more attention if they had been dressed in suits of armor. They were gigantic up close, not like Arnold Schwarzenegger in drag, but instead very beautiful, very feminine, with an odd kind of grateful quality.

Two of the girls, both brunettes, simply were spectacularly beautiful. The one Smadja seated next to Charley was indescribably lovely. She was new at the Latino; a very beautiful head with a body that could have come out of an expensive mail-order catalog, Charley thought, if it had been ordinary merchandise like a statue or something. Her large, golden eyes had a sheen of willfulness in them. But it was willfulness on the playful side, Charley thought the minute he looked at her, but the realization was gone immediately. He didn't have time to analyze what he had seen but he had the distinct feeling for one quick flash that she was definitely some kind of a joker.

Charley was courtly but distant as the representative of the Prizzi family, even while he was deciding that she had to be the most beautiful girl he had ever seen in his life. She was big, an absolute continent of flesh, but after registering this as he stood to greet her, Charley wasn't conscious of it again, even though she never stooped to make herself seem shorter. She had the posture of a fleet admiral on a visit to the White House. She was so elegantly formed that he reasoned, in a convincing new flash, that this was the size people had been meant to be until life had shrunk them backward into midgets.

She was called Mardell La Tour, a very beautiful name, Charley thought.

The two other showgirls, seated with Gennaro and Natale, broke into wild laughter because Gennaro had persuaded Natale to do his thing, Charley explained to Miss La Tour.

"What's that?" Mardell asked Charley.

"He's a walking whoopee cushion," Charley said. "Ain't you new here?"

She shivered violently.

"What's the matter?" Charley said. "You in a draft?"

"Someone at Buckingham Palace — I won't say who — hits me with an icy radio beam when it becomes necessary. It's for my health." Mardell had decided on that line on the spur of the moment because it seemed likely to capture his attention. She achieved what was almost a caricature of British speech. She spoke

19

very much like an English actor named Terry-Thomas.

"Buckingham Palace?"

"I started with the new show on Friday night."

"I have to wind up here about once a month," Charley said. "How come you talk funny?"

"I'm English."

"Whatta you mean?"

"I come from Shaftesbury, England, by way of London and Paris." She pronounced it Shahfssbree.

"Paris?"

"I worked at the Lido."

"No kidding? It's funny I never seen you. Here I mean. I never been to Paris or London, but I been here."

"As I said, I just started. Are you a gangster?"

He stared at her. "That's a pretty old-fashioned word," he said slowly. "How come you asked me that?"

"The girls told me we were expected to sit with gangsters."

"These girls said that?"

"No — somebody in the dressing room."

"Yeah? Well, lemme tell you something—"

"They said the club is owned by gangsters and that gangsters come here to meet other gangsters."

Charley stiffened. "Do we look like gangsters

here at this table?"

"Oh, definitely."

"What would you base that on?"

"The flicks. Telly."

"Telly? The flicks? I happen to be a Brooklyn businessman. Them two over there happen to be New Orleans businessmen. We are Italian descent so we talk the way it sounds to you, and I happen to be from Brooklyn so that adds."

The stouter New Orleans businessman was being served a chef's salad that seemed to be garnished with pork chops. The other one tubaed out a long, basso fart as a measure of repartee. The two girls on either side of him shrieked with laughter.

"I'm so sorry," Mardell said to Charley as if she were apologizing for Natale. "I had no intention of offending you."

"Listen — *you* talk funny. Is that how they talk in Shahfssbree, England?"

"We're nearer Semley, actually."

"Anybody from Brooklyn things I talk natural. But because I think you talk funny doesn't mean I got a right to ask you if you are a hooker or something."

"I am not good at small talk. You see" — she seemed embarrassed — "my mind is always waiting for the next radio beam."

"What?"

"It keeps me from catching leprosy."

"Forget it," he said. "Come on, I'll take you home."

"But I can't."

"Why not?"

"I have another show to do."

"I'll straighten that out."

"I'm sorry, Mr. Partanna, but I can't do that."

"You off Sunday and Monday?"

"Yes."

"Could I take you to dinner Sunday?"

"I have to wash my hair and my smalls and finish a book on Sunday."

"A book?"

"A library book. It's due."

"How about Monday?"

She studied him. "I could do Monday. If we could lunch in my neighborhood."

"Where's that?"

"Chelsea."

"Where?"

"I'm at 148 West Twenty-third Street."

"Great. Even if you lived in Hackensack it would be okay."

He relaxed so suddenly that he almost slipped under the table. Natale did a whistling, high-pitched fart and the two other girls fell apart laughing. "How do you *do* that?" one of them asked, grasping his thigh, sexually excited to find herself seated next to a man with such a sense of humor.

"It depends on the amount of air I swallow," Natale said shyly. "The more air, the bigger the noise."

# 3

Charley spent five days sweating out his passion. Business and social attitudes within his milieu insisted that he be seen as a menacing figure, but that appearance was mainly a professional necessity. Charley had an extremely tender side because he had begun to read magazine fiction in his preteens. A helplessness about beautiful women had grown steadily within him because, like money to the Prizzis, beauty — within the tight definition of beauty which Charley guarded deep in his heart — was the grail for Charley. He wasn't hooked on paintings in museums, big sceneries, the finest examples of courage and fidelity, or the immutable ecstasy of great poetry — his profound feelings for beauty began and ended with beautiful women. This made him one of the more susceptible men in the republic; perhaps on the planet. In others the characteristic might have been called "romantic" or "girl-simple," but Charley's addiction to beauty was bottomless; long before, as he had tumbled out of puberty, the worship of female beauty had become a true aesthetic experience to be repeated over and over again.

From the moment he left Mardell, he couldn't think about anything but that enormous hulk of beauty and grace who didn't even know that she worked for him. He took a lot of cold showers and, when he woke up in the night and the mindless erotic pictures began to slither and entwine inside his head, he got out of bed and stood on the terrace in the darkness, breathing deeply and doing knee-bends and push-ups. At last the day came when he would see her again in the flesh; a mountain of flesh carved into the shape of one of those gorgeous women made of marble who stood in the middle of fountains in Rome.

He dressed carefully on that day. He gargled with stuff guaranteed to eliminate bad breath, even though he had read in a magazine that it was the liver that sent up the noxious fumes if it happened to get out of whack. He wondered if there was a way to have his teeth painted to add pleasure points to his smile, but he had left it too late; there was no time to call the dentist. He put on one tie, then another, until with the third one he caught the effortless knot he was looking for. As he went out the door he began to figure out the best way he could ask her for her picture without sounding like a dope.

He parked the van and went into Mardell's apartment building. It was twelve forty-five on Monday afternoon. When she opened the door she was ready to go; she didn't ask him to come in. His legs could hardly hold him up. He had never seen anything so gigantically beautiful. She was wearing a golden yellow turtleneck sweater, no jewelry. Her hair fell to her shoulders like a bright-gold Cleopatra wig, and her porthole golden eyes let him look back, back, deeply into the willfulness hiding inside, but he shook off to stay pinned down under the visual squashing that the sight of her in daylight, without makeup and away from the Casino Latino, was doing to his willpower — his ebbing willpower — that was supposed to be keeping him from grabbing her.

"You are sensational," he said.

"We had better go." She started out, pulling the door behind her.

He put his hands on her waist and stared into her eyes as if his optic nerves had been frozen, as if he were Scott in the Antarctic in the last few seconds of life. His eyes stayed fixed and glazed, but he was able to bring his arms up behind her back, holding her and pulling her to him as Mohamet may have pulled the mountain in during the last stages of the classical overtake. She came in to him like a ferry easing into a slip. He stood on tiptoe. She bent her knees and sank a few inches, but kept her back straight. They kissed; softly; religiously. The kiss held them for some time. As they broke away, reluctantly, Charley perhaps more reluctant than Mardell, she closed the door behind her and they went down to the street.

They had lunch at an Italian restaurant called Italian Restaurant on Twenty-first Street. "Lemme order," Charley said. Then, as he read the menu, he saw to his dismay that it was some kind of Florentine food, so he ordered steaks.

"I adore steak," Mardell said. "Is that typical Italian food?"

"Whatta you gonna do?" Charley said. "This is a Tuscan restaurant."

"It says Italian Restaurant on the window."

"Tuscany is a little place way in the north of Italy. They don't know about food. Next time I'll get you some real food, in a Sicilian place."

He wiped his forehead with his napkin. "Listen, Mardell, what I believe is that where you start out is how everything is always gonna be. Do you believe that?"

"I – well – I suppose so–"

"So I have to tell you one thing. It's no use trying to hide nothing from you." He inhaled deeply. "I love you, Mardell. That's what it is. Nobody can change that."

"You *love* me?" She spoke of an utter impossibility.

"You're shocked I said that? You don't want that?"

"No. That is, I didn't say that."

"Then whatta you mean?"

"I mean – how can you love me? In total accumulated time you've known me about fifty-five minutes."

"How can I love you?" he said wildly, brushing the drinks waiter away. "How *can't* I love you? You are the most lovable thing I ever seen. You are the most important thing that ever come into my life."

"Charley, I just can't keep up with this."

"Are you a virgin?"

"A *virgin?*"

"You want to know how deep I feel, that's why I asked you that. It doesn't matter if you ain't a virgin. The past is the past. I love you, Mardell."

27

"We have to talk. You don't know anything about me."

"I know what I see. I know what I feel. On some things I'm wrong, things I decide with my head, but I never *felt* anything like this in my life, so I know I can't be wrong. You belong to me, Mardell."

The waiter staggered to the table with two orders of bistecca alla fiorentina surrounded by *strozzapreti,* dumplings made with ricotta cheese, Parmesan cheese, beets, spinach, and egg, served in gravy with more Parmesan cheese. The steaks were as big as suitcases.

"Oh, Charley," she said ecstatically. "Doesn't that look delicious! I'm so *hun*gry!"

# 4

Mardell La Tour, at twenty-three years, one month, was devout about her personal fantasies and had found a way to put them to use. Her best friend, Hattie Blacker, was practically knocking her brains out trying to get a master's in sociology so she could go on to take a doctorate in the behavioral sciences. For the past year, Mardell had been backing up Hattie by researching various forms of human behavior. So far, she had been a trapeze artist named Francie Braden; a professional tennis bum called Lally Ames; a lady mud wrestler in Hamburg, Germany, billed as Gert Schirmer; and a movie press agent in L.A. known as Janet Martin. She didn't need to do those things for a living, but she was determined to help Hattie.

Mardell, a mask name, had been born a Crowell and baptized Grace Willand. She was a graduate of Foxcroft, Bennington, and the Yale School of Drama. Her father was an Assistant Secretary of State for East Asian and Pacific Affairs. Her mother was a painter and sculptor. They were so rich that if they closed an account in just one of the banks that held a small part of their money, it would constitute a run on the bank, forcing it to close. They lived in a large Federalist house in Georgetown that had a cribbage room, two bowling alleys in the basement, and a tunnel to the houses of whoever it might be that would be running for the presidency in '72, '76, and '80, as well as last year, '68, and in the presidential election years before that. They were venerably old money that had owned a large portion of the country for many generations on

29

both sides of the family.

There was nothing gnawing about the need to imbed herself within imaginary lives — i.e., being able to live other lives under the safe umbrella of money, improvising a living, moving, talking sketch of one life then moving on to the next — she merely wanted to help her friend Hattie Blacker shine above all the other members of her class at Columbia, not only because Hattie had really taught her how to play tennis, but also because Hattie had brought Freddie into Mardell's life.

Freddie was the dream man of Grace Crowell's decade. Ever since she had come out in Washington four years ago, Freddie had been either the secret or open target of every girl she knew. In a polygamous society Freddie could easily have had twelve or fourteen wives, all desirable; all knockouts. He was just nonpareil in every department. He was extremely beautiful in a brutishly lovely way. He was as graceful as any defecting Russian ballet dancer. At nineteen she had listed all the marvelous things Freddie was or had (he owned two Houdon busts, for one example), but she hadn't bothered to remember all of them because she was simply too busy remembering Freddie after each time she saw him — which was as often as he could get away from his rather secret job in Washington.

She kept in touch with Washington through an exchange of letters with her mother. Sometimes, to stay in the character she was living currently to help Hattie research her papers, she wrote "case letters" to the people who she felt were closely related, dependent upon, or committed to the imaginary characters whose life she was living at the moment. The letters to the imaginaries were written because they were tools that helped her to *expand* her characterizations. Hattie was entirely too grateful for the research Grace was doing for her, to the point where Grace had had to tell her, "Oh, don't be so wet, Hattie. I was a drama major. All these living impersonations help me, too. I mean — what better training could there be for an actress or a playwright than to live other people's imaginary lives under the conditions in which they might live them?"

Briefly, in the five years since graduating from Foxcroft, Crowell/La Tour had tried coke, astrology, gin, psychedelic mushrooms, eastern religions, jogging, space shoes, transactional therapy, high-protein food, and *W*, which was either a newspaper, a magazine, or a catalog. She had never worked in either London or Paris. She had been in Shaftesbury to get the Sunday newspapers one summer weekend when she and Freddie had been the guests of some people named Weldon.

In fact, the Mardell La Tour identity hadn't existed until she walked into the Casino Latino at show change time and had been hired on the spot. Blocking out the fantasy of this succeeding life as Mardell La Tour, showgirl, she was thinking of becoming a sexual glutton – albeit with only one man, if possible – but then all the way around the barn, just to see what it was like and to be entirely ready and able when and if the great legal moment happened with Freddie.

She was thrilled to meet a genuine hoodlum and to find him to be such a polite man who was so intent on doing what he saw as the right thing. The headwaiter, Mr. Smadja, was a darling. She learned from him that the Latino was owned by the Prizzi family, the nonpareil Mafia family of the United States, or at least *prima inter pares*, as her own father was to the American government. After a while, just keeping her ears open in the dressing room, she discovered that Charley Partanna was the underboss and the enforcer for the family and this knowledge drove her into rigorous disciplines of fantasy.

A week or so after she met Charley for lunch she wrote to her mother:

I have met the most fascinating man in New York. I think I could make him into a wonderful paper for Hattie Blacker. He's what they call in his trade a "hit person," my coworkers tell me, and if you don't know what that is, it is just as well. He's utterly ethnic, really adorable, and is an executive with one of the crime organizations of Brooklyn, which is a borough of New York City. He has *marv*elous manners and, although he is thirty years old, he is working for a high school diploma by attending night school. He has five months to go, making two and a half years of steady hard work in all. He seems to respect the diploma he will get more than the knowledge. He treats me as if I were a tiny, delicate, slightly confused Dresden doll, if your mind can fit me, a Size 16, into such a frame.

Seriously, he could represent a chance for some of the best research I have ever done. Hattie Blacker says that when she gets her doctorate she is going to settle into American tribal sociology. I am thinking seriously about doing a long paper for her on my friend, which is something that really could burnish the Blacker shield.

I had lunch with Edwina, whom you will

remember because she married poor Puffy Witzel aboard that darling little train in Scotland. I see Charles, my crime executive, three nights a week after his school and my work. During the rest of the days and nights I either catch up on my reading or I do a few rounds of the discos with Chandler or Freddie. *That* has reached a most interesting point: Freddie wants me to marry him.

I think there's a novel in Edwina. Three hours before her husband's funeral she had a selection of widow's weeds delivered to her from Bendel's and Mainbocher, at the Campbell Funeral Home on Madison Avenue. She tried on seven outfits right in the room where Puffy was laid out (with the door locked, of course), but finally went out to the crematorium with only her sable coat over a bra and panties. She says she hates being a widow so she certainly isn't going to dress the part.

I am eating a lot of Sicilian food because that is the only food my crime executive friend understands. It seems to be either saffron and sardines – or is it pine nuts and currants and anchovies?

All my love to Daddy,

Warmest and dearest to you,

Gracie

# 5

Vito Daspisa had barricaded himself in his ninth-floor apartment at the beach after a thirty-two-block car chase that started because some wise-guy cop had tried to take Vito in for possession. What got Vito so hot was that the guy was not only on the pad, but whenever he had needed quick money for an abortion or for his car insurance, Vito had always helped him out. So Vito lost his temper. And, the way it worked out, he shot the ungrateful prick. Then, in the car chase that happened right after, a crazy rookie just out of the Academy had stood in the street in front of the car waving his gun like he was Mr. Law-and-Order, so Vito had sideswiped him – what else? – was he supposed to drive up on the sidewalk and waste old ladies?

He made it to his apartment house at the beach, then an army of cops with tear gas and plastic explosives emptied the building of all the tenants except Vito and surrounded him. It was a Technicolor stakeout for the evening news with bullhorns, helmets, Air Force-type searchlights, and snipers on the roofs. A police task force swarmed over the area with assault rifles and bulletproof vests. It was potentially such a big media event in a slow news week in September that the commissioner was there to represent the mayor, whose wife had him pinned down at his literary agent's in Montauk to rest up six weeks before the elections.

When His Honor heard about the Daspisa stakeout, he busted loose and started back to the city behind a motorcycle escort for his rendezvous with the TV cameras at Manhattan Beach. It was not only an election windfall, it was a national promotion windfall for his second book, *Me*, that nobody could have anticipated except that, as the mayor said, when New York was for you it always came through when you needed it.

A crowd of about eight hundred people collected in the open area, forming a semicircle around Vito's apartment house. The three networks were demanding a minimum of two days for the stakeout and a maximum of three. Richard Gallagher, the Deputy Commissioner for Public Information, told them nobody would believe it would take two days to get a punk like Vito out of the building. "All we gotta do is send up two men with plastic. One sticks it on the front door, the other on the back door. We blow the stuff simultaneously, the doors go down and the task force goes in and takes him."

"No good, Commissioner," said Manning, a network contact man. "They might have to take him out on a stretcher. That's no good. He's gotta come out standing up so the viewers can see him. Unless, of course, you shoot him down, which is the other alternative shot."

"Shooting him will work better than just bringing him out, Gordon," the standup reporter said.

"I wanna get you maximum cooperation, but this can't go on more than two nights," Gallagher said. "It ain't fair to the taxpayer, and the mayor will be on our ass. Election Day is practically here, fahcrissake."

The networks agreed to the two days. For a compromise, they said they had to have a little human interest on camera, they couldn't keep shooting nothing.

"Like what?" Gallagher said.

"Like you could get one of his relatives out here and we could interview them."

"Okay," Gallagher said. "But let's get some

things straight here. I gotta have coverage on the mayor, who is breaking his ass to get here, and when he gets here I not only gotta have shots of him tearing up in the car and taking charge, but it's gotta be guaranteed the shots will get on the air."

Late in the afternoon of the second day, Vito wrote a message saying he wanted to talk to Lieutenant Hanly of the Borough Squad. He folded it into a schoolboy airplane and sailed it out of the window to the cops in the street. The cops located Hanly in a massage parlor and had him out at the beach in twenty-five minutes, burping tits.

On the scene, he was passed along the chain of command to the mayor. They stood together, isolated from the rest of the brass, in the over-lighted open area in front of the building, a pregnant two-shot for the networks, while the mayor gave Davey his instructions. "Tell him to stretch it out for at least one more day," the mayor said. "Be solicitous. Ask if he's okay on food, et cetera. Promise him anything. Just tell him you have to come down to check it out with me."

Hanly went up in the elevator alone. He stood against the wall next to Vito's front door, flattened out. Backhand, he rapped on the door with the butt of his service revolver.

"Vito?"

"What?"

"It's me."

"Who the fuck is me?"

"Davey Hanly."

"Whatta you want?"

"What do *I want*? You threw down the air-plane that said you wanted to talk to me."

"I must be punchy. I ain't had no sleep."

"The families of those two cops ain't had no sleep either, you prick."

"Ah – I lost my head. Listen, Davey, whatta you say? You wanna make a deal?"

"A deal?"

"You set it to keep those crazy cops away from me and get me downtown someplace, better yet in New York, and I am gonna lay out the entire Prizzi shit operation on the East Coast for you."

"Jesus, Vito–" Vito was talking about throwing away a big piece of Hanly's bread and butter.

"Whatta you say, Davey?"

"What can I tell you? I'll go down and they'll talk it over."

Hanly went back to the street conscious that the network cameras were covering him, playing it very grave, very troubled, but hopeful for justice. He reported to the mayor on full camera, no sound, saying that Vito was just buying time, but they looked like a couple of conspirators plotting the downfall of mankind. The mayor patted him on the back, dismissing him. Hanly lost himself in the dense crowd packed in the darkness around the building and went into the bar across the street. He went to the last booth where Angelo Partanna was waiting. He sat down opposite Angelo, took off his uniform cap, wiped his forehead and neck with a handkerchief, and said, "He says he'll lay out the whole Prizzi East Coast shit operation if I can get him downtown and he can talk to a lawyer."

Angelo sighed heavily. He got up slowly and walked to a phone booth across the room. He was a tall, scrawny, bald, and relentlessly dapper man in his late fifties. He had brush strokes of white paint on either side of his head above the ears; no hair above that. He was cocoa-dark with a nose like a macaw's beak. There was no jewelry on him, but nobody would ever call him any slob. Angelo was the *consigliere* of the Prizzi family. He was inclined to overvalue cunning as a human quality. It was his conviction that there was no situation imaginable that he couldn't plot his way out of. Even among Sicilians he was viewed charily because of his deviousness. "People look at television," he said to his son Charley, "and they think everybody in the business is an ignorant strong-arm. I never strong-armed nobody in my life. When they see me they think I'm a rich dentist. Always dress quiet. Keep the suit pressed, the shoes shined, and let them think you are a civilian. And always wear a hat when you leave the house."

He took the OUT OF ORDER sign off the mouthpiece of the telephone, put it in his pocket, and dialed Corrado Prizzi's private number.

# 6

Corrado Prizzi sat in his favorite chair gazing dreamily, out of the large window sixteen feet away, at the view of lower Manhattan, which resembled the teeth in the lower jaw of a tyrannosaurus rex, while he absorbed the tenderness of *Aroldo*'s cavatina "Sotto il sol di Siria."

Corrado Prizzi was the inventor of franchised crime; sort of a Sicilian Thomas Edison. His organizational vision had broken the patterns of merely local or regional organized crime and had made his own family an international presence that financed and designed local criminal organization and its enterprises down to the last detail, in the manner of the 803-page manual for the operation of a neighborhood McDonald's. The Prizzi family, because of Corrado's foresight, was in partnership with more than seventy percent of the families working in the United States: Mafia, black, Hispanic, Jewish, cowboy, and Oriental, in such high-yield activities as narcotics, gambling, tax-free gasoline, counterfeit merchandise, pornography, labor racketeering, junk bond financing, prostitution, toxic waste disposal, loan sharking, and extortion. These were industries that required capital to maintain quality and excellence. Corrado Prizzi provided the seed capital, the know-how, and a vastly growing array of political protection.

When he was seventeen Corrado Prizzi became a qualified man. When he emigrated to America with his wife and infant son Vicenzo in the following year, 1915, they were well-to-do compared with other Sicilian immigrants. They had $900 – a big edge which, with his training as a specialist, enabled Corrado to build a family of *compari* that would grow as a syndicate and a kinship unit.

The year after he landed in New York, after

he had established strong bonds with the Irish and Jewish hoodlums in lower Manhattan, he and his family followed the mass movement of immigrant Sicilians to Brooklyn, to the area between the Brooklyn Bridge and the Navy Yard. Corrado organized the lottery and that provided the backlog of operating cash with which he established his legitimate front: an imported cheese and olive oil business and his storefront bank. Originally the bank was there to receive deposits and send money back to the old country. Most of the time, storefront banks like his operated outside the restraints that bound state and national banks, and there were ample opportunities for fraud. There was no doubt that his interest rates on bank loans were high, but so were the risks. He was investing in poverty which could pay back only in small amounts — so much so that he was obliged to establish a small Black Hand unit to ensure collections. Individuals who were unwilling to repay him would suffer the consequences by losses of their peace, their businesses, or their lives. The plain fact was that immigrants who wanted to start up businesses were forced to go to his storefront bank for capital. After a while, in some of the cases, he wrote off part of the loans in exchange for an interest in the businesses. The experience gave him a knowledge of banking that was to profit him in later years.

He established his own ethnic-political machine and, because he was fair, because the immigrants needed someone to tell them how to get started in a strange, new country, he handed out patronage in return for support on Election Day. As he accumulated capital he bought into other political organizations in other parts of Brooklyn and in Manhattan, as an invisible partner of such men as James March (aka Antonio Maggio) and Paul Kelly (aka Paolo Vacarelli), keeping ward and political machines in power; obtaining exemptions from city ordinances for businessmen; arranging bail and obtaining pardons; sponsoring dances, parades, picnics, boat rides, bazaars, and church functions; and adding to the ranks of mourners at funerals.

In 1928, the young man Angelo Partanna, whom Corrado had brought over from Agrigento to run the lottery, bribed a woman clerk in the office of Charles J. O'Connor, the liquor administrator in charge of permits, for the withdrawal of tens of thousands of gallons of prohibited liquor for "medicinal purposes." The stolen permits were serially numbered and had a rubber stamp facsimile of O'Connor's signature. Corrado Prizzi sold the liquor at the official underworld curb exchange that ringed police headquarters along Kenmare, Broome, Grand, and Elizabeth streets in Manhattan and that met day and night to carry out business. In two years, back when the purchasing power of the dollar was ten-to-one against what it would become, Corrado Prizzi made two million dollars, the capital that financed his move into vaster, more widespread operations long before his competitors could get there.

Don Corrado was *mafiusu* – from the Sicilian adjective that has been used since the eighteenth century to describe people and objects as "beautiful" and "excellent." Elsewhere, modern man sought wealth as a means of acquiring material objects; the *mafiusu* sought wealth as a means of commanding obedience and respect from others. Elsewhere, man believed that power follows wealth; Don Corrado knew, in his medieval mind, that wealth comes from power.

The room where he spent most of his time was in a house owned by a Bahamian company, whose shares were held by an *Anstalt* in Liechtenstein. The don didn't own anything but seemed to live very nicely on his Social Security payments. These were, thank heaven, still untaxable in the late 1960s.

He was a pitiably old-looking man though he had only just reached seventy-one. He was small, wore suits that were two sizes too big for him in such a way that he appeared shriveled and unprotected. Angelo Partanna said that the don believed that looking old and feeble gave him an edge and, after his wife died, what was to stop him?

He shuffled when he walked. He smiled wanly when he smiled, which fortunately wasn't often since it was a smile that chilled the bones.

Every room in the don's house was decorated the way he remembered the furnishings of a Sicilian duke's country mansion that he had seen when he was twelve years old, while the duke was away in Paris for the season. He could remember every room he had entered that day as if he were looking at a set of photographs. The room Corrado Prizzi lived in was a replica of a room decorated in 1872, following the decor of the duke's father's palace in Palermo, which had been decorated in 1819. So, while the furnishings of the Prizzi house were not modern in any way, they were rich, if a little worn; fringes, velours, ormolu, and gilt-framed pictures everywhere; carved cherubim, and portraits of Jesus in his many manifestations, as well as several realistic limnings of St. Francis of Assisi.

The telephone rang. Still listening to the

Verdi, he reached out and picked it up.

"Hello?"

"This is Angelo, Corrado. You remember Vito Daspisa who worked with his brother Willie in the—"

"I know him."

"He killed two cops. Now he is inside his apartment out at the beach surrounded by a giant stakeout of cops and television people."

"So?" The don tried to listen to the music and to Angelo Partanna at the same time.

"So he sent for Davey Hanly and he—"

"Hanly?"

"The Borough Squad. The bag man for the Department in Brooklyn."

"Ah."

"He told Hanly he would give him the whole rundown on our East Coast shit operation if Hanly would get him out."

"If *Hanly* would get him out? Vito Daspisa is one of our people."

"Yeah."

"One of our people and he offers to betray us so *they* can get him out? I can't believe it. I took his father in when the Horowitz Novelty Company failed. The father handled punchboards for Frank Costello."

"What do you want me to do?"

"Where are you?"

47

"In a bar across the street from his apartment. I got Hanly with me."

"We gotta take Vito off the payroll, Angelo. Us, not them." He hung up.

Angelo left the phone booth and went back to the table where Hanly was waiting. He sat down heavily. "I am disappointed. This man come to us nine years ago when his brains was running out of his nose because he was getting his head punched off as an Armory fighter. We took him in. This is how he pays us back."

"You're breaking my heart, Angelo. How do you want to handle it?"

"All anybody wants is for this crazy cop-killer to be dead, Davey, but the Department has to get the media credit after all the trouble you guys are going through. Without risking any more cops' lives."

"Yeah? How do we do that?"

"We'll send my son Charley in."

"Charley?"

"Give him a temporary rank of first-grade detective and some name off the department's personnel computer for his protection. Get him an assault rifle. He'll handle everything."

"I'll have to clear that, Angelo."

"Why not? It makes sense."

Hanly left the bar and plunged into the crowd.

## 7

Angelo drove through the traffic from Flatbush to Midwood to get Charley from night school. He, too, was proud of Charley's determination to get a high school diploma. Charley had quit school when he was fifteen to go to work as a helper on an ice truck for what looked like a lot of money to him – forty-eight dollars a week. Louis Palo, a neighborhood guy who was about five years older than Charley, had come off the ice truck to go to work for the Prizzis and he recommended Charley for the job.

Angelo didn't try to stop Charley, but he said, "I hope you ain't gonna be sorry about quitting school." Charley didn't know what Pop was talking about. He left the ice truck when he was sixteen because Pop got him a job as a runner in the counterfeit liquor stamp operation. He was a made man at seventeen (although he made his bones at thirteen under very unusual, but necessary, conditions), the same age his father had been made in Sicily.

After that, his advancement in the environment was assured. From seventeen until twenty-one he worked in Religio Vulpigi's setup, which handled high tech in-flight robberies and the hijacking of negotiable securities. They lifted passenger baggage holding jewels and money on commercial airliners and heavy freight shipments coming through La Guardia, Newark, and Idlewild.

When Charley was twenty-one he was transferred to be the bridge man between the mob-owned racetracks around the country and the racehorses they had to keep buying in England and Ireland at the right prices so there would always be enough to keep running enough races for the bettors to keep pouring the four hundred million dollars a year into the business.

Charley was drafted when he was twenty-four. Eduardo, the don's other son, could have fixed it, but Charley said all the guys his age were going in so he went in. He wound up in Special Forces for fourteen months because he was good with weapons and had high tech skills, then he was blown right out of it in a Cong attack on a U.S. base near Pleiku in the Central Highlands.

Pleiku was the South Vietnamese Army headquarters for patrols against Cong infiltration routes coming down through the jungles from Laos and Cambodia. Charley's detachment was billeted three miles away at Camp Holloway. His outfit guarded a fleet of U.S. transport and observation aircraft and helicopters. The Cong hit at about 2 A.M. on February 7th, 1965, with mortars and heavy automatic fire. Eight Americans died and more than a hundred others were wounded; ten U.S. aircraft were destroyed. Charley had the bone in his right thigh shattered. After four operations, the last two in Washington, his thighbone was replaced with an aluminum rod. He was just turning twenty-seven when he walked out of the hospital and went back to Brooklyn, where the don turned out practically the entire family at the old Palermo Gardens and gave him the party of the year.

When Charley came back from Nam he told Pop he would sign up for night school. Pop was so proud he told the don, and the don had Charley come over to the house so he could tell him he'd done the right thing; he was a real American.

They ate a tremendous lunch. Charley couldn't believe how much a little old guy like the don could put away. The don asked him when he would get his diploma.

"Like in two and a half to three years, *padrino.*"

"Do they have a thing at the night school after you finish the job?"

"I don't know, *padrino*. They never said."

"How are you doing in the school so far?"

"Okay, I guess. I run a B+ average. I was elected Secretary-Treasurer of my class."

"If they have a graduation I wanna know, because me and Vincent are gonna be there. Amalia, too. If they don't have a graduation I gonna ask Eduardo to talk to the head of the Board of Education to have them set one up."

"You pay me tremendous honor, *padrino*."

"Whatta you talkin' about?" the don said. "You are gonna have a high school education, the first soldier we ever put on the street with a high school diploma."

The Luis Muñoz-Marín Junior High School in Midwood operated from 7 to 10 P.M. as a night school. Charley was in a class with eleven other adults; two-thirds were women; six Puerto Ricans, four blacks, a Russian woman from Brighton Beach, and Charley. The teacher was a blocky determined Norwegian from Bay Ridge named Mr. Matson. The desks, meant for twelve- and fourteen-year-olds, were small for a lot of the night class. Charley had to sit in a chair on the far side of the room. He sat there daydreaming about Mardell La Tour.

Tonight could be the night. He had set up a careful pattern after that first lunch. He didn't want her to think he was some kind of a wolf. But enough time had gone by. Enough confidence had been built. He was only human, for God's sake, but tonight could be the night.

He had attacks of dizziness when he thought about Mardell. He found it impossible to imagine her either: (a) naked, or (b) lying down. But he was as eager to know those two things as any astronomer-topographer who had ever sought to map outer space. Not only was she a spectacular girl, she had a body on her that was bringing him to his knees because, with Mardell as it had never been with anybody else, there was no place else to go. Also, there was no denying it, she had an unusual imagination. He had found out what Buckingham Palace was, in the Encyclopaedia Britannica his father had given him on his twelfth birthday. When he found out, he had to decide that Mardell must be some kind of a nut.

The gleaming jewel of the night school class was Señora Roja-Buscando, who sought to answer every question put by Mr. Matson, interrupting the answers by any other student to the point of exasperating Charley so much that he broke his rule of never putting fear into a woman. Night after night, he *poured* fear over the señora, but it had absolutely no effect. She dominated the class, giving advice, scorn, and pity; winning Gold Star after Gold Star. She had four more stars than Charley.

Angelo drove his beat-up Chevy straight to the school, got directions from the office to find Charley's classroom, and stood outside the room staring through the glass pane of the top half of the door, hoping to catch Charley's attention. He had to tap on the glass with a dime. The entire class and Mr. Matson looked at him. Pop made motions at Charley to come out. Charley cleared his throat and spoke to Mr. Matson. "That's my father," he said.

"You better go out."

"You shoo tell your father that he shoon innarupt the class," Señora Roja-Buscando said. "We are serious here. This is no time for grittings."

Pop drove Charley to the beach. On the way he explained what had to be done.

"*Vito?*" Charley cried out. "Vito Das*pisa?* He's my best friend!"

"He's finished, Charley, and he knows it. He wanted to give the entire shit operation to the cops."

"But I know him all my life."

54

"Vito's trouble is he's a hothead when he has a couple lines in him."

"Why does a guy who is a natural wine drinker for hundreds of years go around fooling with that stuff?"

"He's an American, Charley. He is integrating. His old man was just as much of a hothead, and he only took wine. He got himself killed because he lost his temper in a game of pool and peed on the cue ball because he missed a shot."

"Jesus, Pop."

Charley knew Vito from the old neighborhood since they were five years old. When they were teenagers they used to make side money together playing semipro stickball all over south Brooklyn. One summer Vito was the menace at a crap game Charley ran on Sunday mornings at Coney Island. Vito was a natural athlete, a hulk. When he was eighteen he took his shot at being an Armory fighter in the lightweight division, and Charley was his manager. Vito boxed under the name of Dimples Tancredi because if his mother found out what he was doing she would beat the shit out of him. The second time Charley ever did the job on anybody was because of Vito. A gambler named Four-Eyes Ganz had been bothering Vito to throw fights so Ganz could clean up on the bets. Vito had told him to fuck off but he kept coming back. The whole thing got Charley's goat so he slammed Ganz and his bodyguard against the wall in Vito's dressing room and told them if he ever saw them again they would be dead. Like a dummy, Ganz came around five nights later and made the same proposition to Vito, so Charley put them in a car with the Plumber driving, took them out to the southwest part of the Belt Parkway, and gave it to them. Nobody missed them.

Vito was a good-looking kid, but he grew up a little battered on account of the scar tissue, and after a while he got a little punchy from pleasing crowds by taking punches just to show how rugged he was. Little kids could have fun with him by jumping up and down in front of him with their hands held stiffly at their sides and watching him fall over backward on his head. It was part of being punchy.

Every Saturday afternoon when they were thirteen, Charley and Vito used to take Vito's older sister Tessie to the movies and take turns giving her a feel. When they were seventeen they cleared over six hundred dollars. They ran a New Year's Eve party for ten dollars a head, all the beer you could drink, where they had a man who did nothing but sweep up the broken glass and a four-piece orchestra that, it turned out, couldn't play anything but "Sweet Georgia Brown." It was so successful that they did this every New Year's Eve until, the fourth year, two guys were hurt over a woman and a cop almost died. The word was passed down that they had to quit holding the rackets.

After Charley was made, he and Vito went into different kinds of work. Vito was never made so he bodyguarded bookmakers and picked up extra money intimidating building trades people. After about a year, Charley got his father to get Vito a slot with Vito's brother Willie, who ran the controlled substances merchandising for the Prizzis from Miami to Maine. The government called it controlled substances at Eduardo's suggestion because that way the voters who read about it didn't get scared that the whole country might be turning into dope fiends. The people who run up those kinds of statistics said that just calling shit something that it wasn't − controlled substances, a meaningless kind of a name − had increased gross sales of all shit products by 21.3 percent.

Willie's operation was very big because of the tremendous demand for the shit. The people who made up the shit market had to run very fast trying to keep up with their own lives and their credit cards. Grown-ups and kids were working two jobs each at one time to keep up with the mortgages, taxes, toxic waste, dentists' bills, and the rest of the American dream. They had to find something to pull them through from one day to the next. Booze made them sleepy and could get them fired. Pot made them think they felt sexy when they were only exhausted. The media kept saying that cocaine was a recreational drug. So the Prizzis handled the top end on a national basis, took their share, then split the profits with the franchisees, who were the other families across the country.

Vito was third man in the East Coast operation, under Joey Labriola, who everybody suspected of being a *culatino* but didn't say nothing because he was a big part of Willie's operation. *Suspected* Joey was a *culatino*? Joey was either supergay or he was a female transvestite trying to act like a man. But he had Willie's protection and Willie delivered a lot of money, so everybody pretended Joey was a visiting lumberjack.

"What did Vito *do*, fahcrissake, Pop?" Charley asked.

"He killed two cops and then got himself surrounded by about two hundred cops in his own apartment. He tried to make a deal with Davey Hanly to give them our entire shit operation on the East Coast. He has to go down, no matter what," Pop said.

"Aaaah, shit," Charley said.

"We got an Army assault rifle for you. It hits so hard it'll go right through the door, through Vito, and out the back of the building."

Charley remembered Vito swimming in the Gowanus Canal when everybody said it could give typhoid; Vito yelling up Bushwick Avenue at Arcade Annie who was pregnant again, "When you gonna drop it, Annie?" and the laugh he got. He remembered Vito scoring his nineteenth consecutive kayo at the Armory. He thought of Vito doing the Peabody and moving faster, forward or backward, than anybody on the floor.

"He done everything wrong, Charley. He shoulda depended on the Prizzis to get him out, but he had to fink. Eduardo had it all set up. They were gonna bring him out surrounded by twelve state troopers holding an armor plate on his head to protect him from the cops, and even the TV people said it would be the shot of the year. He was gonna be lost inside under a different name until the two cop killings blew over and Eduardo could set up the right kind of a trial. Then, when he was cleared, there would be a job waiting for him as manager of an Ohio track."

"What'll I tell him to get him lined up?"

"Tell him Eduardo made a deal with the mayor and it's fixed so after a couple years inside we'll give him a good job in Vegas."

"He hates Vegas."

"Tell him Louisiana. He ain't going nowheres anyways."

# 8

Davey Hanly had passed the word to Angelo that they wanted the human interest shot to keep the networks sweet, so Angelo called Vito's brother Willie and told him to come over to talk to Vito. "And come alone, you hear? Don't bring Joey."

"Why not?"

"Because there are a buncha TV cameras here! Whatta you think? the don wants everybody to think we're a bunch of *finocchi?*"

"Jesus, Angelo, watch what you're saying."

"Just don't bring Joey."

Willie was an animal who had been taught to wear shoes and a tie. He sold dope like it was the alchemist's lost formula for turning vegetables into gold; he didn't care what it did to anybody, but his profound feelings about Joey were something else. He resented Angelo's attack on Joey so deeply that he could hardly think of anything except getting even. He went out to the beach considering what kind of a club he could find to beat Angelo with and, when finally he was standing in the crowd outside Vito's building, the whole thing came to him. What Vito was doing inside that apartment house was giving him and Joey their big chance to get out and make a whole new life together. It would be like they were married.

He took his instructions from Gallagher and from Manning, the TV guy, nodding to show he understood. He could hear the stand-up reporters on the air live referring to him as the brother of the alleged killer, a respectable wholesale grocer who could not understand where his brother had gone wrong. Willie stood in the clearing that had been made in front of Vito's apartment house, in the floodlights that had turned night into high noon, the avid crowd in a deep, wide semicircle behind him, facing a battalion of more than eleven television cameras, countless still cameras, radio microphones, police brass, and gofers, then he talked into the field telephone the cops had set up in the open space in front of the building with the big crowd all closed in behind him and the network cameras shooting him from the front. After seventeen rings on Vito's number, Vito came on the phone.

"What?" he said.

"Vito? Willie. How you doin'?"

"How'm I *doin*?" Vito screamed. "I'm fuckin' doin' my own funeral."

"Lissen, Vito — you can come out. It's okay."

"Okay? *Okay?* There's two hundred cops down there who gotta get even for their buddies or something. Fuck you, Willie. I ain't coming out." Vito hung up. The rotten language would be beeped out of the tape before it went on the air. Willie looked at Gallagher blankly. Manning, standing beside a TV camera and facing Willie, made revolving motions with his hands for Willie to keep talking.

"For our dead mother's sake, Vito," Willie said into the dead telephone, "throw down your guns and come out here where we can help you. This is your brother. It's Willie. Lissena me."

Five blocks away Rosa Daspisa, who was slugging away at a bottle of muscatel as if it had never given anybody a hangover, watched her husband become an instant media celebrity on the twenty-three-inch screen and went crazy. She streaked out of the apartment in her kimono and kitchen apron, wearing bedroom slippers. She was a swarthy woman who still had a nice figure and a head of black ringlets like Medusa, but the muscatel, over the past couple of years since her husband had become engaged to Joey Labriola, had stepped all over her face.

She burst out of the building, flagged down a cab as soon as she hit the street, and in five minutes she was at Vito's apartment house. She tore through the crowd as if somebody had just handed her the Heisman Trophy and grabbed Willie by the arm. "You fag-lover!" she yelled, tears glazing her cheeks, "whatta you tryna do to me?"

The cameras had moved. Willie shook her off like raindrops. Two cops grabbed her, but Davey Hanly said something to one of the cops, who turned her over to Davey. He pulled her, sobbing, through the crowd, which had lost interest in her, to the bar across the street. He led her to the back of the saloon, where Angelo was seated alone in a booth.

"Siddown," Davey said.

"What's this?" Pop said.

"Mrs. Willie Daspisa." He left them.

Rosa stopped crying because she was fascinated by Angelo's suit. It was gray vicuña, the stuff cumulus clouds are made of, carrying a darker gray herringbone pattern. "That's a beautiful suit," she said.

"What happened, Mrs. Daspisa?" Pop asked gently in Sicilian. There wasn't a more tender man in the environment.

# 9

After Willie dumped his wife he stood at the forward edge of the crowd, where he had a good view of everyone who moved in front of the building. He watched Hanly come out and go in again. Willie sensed that something was happening. They were setting something up, he was sure, because the task force was bunching up outside the building. They must be organizing to take Vito out. He almost jumped straight up when he spotted Charley Partanna on the far side, edging through the crowd to the west entrance of the building. He watched Charley go in, then he had a figure on it. He decided to wait around and see if they brought Vito out feetfirst. If they did, Charley had done the work. Willie grinned. He could now sink the hooks into Angelo for what he called Joey.

When Charley was inside, the stand-up TV reporters, fed by Gallagher, identified him as Detective-Sergeant George Fearons, who was going to try to persuade the suspect to give himself up. Fearons, they reported to an audience later rated at thirty-one percent nationally, was one of the new breed of psychologist cops. He was going in to face, entirely unarmed, an alleged killer, relying on his own knowledge of human motivation to protect himself and to get a hunted man to surrender. Either he would come out with his prisoner in handcuffs or the final assault would be made to bring Daspisa out by force. There was a short break for commercial messages.

Charley picked up the assault rifle from Davey Hanly inside the building, where Hanly was waiting with Sergeant Ueli Munger, the officer in charge of the task force. Munger had been demoted from the rank of captain recently for knocking down two superior officers following a nineteen-hour ordeal of getting a woman down from the high cables on the George Washington Bridge.

"You wanna go through a short course on the weapon?" Munger asked Charley. Charley shook his head. He was getting depressed. Twenty years of hanging around with Vito, and now he had to blow him away. He looked at the rifle and hefted it. It could blow anybody away.

"It's a sweet piece of equipment," Munger said. "It gives about ten rounds a second and each one travels 2,300 feet a second. The beauty part about these babies is that like if the bullet goes in at the shoulder it can come out in the thigh, so if you got ten of them going in every second God knows where they come out."

"You got thirty bullets in the magazine, Charley," Hanly said. "That oughta do it."

Charley took the noisy elevator up to Vito's floor. Riding up, he remembered an article he had read once that said there was only an imaginary connection between the past and the present. The article, written by a big scientist, had asked Charley directly how could there even be a present when it was always, instantaneously, becoming the past. Charley could look back and see all the great times he and Vito had, but, as the magazine article said, those two people didn't exist anymore, they had existed only while those other things he remembered were actually happening – and only when they were happening. The friend of Vito's he had been back in the past wasn't the same Charley Partanna who was going to zotz Vito now. The Vito he would be doing the work on wouldn't be the same Vito he had all the good times with. There were hundreds of Vitos and hundreds of Charleys all existing separately in time, strung out across their memory like beads; spaced out like separate frames of film on a continually running, irreversible reel. He hadn't even met the Vito he was going to have to put away.

Charley didn't flatten himself against the wall. He rang the doorbell of Vito's apartment, admiring the nice, clean hallway, his kind of place.

"Davey?" Vito yelled from behind the door.

"It's Charley."

"Charley Partanna?"

"Who else?"

"Where's Davey?"

"Angelo sent me. He talked to the don."

"How come?"

"Eduardo had everything handled. He had it set so the state troopers were gonna take you out with a two-inch thick armor plate over your head. The cops wouldn'ta been able to touch you. The mayor was gonna lose you for two years, then Eduardo woulda talked to the right judge."

"So — what happened?"

"You blew it, Vito. Eduardo had it all set up for you but you hadda tell Davey you'd give them the Prizzi shit operation."

"How could I blow it? I been right here."

"You talked to Davey, didn't you?"

"Yeah."

"Who do you think Davey talked to when he went back to the street — his mother?"

"Ah, shit — I blew it."

"Yeah."

"I'm all wore out. I shouldn'ta whacked that cop with the car, but Teddy Egan had it coming. Hey, Charley?"

"Yeah."

"Come on in and we'll have a cuppa coffee."

"Why not?"

"All I got is instant."

"Instant is okay."

"Hey — in case I forget it, will you tell them to give out my ring name like when I fought under it. Okay?"

"Absolutely."

Vito checked the load and the safety on his gun. He held it at ready as he took the chain off and unlocked the three dead bolts. His face was sad. What the hell, he figured, he had to do it, it was Charley or himself. Vito flung open the door and fired. The shot went into the ceiling because Vito was flung backward so far and so fast by the force of the rounds that were piling into him and jerking him crazily like he was being pulled everyway by powered steel cables.

The assault rifle was on automatic. Charley had opened it up, holding the rifle waist-high. Vito was slammed back across the entrance hall to crash into the furniture on the far side of the living room. Charley went into the apartment and gave Vito one more burst until the magazine was empty. He said, "Vito?" but there was no answer.

He went back to the main floor. Hanly and Munger were waiting for him.

"From what it sounded like, he'll go quietly now," Hanly said.

"Yeah."

"You gonna bring the TV in?" Munger asked Davey.

"That's the name of the game, ain't it?"

"Listen, Davey," Charley said, "I hadda promise him that you guys would give out his name under his ring name he fought under, Dimples Tancredi."

"Holy shit," Munger said excitedly, "you mean that guy up there was Dimples Tancredi, the great Armory fighter?"

The task force, led by Sergeant Munger — who, the networks revealed, was a courageous Swiss who had been born in Schaffhausen, one of the relatively few in the Department — rushed into the apartment of the alleged killer, just ahead of the NBC camera crews, with guns blazing, subduing and killing the suspect instantly and delivering a terrific camera shot that one network used beginning eight months later in three separate cop series and mini-series. Munger was decorated for valor and eventually repromoted to the rank of captain although subsequently it appeared that that could have happened for reasons of mayoral politics. Almost all of the resolution of the thrilling stakeout was seen on television nation-wide, repeated for the requisite three days, then bumped by a serial murderer who was terrorizing the nation's capital, who in turn was bumped by the hijacking of the Orient Express by a fanatical Middle Eastern sect, all of it covered, day and night, by the *oculus mundi* and nineteen Canadian stations.

# 10

Hanly got Charley out of the building through the back delivery entrance. Charley walked around the block and gradually made his way to the bar across the street from Vito's building.

Pop was sitting in the last booth.

"Okay?" Pop asked.

"Yeah."

Pop got up and went to the telephone booth, took out the OUT OF ORDER sign off the mouthpiece, put it in his pocket, and dialed.

Charley decided he would have time to catch a quick movie before he went to the Latino and picked up Mardell at eleven thirty. He could use a little of Mardell after the work he had just done, if there was such a thing as a little of Mardell. Pop came back from the phone booth.

"The don is prouda you, Charley," he said, smiling broadly.

"Did anybody tell Vincent yet?"

"How could I tell him? He's home, asleep."

"I mean did anybody tell him about the stake-out?"

"It's hard to say. Jesus, you can't imagine what a tiger Vincent used to be."

"I still wouldn't want to be the one who crosses him."

"You wanna have dinner?"

"I ain't really hungry, Pop."

"Can I drop you?"

"I gotta get a cab and go back to the school. My car is still there."

"You done right tonight, Charley. That's all you gotta know, you done right."

71

Charley nodded. "That Vito was sure a crazy guy."

He was waiting for Mardell at the Latino bar on the street level when she came up the stairs from the club at eleven forty. She was surprised to see him. He asked her if she wanted a drink, but she wanted to get out of there. As they moved out to the street he said, "How come the rush?"

"That place is filled with gangsters. They make me nervous."

"Where do you get those ideas?"

"I can tell, Charley. I know the types. They are dangerous people."

"Dangerous? What about me? You said I was a gangster the night we met."

"Oh, I know about you. I had a long talk with Mr. Smadja. He told me."

"He *told* you?"

"He told me you were an absolutely crack salesman, that you could persuade people right off their feet. Can we have a little snack before you take me home, Charley?"

A snack for Mardell was a steak. "Won't a snack make you sleepy?"

"Oh, no. And I'm famished." He took her to Gallagher's.

While she was eating the steak, the Idaho

with the cottage cheese and chives, the side order of onion rings, and the green salad and he was just sitting there just adoring her, she said, "Do a lot of gangsters eat here, Charley?"

"How should I know?"

"That man, two tables on your right."

Charley looked. "That's a priest, fahcrissake."

"They wear disguises."

"Priests?"

"Gangsters."

"Where do you get your information?"

"I am rather well informed, Charley. The Buckingham Palace radio beam that keeps me well also keeps me out of danger."

"Listen, Mardell — I found out what Buckingham Palace is."

"You found out? Everyone knows."

"The Queen of England lives there."

"I know *that*, Charley."

"So? How come the Queen of England is taking care of your health?"

"I — I don't quite understand it. My mother arranged it. But thank heaven she does, and thank heaven it works."

Mardell invited him into her apartment that night, and the whole sky fell on Charley. It was as if he had never known a woman before. He had gotten laid for the first time when he was eleven — Vito's sister Tessie — but he had never met *the* woman. He knew his time would come. He wasn't in any hurry because he was sure it would happen. That was the way it was set up and, in the meantime, he fooled around a little but nothing that would give anybody any ideas. He generally did it outside the neighborhood, because if he knocked up one of the neighborhood girls everybody would make him marry her. When the Prizzis had made him Vincent's *sottocapo* and *vindicatore* he had turned into sort of an instant celebrity in the environment. Women who had probably just admired him from afar now all wanted to fuck him. But this Mardell! There was no way even to think about it. Nothing like it had ever happened to anybody in the history of the world. Everything fit, there was no problem like he had worried he might get himself lost in there. She keened, she wept, she made noises like a lunch whistle over and over again. He couldn't believe that he could ever have kept going the way he kept going. He had seen a television documentary once, about mountain climbers, and that was what he was doing, exactly what he had been doing, rappeling up and down Mardell, his mind like a bowl of Jell-O, his eyes rolling like dice in his head, the world and time and the work on Vito all wiped out because she loved him; she had said it and then she said it again: she loved him. After a couple of hours, they just couldn't move or talk and they fell asleep, holding each other safe from all the dangers.

# 11

Willie Daspisa had not only taken the oath of *omertà* but had made a fortune of money off the Prizzis over the years, plus he walked with a hundred and eighty thousand dollars of Prizzi money when he left. He owed them in more ways than one. If he had said he had escaped into the Witness Protection Program to get away from what he looked like, it would have made more sense than the word which got out — that he did it because he was scared by what had happened to his brother Vito.

After Willie finished singing for the U.S. Attorney, he said he wanted to have a meeting with George F. Mallon, the opposition mayoral candidate. Mallon's campaign was going so badly that he would talk to anybody.

Willie's singing led the Feds to pick up

fourteen key Prizzi shit people between Boston and Miami, and federal indictments were sought on one of the biggest banks on the East Coast for laundering shit money. The indictment, the arraignment, and the trial were slammed through like an express train. Willie and Joey came into the federal courtroom surrounded by U.S. Marshals. They testified against the fourteen Prizzi people. Joey worked like a Trojan to play it very straight, slipping only three or four times into his impersonation of the Sugarplum Fairy, but no cameras were allowed in court anyway so it didn't make any difference. Eventually everybody charged would be found guilty, and everybody would be absolutely clobbered by the judge.

Willie and Joey were kept in a midtown hotel suite off Broadway in the protective custody of a revolving team of U.S. Marshals until the government was ready to move them out to the plastic surgeons, the new pocket litter, and to their new homes and businesses, wherever that would be. While they waited, Mallon came in to listen to what they might have to say.

George F. Mallon was a multimillionaire with a head made of ferroconcrete, "your typical hardheaded businessman," as he often defined himself. He had made his fortune building tabernacles with their attendant dormitories, broadcast studios, gymnasiums, prayer halls, computer installations, office wings and underground passages, money crypts and strong vaults for the hundreds of evangelical television clergymen in the United States. These preachers instructed the country on such things as the Supreme Court and the Constitution; national and international politics; apartheid, democracy in the Philippines and Nicaragua, and Star Wars; Social Security and welfare parasites; narcotics-user tests for all Americans; the pressing First Amendment constitutional right for cigarette companies to advertise; abortion; selective diplomatic representation in China; and the need for prayer, if not abortions, in the schools.

Mallon undertook the construction of these innumerable holy cities by guaranteeing building costs in return for iron-clad mortgage guarantees and a percentage of the electronic pulpit profits. The operations had been successful from the first broadcast. His share of the salvation grosses had put him on the Forbes list among the wealthiest men in America.

He was a wispy, sandy-haired man with a wide mouth and narrow lips. He may have been a bungled-instrument delivery, because his head came to such a point that no hat, other than those designed by Dr. Seuss, would fit him. He was running against everything New Yorkers stood for: corruption, gambling, prostitution, narcotics, high-cost luxury housing, and racism. He had never been in politics before, but he had seen shrewd operators pretending to be country boys, climbing into their pulpits under television makeup, feigning simplicity, to be swept to national heights by crying out to the millions in the unseen congregations for the glory of the Lord and postmarked contributions. He knew what money could do in politics and he had an understanding with the more powerful of the electronic clergy that if he filled public offices they would see that the money and the glory were provided, although he had not taken into account that what had worked so well far out there in the golden fields of the American heartland might be incomprehensible in Gomorrah.

He seemed to be running against the grain of voter prejudice and opinion but, backed by his militant army's evangelical fervor, he cried out against abortion and for prayer in the schools, wishfully believing that the voters would be able to remember what he was saying while they nurtured what they so steadfastly rooted for: corruption, gambling, purer narcotics, high-cost luxury housing, and racism. These voter passions could have been offsetting the righteousness of George F. Mallon's zeal, he realized, since he was far behind the incumbent in every poll.

Monitoring Mallon's candidacy was a normal, even a routine part of Angelo Partanna's job. He maintained a surveillance of the Mallon campaign from the inside by making substantial cash contributions which, by dint of Eduardo Prizzi's solid political connections on all sides, allowed him to plant his people inside the Mallon organization — and elsewhere — to keep tabs on Mallon's plans as well as on members of Mallon's family on the remote chance that they could be used to change Mallon's mind on this campaign issue or that.

Mallon sat down opposite Joey Labriola and stared into his eyes. "You sent for me?" he said.

"Him," Joey said.

George F. Mallon turned to Willie, who was resting on a bed. "What's on your mind?" he asked Willie in as macho a way as a five-foot-six-inch man could assemble, which, in his case, was plenty.

"You wanna talk, get him outta here." Willie pointed to the U.S. Marshal.

"Would you mind?" Mallon asked the marshal.

"These men don't leave my sight," the marshal said. "Those are the U.S. Attorney's orders."

Mallon looked at Willie and lifted his eyebrows. Then he gave a short, abrupt shrug. He said, "Rules are rules."

Willie swung his legs off the bed and faced Mallon. "Did you see the mayor on television the night they gave it to my brother?"

Mallon nodded.

"Did you see that Lieutenant Hanly come out and report to him twice?"

Mallon nodded.

"You thought the cops did the job on him."

Mallon nodded again.

"No way. The Prizzi family done it while the mayor was practically looking."

Mallon was stonily disbelieving. "Why would the police allow such a thing? Your brother was entirely surrounded by almost two hundred policemen."

"They didn't want to risk anybody. Maybe they wanted to save on pensions and insurance."

"That is ridiculous."

"It was business."

"*Business?*"

"My brother probably tried to make a deal to get out of there. He was probably going to give the cops everything he knew about the

Prizzi's East Coast shit operation."

"*Shit* operation?"

"What you like to have the newspapers call controlled substances. *Capeesh?*"

"*Dope?* Narcotics?"

"But the only ones he could work a deal with was the cops. He made his offer to Hanly, the bagman for Brooklyn, so he had to go down."

"Go *down?*" Mallon was horrified.

Joey tittered.

"So the Prizzis sent Charley Partanna in to zotz him," Willie said.

"*Zotz?*"

"Partanna killed my brother."

"The mayor was involved in this?"

"He was standing outside, wasn't he? Hanly reported to him, didn't he? Hanly was inside the building with Charley Partanna, wasn't he?"

"How can you prove such a thing?"

"Not me. You. Grab Hanly. Make him talk. Talk to Munger, the task force sergeant who went into my brother's apartment first, before the cameras. Ask the television guys. They'll know if Vito was standing up when the cops went in. Then, when you got an airtight case together, pick up Charley Partanna. Charley blitzed my brother for the Prizzis."

When Willie finished talking to the U.S. Attorney, the Feds took the Prizzis' stash of $200,000 worth of blow — the cost price, not the street price. After he had finished costing the Prizzis so he could buy his way into the Witness Protection Program, and after he finished paying off Angelo Partanna for saying what he had said about Joey, he and Joey disappeared into the Program with new faces, new prints, and new paper. Before you knew it, they were gone. They were probably selling real estate or Buicks somewhere in Nebraska with both of them now born-again Protestant-Episcopals who could tell a great Irish dialect story.

# 12

When all the information was in, Angelo Partanna brought it to the don.

"Willie Daspisa did this to his own *family*?" the don asked rhetorically.

"He gave them the fourteen people. He threw one of our banks away — they're gonna be hit with a coupla million fine for washing the money which is itself enough of an *infamità*,

Corrado. But he gave Charley to that *premio di consolazione,* George F. Mallon."

"He can't touch Charley. He's got no evidence. Who's gonna talk? Hanly? The task force cop? Never. But just to make sure, sweeten them up a little."

Angelo nodded.

"But you are gonna know if Mallon gets anything heavy on Charley. As soon as you know that, we get Charley outta town. Mallon don't care nothing about Charley, he wants to nail the mayor so he can win the election. But he can't win the election unless he can railroad Charley. When Election Day is over, Charley will be in the clear. I'm gonna think up a way to keep him in the clear."

"I feel better, Corrado."

"Why did Willie do it? I can't believe it when he says he was scared because of what happened to Vito. Vito had nothing to do with him."

"You ever see Joey Labriola?"

"Willie's helper?"

"Yeah. A *finocchio.*"

The don's jaw dropped in disbelief. "A Sicilian?"

"Yeah."

"Willie's second man – Joey Labriola – is a fin*occhio*?"

"Yeah. I mean I seen him plenty of times — you couldn't miss it. I talked to Willie's wife after Vito caught it. She is outta her head because Willie ditched her for a man. I checked her story out, even. Joey told a hairdresser who works for us that him and Willie is as married."

"When?"

"When what?"

"When did you find this out."

"I knew for a long time."

"How come you didn't tell me?"

"Their operation was making money. Why should I tell you crappy little stories like that?"

"Then they just used the job on Willie's brother as an excuse to dump Willie's wife?"

"Yeah."

"They are *finished*!" The don's voice rose as his small fist fell upon the arm of the chair, making so heavy a sound it broke into the strains of Verdi's *Aroldo* which was playing in the background.

The don sat silently as if listening to sage advice, then he said, "Go to see Eduardo. Tell him I want him to get Willie's new address from the Program. If he doesn't understand everything right away, tell him to come to see me."

"Yes, Corrado."

"Is the wife a Sicilian woman?" the don asked.

"Yes."

"Bring her to me after we handle Willie and I will give her revenge. I will give her Willie's thumbs. They are *finished*!"

# 13

No one was able to find Willie and Joey. Eduardo, who was in charge of looking for them, wasn't on the street side of the family. Eduardo not only handled the family's money, but he was the mover of its heavy political influence, the area in which Corrado Prizzi had first tested his breathtaking conception of franchised international criminal operations.

Realizing that no single family could support the demands of politicians on a national level combined with the politicians' demands on the state and municipal levels as well, Corrado Prizzi showed the families the meaning of strength in union. Under his guidance all the families, each contributing a pro rata share according to the amount of political influence that had to be bought, acted as one constituency that was represented by Corrado's younger son, the eminent lawyer-financier, Edward S. Price.

Thirty-two years before, when Eduardo had been accepted by Harvard University, Don Corrado decided that he could serve the Prizzi family best if Eduardo changed his name. During the summer vacation before the first college term started, Eduardo had an operation in Switzerland done by a good plastic surgeon to work out new lines for his nose, which was too large and Arabic for a man whose name was going to be Edward S. Price and who was to go on to become a star graduate of Harvard Law School and then to earn his M.B.A.

Eduardo had come up legitimately through the ranks of the establishment. He just had access to a few billion dollars more to invest, which helped to further his career and his position in the WASP community.

Eduardo had large amounts of untaxed money to work with so, over the years, he had become the great, gray eminence of American politics; the man who had invented the Political Action Committee, which legalized political bribery; the man who had introduced the three-year presidential campaign by as many as eleven candidates roaming in different parts of the country at the same time to divert the public mind from what was happening in the republic; the man with the clout far beyond clout; the briber of governments.

Eduardo operated from the office of the president of the colossal international conglomerate called Barker's Hill Enterprises, which had thirty-one administrative vice-presidents who ran a staff of 7,390 lawyers, accountants, and managers in thirty-seven states and twenty-nine countries overseas, and which handled the supervision of the Prizzi family's investments. Eduardo washed the money, handled the politicians, judges, and law enforcement people, and supervised the annual rollover investment of the tax-free money that poured in from the Prizzi street operation and from its partnerships – franchises with other families – from gambling, narcotics, numbers, pornography, tax-free gasoline, stolen cars; extortion, pornography, recycled postage stamps; prostitution, labor racketeering, illegal meat and alcohol; high tech airline and air terminal robbery, counterfeit credit cards, watches, and currency – into Prizzi-owned insurance companies, defense and government procurement contracts, brokerage houses, toxic waste disposal monopolies, clothing manufacturing, downtown real estate in seventy-six cities, eighty-two hospitals, 1,723 parking lots, two film companies, 9.2 million square feet of shopping centers; hotel chains, electronics manufacturing companies, heavy construction, fifty-three banks, television stations, newspapers, and an airline, then depositing the clean money created by these enterprises into Prizzi-controlled banks and personal loan companies to provide a service for those citizens who preferred not to borrow from shylocks.

But even with everything he had going for him, Eduardo insisted that he couldn't find Willie Daspisa. A lot of times his people gave him credit for being a magician who kept pulling political influence out of the hat, but he knew the muscle he had didn't work all the time, that there was an unreliability about politicians that may have been the quality that kept them in office. Nonetheless, if he stuck to any single job and he pushed enough money across the line, it rarely happened that he couldn't get what he wanted. This time, the reason he couldn't find Willie was that he didn't try.

He was annoyed. After all the work and money he had put into persuading the mayor and the governor to cooperate with his plan to salvage Vito, in an election year, his brother Vincent had just thrown the whole thing away and instead had strong-armed the problem, which was the way Vincent approached everything.

Eduardo either didn't know or didn't want to know that Vito had fucked up and that Corrado Prizzi had authorized what Charley Partanna had had to do. Eduardo wanted to believe that Vincent had thrown his monkey wrench into delicate clockwork and that was that. Subconsciously, Eduardo may have hoped that the whole thing would blow up such a scandal that it would wipe out the entire Prizzi street operation. The family didn't need Vincent, that was Eduardo's belief. Vincent was a visible social embarrassment. Eduardo wasn't going to be the one to find the people who had — albeit unwittingly — done so much toward putting Vincent away.

"What is this, some kind of a radical movement in Washington?" the don asked Angelo Partanna plaintively. "They won't give us the names of two nothings after all we done for them?"

"Yeah."

"Whatta you mean?"

"Getting them two names out of the Program is nothing for Eduardo. If he wants something, they sell it to him."

"We'll wait."

"Corrado, my Charley is involved here. You're sure you explained the whole thing to Eduardo?"

"I got some ideas for Charley. He's gonna be okay. Maybe Eduardo really isn't trying on this one. But if I call him on it what is he gonna tell me? He's gonna say how tough it is and how he's working on it. Not counting Charley, it's not important enough to make trouble."

"It's important. It could put Charley on the hot seat. It could bust up the whole street operation of the family."

"How?"

"It can be turned into a big scandal if Mallon uses what Willie said to get elected. He's a reformer, the worst kind. He'll hound us until he has our top people in the can and he'll scatter the rest. It's a dangerous thing, Corrado."

"If anything goes wrong on Eduardo's end, it's because he's blaming Vincent. They don't understand each other. Let's give Eduardo a little more time. I'll give him a push. Then, if it looks bad, we'll have a real basis for coming down on him."

Angelo had been concerned about the relations between the two Prizzi brothers for some time. Things between them had been getting worse for the past few years. Vincent did not resent Eduardo's education — he understood they had to have a lawyer they could trust — as much as he resented that Prizzi money, made in the streets, had lifted his brother up to a place among the mighty of the earth. Eduardo had acquired the power to run the people who were supposed to have the power. Eduardo moved behind the Prizzi money like a snowplow. Vincent knew that, as the elder son, as the older brother, he should have had the place of precedence.

Eduardo, on the other hand, could hardly contain his contempt for Vincent as a ruffian. Vincent was that lowest human category in Eduardo's lexicon: a strong-arm. Eduardo didn't quite deplore the fact that his family had come up from the streets; that to a large extent — an extent which, in his mind, excluded himself and his father — they were common hoodlums. He could not see the need for continuing the street operations, no matter how much they earned. He could prove that the family didn't need that.

Angelo reminded Vincent as subtly as he could, while yet being sure that Vincent was getting the message, of the operational differences between the two brothers; they were at one of their regular thrice-weekly lunches at Tucci's — the only Italian restaurant Vincent had ever eaten in that gave him indigestion and that made him have to lie down for an hour after each lunch, chewing on Tums for the tummy. To Vincent, because of the zuppa di pesce di Pozzuoli, every lunch was a gourmet experience. For six years, Pop had been eating bread sticks for lunch at Tucci's.

It was a Neapolitan joint, fahcrissake, he told Charley. Pizzas or something they might understand, but they couldn't even make a good *sartù*. While Vincent's two donkeys, the Plumber and Phil Vittimizzare, shoveled the food into themselves at a table across the aisle like the famine was due to start tomorrow, Angelo spoke quietly to Vincent about how the don, after all, had spent his lifetime in total power from the day he started the lottery, three days after he had landed in this country fifty-four years ago. Vincent, Angelo said, was still a relatively young man and, although he should be stricken down for saying it, the plain fact was that the don couldn't live forever and when, in the mercy of God, he had to travel that road upon which all men must go, Vincent would have all the power on the real side, the Sicilian side, of the operation. The rest of the business was for a bunch of American college kids and lawyers anyway, Angelo said. Let them knock themselves out delivering the rest of the country to the family.

"Eduardo would be just another fuckin' lawyer if it wasn't for my operation," Vincent said in his cobblestoned Brooklyn English. "I got him the cash to buy all the action he has going. He hangs out with White House people and senators and tells them what to do. But anybody could be a big shot like that, all the money my operation dumps on him."

No matter how much Angelo talked, Vincent refused to see that he and his brother were two perfect halves of the new America, that they were paving the way together for the time when the third and fourth generation of Prizzis and their franchise holders would own more than thirty percent of the country. They were already the most important single part of the national economy. They generated more running cash, created more credit, more jobs, owned more businesses and controlled more financial institutions and industries, and influenced more government executive, legislative, police, and judicial decisions across the board than any other entity within the American dream on the simple formula of investing and reinvesting the billions of dollars of tax-free income they earned each year from the basest desires of their fellow citizens.

Angelo gave equal time to exploring Eduardo's side of the problem whenever his assignments from the don took him into Eduardo's rarified territory on the other side of the bridge and uptown in the heart of the high-rent district. Eduardo was more statesmanlike about the problem when Angelo presented it to him. "Vincent is a hooligan who thinks smashing people's heads has something to do with power. We could knock off the family's street business tomorrow and, in strict dollar terms, take only about a 9.24 percent loss on capital appreciation in the first three years and, after that, it would drop to less than four percent until, in twelve years, you would never know we had ever had a street operation. And that's on capital appreciation alone. We don't need Vincent's operation. It's an embarrassment. We should expand and develop the franchise operation and let the Hispanics and the blacks do Vincent's dirty work."

Eduardo was a miracle with an American-style nose — something that mystified, even awed, everyone in the family. He was fifty years old. He maintained a succession of young women, all called Baby, all graduates of Foxcroft and Bennington, who seemed to be clones of each other. Eduardo himself was entirely tailored. His hair was tailored. It couldn't possibly fit anyone else. His teeth, as well, were tailored, and his speech, and certainly his nose.

When he wasn't talking in family councils or at weddings in Brooklyn, his diction (tailored by phonograph records taken from videotapes of old William F. Buckley, Jr., television shows) had no basis in any other identifiable accent or speech pattern of any English-speaking country of the world. The sounds, although originally manufactured by someone else, were now Eduardo's own.

One morning, at an early meeting in Eduardo's four-floor mansion-apartment, which rose in fourteen-foot increments fifty-eight storeys above Fifth Avenue in New York, Angelo had come upon him in that more than adequately heated palace wearing an ankle-length ermine dressing gown whose edgings were piped in black mink. He was smoking a Davidoff cigar which, if he had bought it at retail, would have cost $12.40. Angelo, who was worried about what could happen to Charley if George F. Mallon weren't stopped in his tracks, brought up the subject of finding Willie and Joey, a matter which Eduardo eluded blithely, passing on it in his own interest.

"Let me tell you something else, Angelo," he said with that crazing diction. "Within twenty-five years nobody is going to remember that we were ever an immigrant family. The calendar takes care of everything. Think about the robber barons of the 1870s — the Astors, the Vanderbilts, the Rockefellers, the Mellons, and the rest. They all began as hoodlums. Look at the Irish and the Jews when they came to this country — all hoodlums. Everybody will forget where we came from — our names will become anglicized through marriage and by deed poll — and we'll be the leaders of society. As long as our money holds out — which, the way we're going, will be forever. In twenty-five years we'll be old money, and because we have more money than any of them we'll be more respectable than any of them."

# 14

Maerose Prizzi, Vincent's daughter, graduated from Manhattanville five months before the don made Charley her father's underboss. She was one of the women in the environment who felt drawn toward Charley because of his new status but not because she had always admired him from afar. If she knew he was alive before he became the family's underboss and *vindicatore* — and she vaguely thought she must have, because after all he was Angelo Partanna's son – in her mind he was just another family soldier.

Maerose had been educated by the nuns so she understood both elemental and sophisticated power. Perhaps this understanding derived from her being a student of her grandfather's bearing. She had a thirst for power that was worse than anyone's thirst for water after being stranded in a desert for a week.

She was eight years younger than Charley and she was a Prizzi, so they didn't turn up at the same places very often except at weddings and funerals.

When she graduated her grandfather gave her five points in the restaurant linen supply industry to assure her cash flow, and fifteen points in a going interior decorating business in New York, not only because decorating was what she wanted to do, but because the Prizzis owned two big antique reproduction furniture factories in North Carolina and a big upholstery fabrics company near Florence. In New York, and to her clients and acquaintances, she was known as Mary Price, niece of the industrialist-financier, Edward S. Price. No one in Brooklyn except her grandfather, certainly not her father, knew her *nome di battaglia*. When she graduated from college she had it made legal, using one of her Uncle Eduardo's law firms, but the name change was their little secret as far as her father was concerned.

She had a feeling for color; like her grandfather, she knew money, and by reading in the New York Public Library at night for two months, working with the craftsmen of North Carolina and Florence (who were sent to New York), and listening carefully to an elderly queen who had once been an Oscar-winning set dresser in Hollywood whom Angelo found for her, she was able to sound like a professional equal of her two partners. After a while she bought one of them out and dominated the survivor. Eventually she would be the sole stockholder of a thriving business that operated in New York, Beverly Hills, and London with a little help from her friends.

Maerose was a tall, gorgeous grabber who wore clothes with the assurance and style that Marilyn Monroe had worn her ass. She was the most classically Sicilian Prizzi of them all; a tall, cool aristocrat risen from a lump like Vincent and a line of Arab Greek Phoenician Sicilians; ancient, with a nose like a Saracen, passionate and unremitting, having the sexually inquisitive eyes of a Bedouin woman in purdah. She had the pitiless lower face of her grandfather — giving fear generously — but as the upper face emerged the slap of fear became the command of authority. She was the definition of serenity and total adjustment on her surfaces, but underneath, in the bottomless crevices of her boiling ambition, she was like the center of the placid earth, eruptive.

After Manhattanville, although she kept an unannounced apartment in New York on Thirty-seventh Street off Park, she lived at home with her father and her then sixteen-year-old sister, Teresa, in her father's house in Bensonhurst, two streets away from Angelo Partanna's house. She had an occasional fling with two or three clients in New York, but in Brooklyn she was strictly virgin territory.

When she was in New York, working with clients or seeing friends, she spoke with the grammatical elegance and diction of a woman on whom many years of higher education had been lavished. But when she was in Brooklyn, speaking to anyone — her father, her grandfather, anyone in her family because, outside her family and its extensions, she had no interest in having friends — she spoke the street language with a heavy Brooklyn-Italian pronunciation and phrasing.

Maerose liked to drink. That was anathema to her family so when she drank she drank in New York. There was usually a filled glass of champagne on the desk in her office, not for effect but because she was always pitched so that she needed a drink.

She had been thinking about what she really wanted to do since she had been twelve years old. She wanted to take over, run, and control both sides of her family's business operations: the street side where her father held the power and the political/investment side where her Uncle Eduardo lived. She by no means resented having been born a woman, holding however that acceptance only for as long as being a woman didn't block her way in taking over both sides of the Prizzi operation someday. What was implicit in her plan to take over both, and what therefore exalted it to an extreme, was one clear fact: she would need to replace her grandfather as head of the family. Her reasoning had refined itself into a fairly straight line. Her grandfather was an old man; he had to die soon. Her father was a sick man, he couldn't last too long. Eduardo was healthy and younger than her father so he would have to be taken from the inside. She was going to have to continue to cultivate Eduardo, as she had been doing since she was fifteen, and after establishing her own decorating branches in Palm Beach and Washington she planned to sell them to Eduardo, giving him an idea of how well she understood business. Then she would have her grandfather persuade Eduardo to take her into Barker's Hill Enterprises as his assistant, so that gradually, over, say, a ten-year period during which he got older and older, she could undermine him with her grandfather and any other key elements of the family's hierarchy.

Until she spotted Charley she knew the weak link in her plan was the street side of the family operation. Her father, the Boss of the street side, would never allow her, a woman, to have anything to do with the family business. It would be necessary for her to wear him down by going back at him again and again just to get him to talk about the intricacies of the street operation. Out of nowhere, Charley Partanna was made her father's underboss and *vindicatore*. Her grandfather respected Charley. Charley had a big future in the family. Charley was going to have a lot of power. Therefore, she was going to have to marry Charley in order to take him over and control the street side, which fed the money to Eduardo so that, when she took over from Eduardo in say ten or fifteen years, she would control both sides of the family's operations. Everyone would have to call her Donna Mae, the first woman in all history to stand at the head of a Mafia family. Maybe you had to be slightly mad to be able to continue to live with such an ambition. Any Sicilian man could have told her it was the impossible dream.

She had her first clear shot at Charley at her sister Teresa's seventeenth birthday party. Charley Partanna was there as a feudal duty. Teresa was a Prizzi. Everyone whose surname was either Prizzi, Sestero, Partanna, or Garrone was there; men, women, and children. At the proper time her grandfather, in a show of great age, would shuffle to the microphone and make a speech. The way he did this was whisper into Vincent's ear in Sicilian, then Vincent spoke it into the microphone in Brooklynese, dumping the words out of the depths of his stomach the way a piled wheelbarrow is emptied by upending it. Then the don would hand over the traditional annual birthday check of one thousand dollars to Vincent and would beckon Teresa to the stage and hand the check to her. She would kiss her grandfather, her father, and her uncle Eduardo, in the order prescribed by Vincent. The four-piece band, all bald or white-haired men who had been playing at the Prizzi parties for fifty-one years, would then play "Happy Birthday to You" and all the Prizzis, Sesteros, Partannas, and Garrones would sing out the words. Vincent would lead Teresa to the dance floor. The band would play "The Anniversary Waltz" and, after one turn of the floor, Patsy Garrone, Teresa's *fidanzato*, would cut in and then everyone would join in the dancing.

Maerose made sure she was standing next to Charley Partanna during the singing, so that when the band began the dance music all she had to do was to say, "Come on, Charley. Let's dance."

"Jeez, Mae," Charley said. "I ain't danced since Rocco's anniversary."

"Whadda you do on Saturday night? Raise pigeons? Come on!" She pulled him onto the dance floor. "Hey!" she said after a few turns. "You're a terrific dancer."

"I put $840 into Arthur Murray's to learn how to do it right."

"Yeah?"

"I do rhumba, samba, mambo, waltz, and fox-trot."

"No lindy? No Peabody?"

"I could always do them."

"I heard you went to night school."

"Not for dancing."

"How come I never see you around?"

He shrugged. "I'm around. You go to New York."

"Why don't you come over to the house for dinner?"

"Vincent sees me all day."

"How about lunch Sunday? Poppa has to eat lunch on the don's boat Sundays."

"Well—"

"Where are you living?"

"I took Vito Daspisa's place."

"Oh. Yeah?"

"It's a great apartment. If I didn't take it somebody woulda."

"Vito was certainly dispossessed, wasn't he?"

"Yeah."

"Did you have a decorator?"

"What?"

"That's what I do in New York."

"Yeah?"

"Why don't I decorate your apartment?"

"Whatta you mean?"

"I mean the right colors, so — no matter how you feel when you walk in or when you wake up — when you are there you feel better."

"That could be a neat trick."

"You might have to throw out all the furniture."

"Jesus, you want colored furniture?"

"The shapes have to harmonize with the colors. That's how we lock in the perfect."

They danced together every third dance because Maerose appeared beside him and asked him to dance. She was dancing with her father while Charley went to the john then stood with Pop drinking a root beer and watching the dancing.

"Whatta you," Pop said, "discovering Maerose after all these years?"

"She's gonna decorate my apartment. We gotta meet someplace. Dancing is holding a meeting."

"You are holding all right," Pop grinned. "But it ain't no meeting."

Maerose came out to Charley's apartment the following Sunday morning to see the layout. They toured the four rooms, she made a dozen pages of notes, and he gave her the keys to the apartment. "The whole thing is in your hands," he said. "It's up to you how you fill up this place."

"It's gonna take about four weeks, Charley."

"I'll move in with Pop."

"We gotta have meetings so I can lay out the progress reports."

"We don't need meetings. Whatever you want, do it."

"I wanna have meetings."

"Okay. How's about four o'clock next Thursday?"

"What's four o'clock? What's wrong with the nighttime?"

"I got things I gotta do."

Her voice went hard. "You gotta girl?"

He shrugged.

"You have to see her one hundred percent of the nights?"

"Whenever. Anyway, I got a thing I gotta do for Vincent in Baltimore."

"The Social Security thing?"

"How come you know about that?"

"I'm a Prizzi, remember? Whatta you think my father and me talk about, his golf?"

"Vincent plays *golf*?"

"I shoulda said polo. When are you going to Baltimore?"

"Ask Vincent. He didn't tell me yet."

"I want you to take me to dinner Thursday night." There was a hard edge to her voice; nothing absolutely insistent but hard.

Charley couldn't figure out what was happening to him. This was Corrado Prizzi's granddaughter. But she was acting very horny. What was he supposed to do? Tell her to get outta here? This was getting to be such a tricky situation that he knew it was going to make trouble somehow and that sooner or later he was going to have to talk to Pop about it.

"That would be great," Charley said reluctantly, "but I got another job to do. The family is giving me one of Eduardo's private jets and

106

I gotta go in and out, talking to the other families about putting all their people on the lookout for Willie Daspisa."

"Eduardo can't find him in the Program?"

"No."

"Okay, Charley. You do your work, I'll do mine. When you get back from whatever you gotta do I'll have your place finished and we can celebrate."

Maerose had viewed Charley as an instrument to further her plans until he made it absolutely plain that as far as he was concerned she shouldn't have even existed. She had never been brushed in her life. Men fell all over themselves if she smiled at them; men who didn't even know she was Corrado Prizzi's granddaughter. Charley was falling all over himself to get away from her. He treated her as if she were her Aunt Amalia, a woman in the Prizzi family whom he had to be polite to because she was the don's favorite daughter. Nothing like this had ever happened to her before. When she felt like it, she told men what she wanted and they delivered, then she let them get lost. She was a Prizzi and she had a life ahead of her. Charley would have been useful – not irreplaceable, but useful. Until he had turned her down flatly for dinner and everything else, he had been just another pleasant guy, a lightweight who could have been more useful than other men because she would have been able to build on him when she married him. Now she saw he was going to take a little training. The thought of his resistance was an aphrodisiac but it also cut about sixteen feet off her height.

She didn't believe he had another woman. From what she heard around, Charley had always played women very casually or in intense bursts that burned them up. Then, after a pause, he moved on. He was probably in the burnout phase now so she would let it run its course. But in another way, if he wasn't ever going to get the hots for her, it could be a problem. She was going to have to think about how to heat him up.

# 15

The first time Charley saw that something was definitely out of whack with Mardell was when he told her he was going to have to be out of town for a few days on a business trip. From the beginning he had figured she was a little nuts, the way he would have accepted it if she stuttered or had one leg shorter than the other. He had even taken the business she had handed him on the first night they met — about radio beams and Buckingham Palace — in his stride, like it was her idea of some kind of a joke. But when he said he had to go out of town, she went to pieces right before his eyes. She got a grip on his wrist that he couldn't break without hurting her, and she stared away from him, straight at the wall of her apartment, absolutely silent, tears rolling down her face.

"What is it? What's the matter?"

She wouldn't answer. Gently, but with great difficulty, he pried her fingers loose from his wrist. He pulled up a straight-back chair and sat beside her. They were both naked after two hours of making love.

"Talk to me," he said. "What is it?"

"You'll never come back," she said.

"Whatta you talking? I'll be back in three days. I'm going on the company jet. Just me and the pilots."

She shook her head, stared, and wept.

"Mardell, fahcrissake, where do you get ideas like this?"

"That's how my father left my mother. I can't talk about it, Charley."

It took him almost an hour to get the story out of her. It was about as lousy a story as he had ever heard. Her father had raped her when she was twelve then had disappeared. She got a baby out of the rape and her mother made her give the baby away for adoption. She had never understood any of it. Now it all came down to the kick in the head that, if Charley went away, he would never come back, either, and if he didn't come back she was afraid it would make her pregnant. They wept together. They went back to bed. Charley didn't talk anymore about needing to go away for a couple of days. He reorganized the trip so that he went in and out of New York on the jet, leaving early in the morning for the distant cities and coming back at night sometimes just in time to go straight to the Latino to pick her up after the show.

When Charley told her that he had to travel out of town, Mardell knew it was her chance to add to the dimensions of the character she was playing. It would help Hattie Blacker authenticate the case history of the woman Mardell La Tour. For her own purposes, it was becoming clear to her that with the amount of detail she had piled up over the past year and a half on the other case histories, and the detail she was accumulating as the mistress of a very successful *mafioso,* that someday she might want to write her own autobiography into which she had already built so much drama, conflict, and suffering.

Charley was wonderful about the all-out way he supplied the responses to the lines she improvised within the character. He deserved credit and, when the autobiography was published, she was going to see that he got it.

Charley saw the heads of six families on a day-trip basis. He brought copies of the pictures of Willie and Joey that had been taken on a family picnic to Indian Point three summers ago when the don had rented an excursion boat from the Hudson River Line and everybody had such a wonderful time that three of the girls who had gotten pregnant from the picnic had become brides.

"Chances are the pictures don't mean nothing, Charley," Sal Partinico said in Detroit. "You go in the Program, they change your face if you want it."

"We gotta start someplace," Charley said. "I want to get all the people in the country looking for them. Joey is very, very gay. Willie is a beast. The people can maybe put that together."

"If we can help, we wanna help," Partinico said. "But don't expect too much. There are a lot of beasts around."

When he got back to New York after the sixth meeting, Charley knew it wasn't going to work. "Willie probably looks like Calvin Coolidge now that the Program's plastic surgeons are finished with him," he said to Pop.

"We gotta light a fire under Eduardo. Things are too quiet with George F. Mallon," Pop said. "And Mallon's been working Davey Hanly over. They been giving it to Munger. They got depositions from the camera crew that followed Munger into Vito's — they ain't got nothing they can go on yet, but that could be even worse. Mallon could decide to pick you up."

"He ain't got nothing to go on, Pop. Not unless Davey or Munger spill."

"My inside people report out twice a day. I got two people on his campaign staff and one in his house. We gotta be ready. If anything happens, if somebody tells Mallon something — anything that lets him even begin to pin Vito on you — then we gotta get you outta town until the election is over and Mallon is sent back to building television churches."

Charley talked to Maerose the three times that she called the Laundry during the next two weeks to report progress on the apartment. Charley had always liked Maerose in the way the French feel about the British Queen: with a distantly feudal, hopeless fealty and devotion. She was Corrado Prizzi's granddaughter, which made her not only sacred but maybe even a little dangerous. The only time he had ever thought about her until she had come into his life as his interior decorator was as the little kid he remembered dropping bags of water on people in the street from the third floor of her father's house, which to Vincent was the funniest thing he ever saw until she dropped one on him. Her mother had been alive then, Charley remembered, or else Vincent might have lost his head and shot the kid.

Things had been developing differently lately. She wasn't a little kid anymore, and even Charley was beginning to understand that she was locking her teeth into him, and if he didn't do someting about it soon he would never be able to get her to let go. He would get back to Pop's house at night and find little notes from her saying she had darned his socks. Then, before he could get his hat off, she would phone him and ask him if he'd found the socks. He said, "Whatta you wanna sew socks for? They get holes, I throw them away."

She said, "Oh, Charley," and he imagined

she was shaking her head and smiling mysteriously.

She talked to his father about things he liked to eat and when Charley got home from the Laundry he would find a little note saying that there was some *sarde a beccaficu* in the refrigerator, or something like that. He would have to call her to thank her, and do it before he got his hat off, because if he didn't, she called him. She had other little presents for him. "Jesus, Mae," he would tell her, "I'm supposed to be the one who gives you the presents."

"So? Go ahead."

She gave him a cordless telephone for his terrace and a natural noises machine for beside his bed. It could make sounds like the ocean, waterfalls, or rain in two strengths. She gave him an electronic horse-race analyzer even though it was a known fact that he went to the races only once a year, bet only on sure-thing information, and never put a bet down away from the track because let-the-civilians-have-it was how he saw it.

He was forced to give her a bottle of perfume but it was the wrong kind. "Whatta you mean, not subtle?" he asked her on the telephone. "Either it smells or it don't."

He had to have lunch with her one Tuesday because she said she had to show him some fabrics, that it was a matter of what he was going to have to live with, but the lunch worked out okay because he was always on the lookout for new food ideas, and in the little Sicilian joint she found for them on the Lower West Side in New York he had stumbled on a menu item called a Crown of Thorns, a nest of spaghetti woven into an open-topped toque which had pointy olives and red pimentos imbedded in it. He was going to make it for Easter and send it to Father Passanante at the rectory of Santa Grazia di Traghetto in his mother's name.

Five days later, she talked him into going out to the apartment. The job was finished and she said they had to see it together. He had to say yes, even though it was the middle of the afternoon on a working day, because she was insistent about it on the telephone and, after all, if she had finished the job she rated it to have him look at the work with her. He also felt pretty good because Mardell had developed a much more positive attitude since that terrible afternoon when she broke down so pathetically because he said he had to go out of town.

Mae was actually glowing the way women are supposed to glow when they are pregnant, which she absolutely could not have been on his account. She had come out to the Laundry in a cab, but they switched to Charley's van for the ride out to the beach. She was wearing something white and filmy, which didn't seem right somehow for a raw November day as they drove through a sleet storm but, as Maerose saw it, it made her look like a bride, which was part of the central idea. Riding out in the van with the swivel seats, the two phones, front and back, the icebox, the stereo TV, and the pile carpet, she held a single long-stemmed red rose in her hand. "I should have it in my teeth," she said, "but we couldn't talk."

She unlocked the apartment door and threw it open upon the small entrance hall, which she had done in cream and beige. There was a V'Soske throw rug in eight shades of caramel and green on the floor. The Japanese prints on the walls had beige leather frames. The single half-wall facing the door held a bowl of brown and green silk orchids made in Taiwan by a Prizzi company. The lighting was soft.

"Hey," Charley said. "Is this the right floor?"

"Carry me over the threshold, Charley," Mae commanded.

Charley had gone ahead of her into the apartment. "Holy Jesus, Mae," he said, "Vito should see this. You really done a terrific thing here."

Vito's old furniture was gone. It had been picked up by the Salvation Army. Brand-new stuff like he had never seen in his life outside a two-dollar magazine had taken its place, all of it in beautiful, living color. "How'd you ever figure out how to do this?" he asked.

She was still standing outside the apartment. "Charley?"

He turned to face her.

"Carry me in," she ordered.

They stared at each other for many seconds before he understood what she was telling him. He crossed the room and lifted her into his arms. Jesus, he thought randomly, thank God she ain't Mardell, we'd go through the floor. I'm gonna have to work out with the barbells.

He kicked the door shut and stared down at her face, so close to his − her nostrils flaring in and out like a swan's wings, her enormous black eyes glazed with lust as she stared up at him − that he kissed her and she held him there, arms around his neck. It wasn't so bad was the sensation he got, so, being very healthy and in the prime of his life, he staggered with her into the bedroom, laid her down on the bed, and then he laid her.

It was tremendous, even if he did keep remembering Mardell in brilliant, passing flashes. It was like being locked in a mailbag with eleven boa constrictors. Several times he thought the whole ceiling had fallen on him. His head came to a point where it suddenly melted and flopped all over his shoulders and out all over the bed. His toes fell off. Then, when it was over, it hit him what he had done. He had laid a Prizzi and, depending on what attitude she took, what was he going to do about that?

# 16

To keep everything in the character of Mardell La Tour, Grace wrote a letter to Mardell's imaginary mother in Shaftesbury. She was painstaking. She wrote a draft then made a second corrected copy for mailing. She made up the address. The address wasn't important so long as it went to Shaftesbury, England. The letter would go to the dead letter office anyway.

Dear Mum,

I've been following the weather in England every day in the *New York Times* and it looks like you'll never get out of your wellies. Not that New York is any tropical paradise. I got a job selling fourteen colors of shoe polish at Woolworth's. Oh, yes, they have Woolworth's here, as well. The pay isn't tremendous. I still have to cut out soles made out of newspaper for the insides of my shoes to keep my feet dry. I moved to a nice new flat. I can hardly believe that Brenda and Joe were due to come back to work on Saturday but never arrived. The fact that they turned up on Monday, collected six pounds from the post office, and spent all of it on a piglet leaves me quite surprised. Drink is in the offing. But who will go bail for Joe this time? I now suspect that the yarn about the baby dying was all a louse. Sarah writes that Hugo woke up early one morning and wrote all over the walls with Sally's lipstick and emptied her Floris into her boots, yet he thinks he can go back there on another holiday. Emma Cole is not well and Arthur Shears has gone to Youngstown, Ohio, which is in America. I share your bewilderment over why Shirley Parker does nothing but wash blankets. I dreamed the other night that I did not get to play Father Christmas and it depressed me, although I don't know why. I carry with me wherever I go the fond memory of your sweet voice singing "The Death of Queen Adelaide."

Old England may weep, her bright
  hopes are fled,
The friend of the poor is no more,
For Adelaide now is among the poor
  dead,
And her loss we shall sadly deplore.
For though noble her birth, and high
  was her station,
Their wants she relieved without
  ostentation,
But now she is gone, God bless her!
God bless her! God bless her!
But now she is gone, God bless her.

In your next letter tell me if you can use
more of the wizard denture stickum which
is on sale here. Many American celebrities
wear it and boast about it on the telly.

With love and kisses,
Your daughter,

Margaret

XXXXXXXXXXXXXXXXXX

## 17

Maerose behaved much, much worse than Charley ever thought any woman could after a simple roll in the hay. As soon as they recovered from it, she carried on like she had lost her mind. She made plans for them to be together for every hour of the day and night when he wasn't either working at the Laundry or sleeping. She wanted to go to Baltimore with him when he went to Baltimore. She talked like she was on some kind of hop about how she had never dreamed anything could be so wonderful; about how she realized all at once that she had never been in love before in her life. She demanded to know if he loved her, then before he could answer, thank God, she wanted to know when they should tell Vincent and the don. Tell them what? Charley thought. That he had banged their daughter and granddaughter? Tell Vincent a thing like that and Vincent would zotz him. Charley tried smiling his way out of it, but he just didn't have the experience, he was totally outclassed. What had seemed to come out of left field was a big boulder Maerose had thrown at him. He didn't know how to defend himself, but she knew exactly what was happening.

Somehow they got dressed again and made it down to the van and Charley still hadn't committed himself, but he had no idea how he had done it. "Oh, Charley," she said as they were driving across south Brooklyn to Vincent's house in Bensonhurst, "Poppa is gonna be so happy."

"Happy?"

"A union of the two families who made the whole Prizzi presence in America possible. Corrado Prizzi's granddaughter and the son of his oldest friend, his *consigliere.*"

"Union?"

"Let's keep it a secret just a little while longer. Let's live inside this golden happiness for at least a few more days before we tell my father."

"Are you – are you saying we're engaged, Mae?"

She turned to him with her eyes shining. "Isn't that what you wanted? To share one life together, for me to have your children – isn't that what you wanted?"

"Jesus, Mae, everything happened so fast, I

can't really think. It's such a new idea to me."

"New? Then what were you thinking about when you – when you – took me – today? Did you think that I was just some–"

"No! No, no! But it happened so fast. I'm just saying yes – you're right – let's wait a little while before we tell Vincent."

"Oh, my darling."

Charley had been living at his father's house on Eighty-first Street in Bensonhurst while the apartment was being decorated. It was the place Charley thought of as home; where his mother had taught him to cook and to respect the meaning of cleanliness. While he waited for Pop to come home Charley made *pumaruoro o gratte* – baked tomatoes filled with anchovies, minced salami, capers and bread crumbs – and he laid out the cylindrical tubes of hard pastry flavored with spice, coffee, cocoa, and lemon for the cannoli, then filled them with ricotta cheese and sugar flavored with vanilla so he and Pop could have a light supper while they talked. He kept looking at the clock, then he went into the living room and vacuumed the tops of the moldings and the picture frames because the girl could never seem to remember to do that. Pop got home at about a quarter to eight. He was knocked out that Charley had made two of his favorites for dinner.

Charley didn't know how to talk about what was happening to him. He couldn't get it together at dinner. Afterward, they went into the parlor with the overstuffed chairs, the lampshades with the long golden fringes, the upright piano his mother used to play, and the beer steins lined up all around the room on the shelf that was the ceiling molding. When he was a small boy, Charley had wanted to take the steins down to study them up close, but his mother always said they looked better from a distance. He still looked up to see them whenever he came into the room.

"Pop?"

"Yeah?"

"I gotta talk to you."

"Whatsa matta?"

"I been going over it in my head and I can't hardly figure out how it happened, but Maerose Prizzi thinks her and me is engaged."

"En*gaged*?"

"Like engaged to be married."

"You and Maerose? Well, Jesus. That's terrific. What's the problem?"

"Pop, I — I don't know how — I mean — shit, Pop — one minute we hardly knew each other and the next minute she was saying how happy Vincent and the don are gonna be because we are engaged."

"Whatta you mean, Charley?"

"She decorated my apartment. So today it was finished so she said we hadda go out and look at it."

"So?"

"So we looked at it. It was terrific. Then she says, Carry me across the threshold, Charley. She was dressed all in white. She had a rose in her hand."

"Like a bride?"

"Yeah. So I lifted her up and carried her across — I closed the door — then I look at her and she's getting all hot so I don't think, I do what anybody would do, I take her in the bedroom and I — yeah."

"You mean—"

"Yeah."

"Maerose *Prizzi*?"

"Yeah."

"And now you are wondering why she says you and her is engaged?"

"Pop, listen—"

"What's wrong with being engaged to Corrado Prizzi's granddaughter? You'll inherit the earth! In a couple years you'll be Boss. Whatta you so edgy about?"

"I don't love her."

"So you'll get to love her. She's lovable! She's

gorgeous! She's talented! Tell me something she isn't."

"She isn't the woman for me. I'm in love with somebody else."

Pop's jaw dropped. "No kidding?"

"Would I kid you? About a thing as important as this? What am I supposed to do?"

"There are things about Vincent you don't know, Charley. When he was young. Believe me, Vincent can be an animal and he is all fucked up when it comes to honor. There was a guy who Vincent said peed on his honor who went to the movies. He sits in the back row. Vincent grabs the first thing he can find, a hammer, and he goes inna movie house. He hits the guy onna head with the claw end of the hammer and it goes right through. Vincent is very touchy when it comes to honor."

"It don't need to come to that."

"The way Vincent is out of his head about honor, that's how the don feels about gratitude, only he calls it disloyalty. If Mae tells them she is engaged to you, even if she doesn't say nothing about how she got engaged to you, then if you try to say you ain't engaged to her you're gonna have Vincent on your ass about honor and the don all over you about disloyalty. I don't know which is worse."

"I can't dump my main woman, Pop. There

are very tricky reasons."

"What reasons are better than staying alive?"

"I can't, Pop. I'm telling you."

"Who is this woman?"

"She's in the show at the Latino. She thinks I'm a salesman."

"What's her name?"

"Mardell La Tour."

"What's her real name?"

"Mulligan."

"Mardell — it's probably Margaret. Call her Margaret and see what happens."

"I like the Mardell better. She's English."

"English descent?"

"From England."

"Mulligan don't sound English."

"She oughta know. She's from Shahffsbree, England. You should see how they spell it. I looked it up. It's not near anything. Her father who left them when she was twelve died of leprosy, her mother told her."

"That's unusual."

"She believes it. Nobody can talk her out of it. I tell her the mother said the father was a leper just as her way of saying he was the worst. She don't even hear me."

"What has all that got to do with Vincent maybe putting out a contract on you?"

"Because she goes to pieces if I say I'm gonna

be away for a couple of days. I can't walk out on her. I'm afraid of what she'll do to herself. She's a little crazy, Mardell, but tremendous. A valuable woman. She can't cook, but she tries. I tell her, please, it's not you. I can't figure out how she fits in the bathtub she's got. I gotta tell you, Pop. She breaks my heart sometimes."

"She could be acting. Women are funny."

"No. She's always worrying. Jesus, sometimes she puts different-colored shoes on."

"She wears colored shoes?"

"I tell her, listen — if anybody gives you any trouble, I'll drop him off a bridge. Whatta you worried about, I say to her. She says, Who's worried, I'm not worried. I ask her, How come you put different-colored shoes on?"

"We gotta face up to this, Charley."

"It finally comes out that she thinks she isn't good enough for people. I couldn't even figure out what she was talking about. A beautiful girl, a funny girl, a smart girl in a lotta ways. How can she think she isn't good enough?"

"I knew a woman once who thought she was a shit because all her life her mother told her she was a shit."

"I grab her. I say — you want twenny-five thousand dollars cash? How many people you think you ain't good enough for are walking

128

around with twenny-five thousand dollars cash?"

"What did she say?"

"She said, How long is it since I put different-colored shoes on? I don't think like I used to think anymore. You know why? Because you love me and anybody who has a man like you to love them has to know they are good enough for anybody in the world."

"You got a problem."

"I ask her how come she forgets to eat if I don't tell her to eat?"

"She is certainly different."

"I think she is also a little crazy. She does a special number on radio beams you wouldn't believe."

"I'd believe it. You got George F. Mallon trying to work up a case to send you to the hot seat. You are fooling around with peeing on Vincent Prizzi's honor and Corrado Prizzi's idea of what is loyal. What you need is a good radio beam. You'll be lucky if you don't catch cancer."

# 18

For her Mardell characterization she developed certain quirks. As Mardell, she fell off chairs. She forgot to turn off shower baths. She told Charley she had left the apartment with a handful of change in her purse then had to walk through the night streets to the subway from the Latino on her stilt heels because she was too proud to ask anybody for cab fare.

Charley bawled the shit out of her, but he couldn't see that it made any difference. It wasn't until he figured out that she had to be worried all the time to behave the way she did that he let up on her. In the short time he had known her he paid more attention to her than he had paid to anyone else in his entire life.

He decided to make Baltimore a test case with Mardell. He knew he was going to have to go there for two days, and what made up his mind about taking a stand on such a nothing trip, as far as being separated from her was concerned, was a Sunday afternoon when he offered to go out and get her a pack of cigarettes and she began the blank-eyed stare and the crying.

"Fahcrissake, Mardell, I'm only going out for a pack of cigarettes."

"That's how my father left my mother, Charley. And he never came back."

"Then go and get your own cigarettes. Do I want cigarettes? I don't even smoke."

"That is what occurred to me, Charley. That is what set me off. I know you don't smoke and I am grateful to you for volunteering, but it reminded me of what my father did. You don't need to get me cigarettes, I'm going to give up smoking."

"Listen, Mardell, even you gotta know that I gotta have some consideration here. How do you think I feel? I tell you I love you, I do everything I can think of to prove I love you, but you don't want it. You don't trust me."

"Charley!"

"Never mind. Just lissena me. I am talking respect here. When I tell you that I gotta go outta town for a coupla days, I am telling you a very normal thing. It's business. I gotta make a living. I don't do what I'm supposed to do and I get fired. You want me to get fired?"

She bit her lower lip and shook her head.

"Now lissena me, Mardell. I gotta go to Baltimore on guvvamint business. My company has a big contract with the guvvamint."

"Baltimore? People commute to Baltimore."

"Not when they gotta do what I gotta do. I am gonna call you three times a day — in the morning when I wake up, at lunchtime, then after your last show at night. Two days then I'm home witchew again. Six long-distance telephone calls. Are you gonna accept that or are you gonna cry and show me you don't trust me and you don't respect me?"

She nodded. She rushed into his arms almost knocking him to the floor, the sofa catching him as he went down. "It's all right. Buckingham Palace says it's all right. It just came in on the beam."

Charley didn't remember sleeping much that night but he felt too weak to get out of bed and read a magazine. His whole life had changed. He was stuck with the two most beautiful women in the time warp. It was as if some science fiction magazine had pulled him inside. Maerose and the radio beam. The don's granddaughter and Buckingham Palace. It was too much from no matter where he looked at it. If Italian-type guys should marry Italian-type women, then he had got himself the most gorgeous, the smartest, the best-connected wop dame since Edda Mussolini. He couldn't think of anything tremendous she didn't have. She had class; she had education; she was so beautiful it made him dizzy; and how she had ever learned to do what she could do on a bed he didn't want to know. Jesus — blue-black hair, eyes like a sex-crazed belly dancer crossed with Albert Einstein, and a body that, although it was different from Mardell's, was a body so far beyond his lifetime ambitions for a body that it made him want to adjust his clothing whenever he thought about it.

How come I never felt like this about her before, he thought. Because I never saw her that way, that's why. If only I got started on Maerose before the time I took Gennaro Fustino to the Latino none of this would have happened. But Maerose Prizzi was too far beyond his reach until she decided she was going to have to make the first move.

Worse, he thought, sitting inside his cup and making it runneth over was Mardell, a mountain of loving movements. She had hair like radishes floating in honey, an ass you could play handball on, toenails like canoe paddles, and golden eyes that were so big and scared that sometimes when he looked at her he almost busted out crying. He lost himself in Mardell and he saw himself in Maerose. Maybe the Arabs were right with their rules that it was okay to have a couple of wives — but who told the wives? That was the kicker — who told the wives?

Mardell was the biggest problem but, in a mysterious way, she brought him satisfaction. What am I, he wondered, somebody who walks around feeling so guilty about something or other that I need Mardell to make things rough for me so I know I done my penance and I can feel better about everything? But what did he have to feel guilty about? He lived right. He had never done anything to feel guilty about in his entire life.

As he thought about Mardell's specialness, he came up with an answer. The reason he got so much satisfaction out of her was that he had to give her more than Maerose asked him to give. Not that Mardell ever asked for anything. She just stood there, whacked up and helpless. Anybody would have tried to help her. She was probably nuts. So she needed him.

He had read about that in a lot of magazines. He had always thought that the women in the magazine stories framed it that way so the guy would cave in. But Mardell didn't have the head on her to figure out things like that. Mardell just happened to be a natural problem. She was a freak, actually.

Maerose had read all the magazine stories and had figured out how to use them. She was almost too sane, but the main difference between her and Mardell was that Mae was insulated against the shocks of the world and Mardell had nothing but him to protect her.

He decided he knew two things: one, there was absolutely nothing good about the entire situation; two, he didn't see how he was going to get out of it without totaling Mardell. He was in an impossible situation. Two women were out of their minds about him. Two terrific women were breaking their hearts because they were so in love with him they couldn't stand it. He couldn't save both of them. He was going to have to choose one or the other, but his terrible anxiety was for Mardell. Maybe for Maerose, too, but more for Mardell, because he knew in his heart she was capable of killing herself if she lost him.

# 19

Charley's work in Baltimore was to put the fear into the three Social Security administrators who came over from Washington for the meeting and who had already been bribed and handled by Pop.

From the time he had been a kid, Charley had generated fear. At first it wasn't something he had known he was doing, and after a while it became just another skill; a part of policy. If people weren't doing right, they felt the fear and tried to shape up. The fear made people judge Charley's seriousness about his work and made them more respectful. His father had made it clear to him that a man who is feared does not receive challenges to his honor and that the shield that fear creates covers everyone who is close to him. So, as he saw how hosing out fear could save time and get better results, he polished his techniques and encouraged his own awesome reputation. Techniques or not, Charley was basically a frightening man without even trying, forget the techniques, except maybe to women. His job in Baltimore was to frighten the three SSA civilians so that they wouldn't be able to open their mouths if anything went wrong, which, because Pop had set it up, could not possibly go wrong.

Pop had been working on the SSA people for four months and now everything was ready to go. The don wanted Charley to talk to the people and hose the fear all over them so that they understood in their hearts that if they fucked up now that they had made a deal, they were the ones who were going to have to go down.

They had the meeting at the John Arundell Hotel in Baltimore, and for the first time in his life Charley ate turtle soup. The SSA guys were tickled that he liked it so much. They said it was native American cooking. Charley was amazed; he thought hamburgers were native American cooking. "What is the TV dinner," he asked them, "if turtle soup is native American cooking?"

In the meeting Religio's man worked with two of the SSA technicians while Charley set up the delivery arrangements with the third for the 19,556 Social Security checks for an average of approximately $530 a check, to be collated by state and city and street of destination as they came off the presses. The computer would blank out while they were coming off, then wake up again when the series was finished. When the beefs started to come in from the SSA recipients who hadn't gotten that month's check and the government backtracked on it, all they would find out was that somehow the computer had spun its wheels and had not printed that particular run of 19,556 checks, out of millions of checks. With any luck, they would decide the checks had never been printed at all. So they'd print them up again and send them out.

The franchisees would have to move fast to turn the checks into cash before anybody figured out that the government had been ripped off when the canceled checks started to come back. The three SSA guys would have to sweat out what they called mass loss procedure, but the way it turned out, nobody caught on.

The checks were shipped out at government expense, marked as paper stock, to the distribution point Pop had set up in New Jersey. From there the checks went out to the Prizzi franchise cities around the country, where they were cashed in 819 banks. The Prizzis made a gross of $10,335,000 on the deal, a good score when it was considered that they had to pay out only $337,843 for the cooperation of the three SSA people, but it really was a pittance compared to the taxes they had avoided and the money they had pocketed on six or seven hundred billion dollars' worth of tax-free business they had done over the years because they had trained the politicians to pretend it would be dishonorable to collect taxes on illegal money earned by the citizens. Charley was beside himself with admiration. It was the don's own dodge.

When he got back to the Laundry, Charley told Vincent and the Plumber about the turtle soup, but they didn't believe him.

# 20

Three weeks after Charley met Mardell at the Latino, the regular show change rolled around and she was booked with the other five showgirls and the headliners into one of the three Prizzi hotels in Vegas. She was almost hysterical when she told him the news because she found that the best way to handle the Mardell situations was to fall deeply into Stanislavsky's teachings and let the Method carry her reaction to new and threatening situations.

"What are we going to *do*, Charley?" she asked him, swinging on the lapels of his jacket, rounding out her performance as Mardell La Tour even though, during the two days he had spent away from her in Baltimore, she had had a wonderful time in New York, lunching with Freddie, ardent Freddie, going over her notes on Charley excitedly with Hattie Blacker, and dissuading Edwina from moving in with a large colored man on Washington Heights.

"I can get out there every weekend," Charley said tentatively.

"No!"

"I work in New York, Mardell. You know that. The weekend is the only time."

"Then I'll die."

"Come on!" Jesus, Charley thought, at first it may be very satisfying to have two beautiful women so crazy about you, but after a while it gets to be a real pain in the ass.

"From Vegas they send us to Miami, then to Kentucky, then to Atlantic City. It will be twelve weeks before I get back here. I can't live through that." She had no intention of leaving New York to go to that awful Las Vegas. The season was about to start in New York. Everyone who was anyone would be there: Freddie especially.

She immersed herself in the Method, thought hard about her beloved dachshund, Pepper, who died at age fourteen, and tears filled her eyes. "This is why I never went with anybody, Charley. No one until you. Never. We should never have gone to lunch that first time. I thought you would be safe *com*pany because I thought you were a gangster — how could I ever have thought you were a gangster? — but you became so dear to me, so sweet, that before I knew it I let my guard down and I was in love with you for the rest of my life. I'll never survive it, Charley, if I have to go to Las Vegas and you have to stay in New York."

"Ah — what the hell, Mardell — why should you work? I got enough. You can stay right here in New York and everything will be the same except you won't needa go to work every night."

"I couldn't do that."

"Why not?"

"I'd be a kept woman."

"So? It's better than working."

"I simply couldn't. I'm going to start tomorrow morning and find myself a job in New York."

"What can you do, except in show business?"

"I could be a model."

"You might be a little big to be a model.

Lissen, lemme work on it. Lemme get back to you. I'll figure something out."

The next morning Charley asked Pop who they knew in show business. Pop said, "Name it, you got it. Whatta you need it for?"

Charley told him a slightly revised story of how the Latino was going to transfer Mardell to Vegas but how he had decided he would rather not have her leave New York so he wanted to find an agent who could get her some local work.

"I'll tell Juley to hold her over in the new show until you can get something set, but while all this is going on, are you thinking about Vincent and how he looks at his daughter's honor?"

"I'm thinking about it."

"He is a *maniaco*, Vincent. You don't know."

Mardell refused to be held over. "Absolutely not, Charley. Every girl on the circuit would say that I am a dyed-in-the-wool gangster's moll, that my torpedo — or whatever it is they call people like that — just told the management that I had to stay in New York and they had to do it."

"You're making it very hard, Mardell."

"Anyway, how is it you are able to do that?"

"My Uncle Harold works in the agency that

142

books the shows into the Latino. It's really a little favor for him. Don't take it so big."

The Caltanissettas, a New York family that operated out of East Harlem and had brought extortion, arson, and faked malpractice litigation to a fine art, were franchisees of the Prizzis in the counterfeit credit card action. They owned a large theatrical booking agency and they sent Charley to Marty Pomerantz, a small independent agent.

Pomerantz was a mild, little guy who parted his hair in the back and who brought his vegetarian dog to his office on the third floor of the old General Motors Building at Fifty-seventh and Broadway. He had a sixty-six-year-old secretary who wore elastic stockings. Pomerantz had been around the business for a long time. Charley laid out the proposition to him.

"She is a beautiful girl with showgirl experience at the Latino and with Miss Bluebell in Europe, all over Europe."

"Miss Bluebell is very classy."

"The idea I got, I don't want her to work outta town. She strips down great and she could score big as a novelty act."

"It costs to build an act."

"Whatever. Also, she'll pay you the regular ten percent plus — just between you and me —

I'll pay you ten percent more."

"I just keep booking her in the metropolitan area?"

"Just so she can get home every night."

"Burlesque is okay?"

"Why not?"

"All right. Lemme look at her. Then we'll find somebody who can design an act."

It all worked out, and even including musical arrangements, costumes, the two piano players, transportation, and the extra ten to Pomerantz, it only cost Charley six hundred dollars a week and some change.

But he knew he hadn't solved the real problem. Now that she had decided they were engaged, Maerose showed up at his apartment about three nights a week and he had to work Mardell in around her on the other nights. He must have been doing something right. Both women seemed to be very happy, but the day was going to come when he was going to have to have the cake or not eat it.

There were three weeks until Election Day.

# 21

George F. Mallon knew he was running behind the mayor in the election race. The media reported it that way; the polls proved it. Every sampling his public opinion people took showed that he was doing absolutely the opposite of what the voters of the City of New York wanted when he campaigned against corruption, gambling, narcotics, high-rent luxury housing, and racism. He soft-pedaled his antiabortion and school prayer messages until they were almost nonexistent. He gradually persuaded his backers in the Electronic Evangelical Church to go silent in his support. He knew that somehow he had to effect an about-face. There had been a time when he had wanted to wipe the hoodlum element from the city entirely, but he was beginning to understand how much New Yorkers depended upon them for their comforts and conveniences, and he was starting to see that maybe a large dollar could be made there.

The wanton murder of Vito Daspisa, while

the New York Police Department and the mayor of the City of New York simply looked on, seemed to have something to do with the way money was made in high office. But as a religious leader, Mallon could not believe that anyone would really seek to profit from such a brutal killing.

Surely, George F. Mallon asked his closest counselors, even the people of New York would not endorse something like that when they went to the polls on Election Day. His aides, recruited from tabernacles in North Carolina and Georgia, agreed with that. The conclusion was that the voters would admire the mayor for protecting his assets, but they most certainly would not condone the outright murder.

It was agreed that, if they could build an airtight case against the Charles Partanna whom Willie Daspisa had identified as his brother's killer on behalf of organized crime in New York and on behalf of its partners – the mayor and the police – and if this were sprung on the public in the week immediately prior to the election, they would have created George F. Mallon's single and best chance to win the mayoralty.

Trusted U.S. Marshals would have to make the Partanna arrest in the company of several hundred media people and their television cameras at dawn of the Monday eight days before Election Day, to electrify the voters of the city by exposing the mayor, George F. Mallon's opponent, as being a part of the organized crime that was inflicting murder, gambling, and narcotics on the City of New York. If, on the other hand, they were to demand the arrest of Charles Partanna before they had built an absolutely airtight case against him, then the mayor, the police, civic leaders, and the media would all accuse George F. Mallon of attempting to deceive the voters by exploiting their fears in making wild charges out of desperation to get attention for his cause.

"We have five, possibly six, witnesses who can establish the case for us," Mallon said to his staff at a secret meeting in the Disrobing Room of the Church of the Immaculate Recorder, an evangelical holding company which was preparing to go public in an offering of shares and debentures on behalf of the combined electronic churches of America, in whose stock issue George F. Mallon was a founder-partner. "We have Lieutenant Hanly and Sergeant Munger of the Police Department. Former Detective Sergeant George Fearons, and that NBC television camera crew. They'll break under questioning, so I say, let's bring them in."

"These people should be secretly photographed, and their voice recorded, while you are interrogating them, Chief," said Clarette Hines, Mallon's shadow Secretary of State. "We can cut that into a terrific little fifteen-minute documentary and into a series of two- and three-minute spots for flashing on the morning talk shows."

Mallon cross-examined police Lieutenant David Hanly first. The mayor and the Department had to allow Hanly to talk to Mallon. If they refused, it could be more embarrassing in the end. Nobody was worried about how Hanly would handle himself, and Pop made sure of that by seeing that a golden envelope was passed to Hanly. When it came around to Munger, Hanly coached him until he was cross-eyed, and the mayor passed the word down that if he did right his captaincy would be restored.

Under Mallon's questioning, Hanly readily admitted that he had been on the scene before the actual murder of Vito Daspisa had happened.

"Why were you there, Lieutenant? Surely your duties as head of the Borough Squad did not require that you attend the stakeout of a fugitive?"

"I was on my way home. My radio unit picked up the action. One of the policemen murdered by Vito Daspisa was a coworker of mine and a good friend. I wanted to be part of bringing in Daspisa."

"But of all the police officers there, as soon as you arrived on the scene, you, rather than any other police officer, went to the apartment in that building where Daspisa was holed up, and *you* spoke to him."

"Vito sent down a written message. The TV cameras caught it as it came down from his window. He specifically asked for me."

"There is television footage showing you entering the building alone, describing what you were going to do, and showing you as you came down to the street after talking to Daspisa."

"I tried to speak to him. I didn't have any luck."

"I put it to you that you and Daspisa talked about the narcotics business."

"You couldn't be more mistaken, Mr. Mallon."

"Then what *did* you talk about?"

"He said he wanted to talk to his brother Willie."

"But when you came down after — as you say — *try*ing to speak to him, you reported immediately to the mayor, did you not?"

"I don't remember that."

"The meeting was recorded by the network

TV cameras, Lieutenant."

"He was in charge on the scene. I told him the suspect had refused to talk to me."

"But he refused to talk to you and Detective Sergeant George Fearons was sent in."

"That's right."

"You knew Detective Fearons?"

"Not personally, no."

"But you and Sergeant Munger, who was in charge of the task force, did brief him in the lobby of Daspisa's building and issue an assault rifle to him?"

"No."

"You didn't brief him?"

"We didn't issue him any assault rifle. Fearons was a psychology major. He went up to apply psychology on Daspisa."

"He identified himself as Detective George Fearons?"

"Why would that be necessary? He was a police detective. He was known in the Department as a psychologist."

"I put it to you, Lieutenant, that George Fearons retired from the New York Police Department three years ago and is now a professional eater in Montreal."

"A professional eater?"

"He eats enormous continual meals in the windows of Montreal restaurants for a living."

"That's impossible. He is too young to retire and he is too thin to ever have eaten like that."

"I put it to you that the man you briefed was not George Fearons but Charles Partanna, a Mafia hit man who, following your briefing, went upstairs to Vito Daspisa's apartment and shot him dead."

"It was Detective Fearons that we briefed. And after Detective Fearons came back down from the Daspisa apartment, Sergeant Munger and his task force went up and, after forcing entry to the Daspisa apartment, shot him in self-defense after he had opened fire on them."

"Do you intend to stick to that story, Lieutenant?"

"That is what happened."

"If you intend to stick to that story, you are going to have to tell it again in a court of law under oath. That is all, Lieutenant."

The cross-examination of Ueli Munger supported Hanly's statement.

Chester Singleton, the NBC cameraman who followed the task force into the apartment, told Mallon's examining team that it was his impression that the task force had not had to force entry into the Daspisa apartment but that the door was wide open. Also, he said, he had a clear memory of seeing Daspisa in several pieces on the floor, walls, and ceiling of the living room of the apartment, before the task force began to shoot at him as he lay on the floor.

After Singleton left the examining room, Mallon and his aides came to their unanimous decision: there was no doubt in their minds that Hanly and Munger had been lying. The fact that Fearons was in Montreal and could be brought to New York to testify that he had not left Montreal for three years would be damning evidence, which would permit the District Attorney to move in on Hanly and Munger and crack them wide open. Singleton's testimony would establish that Daspisa had been shot to death by someone who the New York Police Department claimed was George Fearons but who could not be. The lawyers on the staff agreed that there was enough evidence to seek a sealed Grand Jury indictment of Charles Partanna and that the facts of this indictment should be made public on the Monday eight days before the election. At that time George F. Mallon and his team of U.S. Marshals and the accompanying media would move in to arrest him.

# 22

Vincent called a meeting with Angelo and Charley Partanna. He was reading a newspaper when they came into the office and sat down. "Listen to this shit they hand out," he said indignantly. He read aloud, " 'The Presidential Commission said today that Asian organized crime groups threaten to become a fixture in America's mainstream economy.' We are taking out five hundred billions a year and all of a sudden this nickel-and-dime buncha Chinks are a threat. Lissena this, fahcrissake — 'The Bamboo Gang came to the United States from Taiwan because of the pressure being placed upon them by Taiwanese law enforcement.' Did you ever hear such shit? The entire Taiwan government is a hunnert percent hoodlum. It was founded by the Green Gang outta Shanghai. The Taiwan president is a top Green Gang hoodlum, Chiang Kai-shek. So why do they hand out shit like this?"

"We used to make buys from them," Pop said.

"Anyway, that ain't what I got you in here for. Charley, you remember Little Jaimito Arrasar?"

"The South American guy, the supplier."

"He is short-weighting us. I want you to fly to Miami and give it to him."

"Jaimito moves around with four bodyguards," Pop said.

"How do you wanna handle it, Charley?"

"Send the Plumber and Phil down ahead of me to lay out where he goes and where he'll be."

"Five guys. If even the three of youse jump them, it's gonna make a helluva racket," Pop said.

"I can handle it," Charley said. "I don't need them two for the hits."

"Five guys? No way."

"I can do it with a coupla cyanide grenades."

"Where you gonna get cyanide grenades?"

"Religio's outfit can make them or steal them from the Army. Just have somebody in the high tech unit deliver them to me on the plane so I don't have to take them through security at the airport."

Vincent sighed. "I can't understand it. Jaimito is clearing a nice steady five and a half millions a week but he has to short-weight us."

"A thief is a thief," Pop said.

154

"Jaimito's a nice little guy," Charley said, "so suppose he don't know that his people are short-weighting us. I mean, it could be policy in Colombia before it ever gets to Miami. If we zotz Jaimito we could be hitting the wrong guy."

Vincent and Pop looked at each other in bewilderment. "What's the difference?" Vincent said.

"The thing is they'll get the message, Charley," Pop said. "The next time they won't offend such a big customer. The whole goodwill thing would be threatened."

While he waited for the nod from Miami, Charley worked with Religio's technicians on locks and electronic release mechanisms, so when the Plumber called in and said everything was ready, Charley was ready.

He flew down from New York with Mardell. She had put so much pressure on him that he had to take her. She wasn't working. She was waiting for the act to be written, so she couldn't rehearse yet, and the costumes were still being made. (Also, although she didn't tell him that, the New York season had not gotten under way yet.)

When he told her he would have to be away for a couple of days, she stopped eating. She ran a fever of 104 by taking the medicine that Edwina always took when she wanted to drive her temperature up. She sat in her underwear and stared at the wall. It was a big pain in the ass. Then after he told her she could go with him to Florida, he had to handle the other end of the deal: Maerose.

While Mardell packed, Maerose spent the night at the beach and she got up at dawn to make him a big breakfast so he would know she cared and would be grateful. After the big breakfast, she ran him back to the bed and held him in such a scissors lock around his waist that he thought she wanted the whole breakfast back. She packed his suitcase for him, but thank God she had an early appointment at her office so she didn't insist on riding to the airport with him.

He was driven to the plane by Zingo Pappaloush, his prospective father-in-law's own driver, so he certainly couldn't take Mardell out to the plane in the same car. He had a limousine service pick Mardell up and he got away with it because she knew he lived all the way out in Brooklyn. They had assigned seats on the plane, so that was where they joined up and where a short man in white coveralls carrying the airline's name across the back walked down the aisle and dropped a small package into Charley's lap.

"I'm so excited, Charley. I've never been to Florida."

"It's very nice."

"I'm going to have to buy a bathing costume."

"A what?"

"A bathing suit."

"So long as you don't wear it."

"What do you mean?"

"I don't wanna be killed in the riot when they see you come out in a bathing suit."

She gave him a playful shove, which numbed his arm and almost knocked him into the aisle. "Oh, you!" she said happily.

"We are in a nice hotel at the best end of the beach, so anything you want during the day, just pick up the phone and tell them."

"Where will you be?" she asked anxiously.

"I gotta work. I am a nine-to-fiver just like anybody else. I kiss you goodbye in the morning and I go out. Then I come home and we do whatever you wanna do."

"It's all right, Charley. I feel secure."

Jaimito was at the Bolívar. The Plumber had fixed up Charley's reservation. At eight o'clock in the morning, Charley installed himself in the penthouse suite across the hall from Jaimito's apartment; they were the only two apartments

157

on the floor. He changed into a T-shirt and a white jumpsuit — which was what the hotel's handymen wore — and at a quarter to ten he sat in a chair and looked through the hole he had bored in the door, until Jaimito and the four men left the suite and went down the hall to the elevator. Charley waited ten minutes, then he went across the hall and removed the lock from the front door of Jaimito's suite. He replaced it with a remote-control lock and tested it. He went into the suite and put identical locks tied to the same circuit box into the sliding door to the terrace and the only other inside door, which led from the living room to a hall that gave access to the bedrooms.

He hung a DO NOT DISTURB sign on the doorknob, put a gas mask over his nose and mouth, got up on a light aluminum stepladder with some difficulty because of the leg he had got out of the war, and fixed the grenades to each of the chandeliers at either end of the room. They were suspended on release wires that were controlled from his circuit box. Upon being released, the grenades would drop to face level on copper wire, and that would pull the pins in the grenades, liberating the cyanide gas.

While he worked, the other door opened and a small blonde with black eyebrows came into the room wearing a short nightgown. She was about nineteen, and very wise-looking. The Plumber's survey had missed her. "Whatta you doing up there?" she said sharply. "Why you got that thing on you face?" She walked over beside the ladder and stared up at him.

He kicked her on the point of her chin with his good leg, hoping he wouldn't fall on his ass. He climbed down from the ladder, stripped off her panty hose, and used them to tie her hands and feet together behind her back. He dragged her along the bedroom hall to the second bedroom, jammed a big ball of Kleenex into her mouth to keep her quiet, and dumped her in a closet. He returned to the living room and cleaned everything up before he took the DO NOT DISTURB sign off the door and went back to the apartment across the hall at twelve ten in the afternoon.

He waited in the apartment across the hall. At three twenty he could hear the five men returning down the hall, making Spanish noises like a pet shop in a fire. Charley broke the electronic connection with the door to the suite and thus released the lock, so when the first goon got there he said, "Hey, boss, the maid forgot to lock the door."

"You guys go in first," Jaimito said in Spanish.

Charley watched through the peephole as all

five men disappeared into the suite and shut the door. He activated the remote electronic locks on all three doors. Then he triggered the chandelier mechanism that released the grenades and pulled the pins. He waited twenty minutes, then he slipped the gas mask over his face and went into the apartment. The five bodies were sprawled around the room, on chairs and on the floor. Charley released the lock on the terrace door and opened it wide to let the ocean breeze ventilate the room so that when the night chambermaid came in to turn the beds down, the air in the room wouldn't make her sick.

He was back at his hotel with Mardell at six thirty. Mardell was preoccupied. Her voice sounded far away.

"Did you have a good day at the office?" she asked.

"Very good."

"That's nice."

"Did you have a good day?"

"I had lunch at the pool." She spoke listlessly. "Some men wanted to join me so I picked up a priest and that kept them away."

"Did he give you any trouble?"

She tried to laugh but she had something else on her mind. "No. Where shall we have dinner?"

They ate a big seafood dinner at a place the bell captain recommended.

"How come you're so quiet?" Charley said.

"I'm eating."

They got back to the hotel early. While they were getting ready for bed, Mardell decided to talk.

"A woman called you today."

"Yeah? Who?"

"She said her name was Maerose Prizzi."

He was stepping out of his trousers and he had his back to her.

"She wanted to know what I was doing in your room."

"It must have been some crazy woman."

"She said she was engaged to be married to you."

He turned to face Mardell, in his boxer shorts and Paris garters. "She said that?"

"Yes."

"She had no right to say that. I never said I was engaged to her."

"Who is she, Charley?" Mardell asked as if she were talking over the recipe for a ham sandwich.

"She's the granddaughter of the man I work for. She's much younger than me."

"How much younger? About twenty years? Is she about ten, Charley?"

"Listen — I know her all my life. I mean, she's had one of those schoolgirl crushes from way back."

"Then you are not engaged to marry her."

"Engaged? To Maerose Prizzi?"

"You've got to arm me with all the facts, Charley."

"I don't get what you mean."

"She said she was going to call me when we get back to New York. She wants to come to see me."

"She's behaving like a kid who is trying to make trouble! I mean, I'm going to have to talk to her grandfather about this. You certainly don't think I could bring you with me to Miami if I was engaged to another woman."

"That has happened. Men do things like that."

"Mardell — she's like a *rel*ative to me." He gave God a chance to strike him down. "I mean, like a second cousin — or a kid sister."

Mardell got into bed, took two sleeping pills, shaking them out of the vial elaborately, snapping out the light on her night table and lay on her side, facing away from the other side of the bed. "Don't talk to me anymore, Charley. The only way to settle this is to sit down, all three of us, all together."

Charley jammed himself into his pajamas and stamped off into the living room. He dropped into a chair, lit a big cigar, and stared at a racing form. He suddenly knew what Vito had felt like when he threw the bolts on that door and flung it open. He was a condemned man.

# 23

Maerose appeared to be looking out the window of her office, which faced a pleasantly landscaped backyard behind the double brownstone her company occupied in Turtle Bay, but she was really looking into her mind and seeing Charley. Her face was blank, her eyes were like the Xs in the eyes of a cartoon character after it has been wonked over the head with a fact of life. She couldn't believe it. She had called the Prizzi hotel in Miami Beach, she had asked for Mr. Charles A. Partanna, and a woman had answered. Her reaction had been one of impatience when she assumed the goddam telephone operator had given her the wrong room. She found out. The woman's voice, very British, wanted to know who was calling Mr. Partanna, and Maerose's reaction had been, who the hell was this, asking her that question in that tone of voice as if Maerose didn't have any right to call Mr. Partanna wherever he was.

"Put him on the phone."

"Mr. Partanna is not here."

"Where is he?"

"He's at his office."

It was one of those *superior* Limey voices. Charley's office! "Who is this?"

"This is Mrs. Partanna."

The shock of those words was like an icy sword thrust into Maerose's bowels. *"Missus* Partanna? When did *that* happen?"

"To whom am I speaking?"

"This is Miss Maerose Prizzi. Please remember that name so that you can get it right when you tell Mr. Partanna I called. I am Mr. Partanna's fiancée."

It was the broad's turn to take the kick in the head. She gasped. She made a light geek sound. "His fian*cée?*"

"What's your name?"

"Mardell La Tour."

"Listen, Miss La Tour. I'm calling from New York, or else I'd come over there and we could *both* break a couple of chairs over that son of a bitch's head. Where do you live?"

"In − in New York."

"Where?"

"148 West Twenty-third."

"When do you get back?"

"Monday, I suppose. But, really, Miss Prizzi—"

"You and I will have a little talk. I'll call you."

Maerose was still shaken up from the call that had produced a woman in Charley Partanna's hotel room in Miami almost a half hour ago. The moment she hung up on Mardell she put private detectives on it in Miami and in New York, and she knew they were going to come up with absolute, incontrovertible proof that Charley had been two-timing her with the woman all along. She had to break his back. He had to know that if he had done such a thing to her she would have to demolish him.

She knew from pumping her father that Charley was in Miami to handle a problem with a schmeck producer, but he had told the woman that he had to go to an office, not that he would have told her why he was there no matter what, but the point was, she couldn't be in the environment because any woman in the environment knew that men like Charley didn't have an office when they went to Miami. Anyway, she certainly couldn't be in the environment talking the way she did. She sounded like C. Aubrey Smith.

Maybe she was some local talent Charley had picked up or someone Casco Fidele's people had fixed him up with. That she could talk herself into accepting. That was something men had been known to do on the road. But if he had taken that woman with him all the way from New York when he had never so much as had the courtesy of inviting her to Baltimore when he went, even if he knew she couldn't come because she had a business to run, she was going to have to — she swallowed bitterly — she was going to have to find out how she could put out a contract on him.

She knew she couldn't do it. Making the threat inside her head made her feel a little better, but if she had Charley handled she would be just like her father, and anything was better than that.

She needed Charley. All her plans depended on Charley. Finding out that he had a woman with him in Miami only made the whole feeling sharper, more disemboweling. He was a devious no-good son of a bitch, and what was she going to do? She was a Prizzi. He knew all about her being a Prizzi, better than most of the people in the world, and yet he had done this to her.

She knew Angelo Partanna would know about

the woman, because he knew what Charley was going to do before Charley himself thought of doing it, but she didn't know how to ask him without opening up the whole can of worms.

She knew one thing. She had to nail Charley to the stage. She had to take away his options and make him see the uselessness of hanging around with a woman like that or any woman except Maerose Prizzi. He had to understand that he had committed himself to a Prizzi, he was engaged to be married to a Prizzi, even if she had never insisted that they make it formal, or even that he acknowledge that they were engaged. He had to be made to understand that he couldn't just travel around the country with any broad he wanted to lay his hands on as if they were in central China, for Christ's sake. He was in Miami. Everybody knew him. His out was that nobody knew that he was engaged to Corrado Prizzi's granddaughter. In order to nail him to the floor where he stood, she would have to make it official, she would have to let the world know to whom he belonged. She was going to have to tell her father and her grandfather that they were engaged. She could hardly bring herself to do it because, once she did it, if Charley kept it up the way he was doing with other women, they would drop him in cement.

Also, it wrecked her timetable. She wanted to get the business established in Washington as solidly as it was set in New York so that, right after her engagement to Charley was made official, at the red-hot crucial moment, at the peak of the good news, she could ask her grandfather to tell Eduardo that Eduardo should take her on in his office and she could sell him the decorating business as a going proposition for a large hunk of cash, then settle down on the long-term basis to learn Eduardo's operation, to undermine him with the family, and finally to take his place.

She began to have certain doubts about being able to make this whole thing stick about being engaged to Charley. Charley never called her to ask her out. She always had to call him. Charley never lured her into bed. Every time it happened she'd had to make elaborate arrangements to set it up. Sooner or later she was going to run out of stories to tell him just to get his clothes off and the door locked. Tears welled up in her beautiful dark eyes. She couldn't give him up. That would wreck her plans to work her way into a position to be able to run the whole Prizzi family someday. Every time they were together he became more hers, and she knew — she absolutely *knew* — that after ten or twelve more times *he* would start being the aggressor. *He* would call her for dinner. *He* would be the one who thought up the plots and did the sweet-talking to get them into bed. With the kind of money and power that was at stake, they be*longed* together.

But for all the other reasons, all the reasons she had started out with, Charley was an important link in her life chain. They had to be the new blood together, the new power team. Charley was only her father's underboss now, but by the time she was in a position to knock Eduardo out of his seat at the head of the legit Prizzi enterprises, her father would surely be finished, either dead or retired, and Charley would be the Boss of the Prizzi street operation, with all the muscle of a boss, which would be the final clincher to back her play when the time came to cut Eduardo down.

She took up the phone and dialed.

"Aunt Amalia? Maerose. Could you get me in to see him some time this afternoon?"

"Whatsamatta, Mae?" Amalia's voice was anxious.

"I want to tell him that I am gonna marry Charley Partanna."

"Mae! Mae, that's wonderful! You will make him so happy!"

"I want to tell him first. I haven't even told my father yet."

169

"But Charley will tell Angelo—"

"Charley won't open his mouth. Will you get me in, Aunt Amalia?"

"Come on over here at half past four. This is the happiest day of my life."

Maerose put on a green tweed Lovat dress with a green sweater and green woollen stockings. She wore flat-heeled shoes and very little makeup to create a little-girl effect. After she was completely dressed she changed her mind. There was a better way to look like a little girl for her grandfather. She took off the dress and put on a kilt with the Fraser plaid and a Shetland pullover, then a tartan tam-o'-shanter with a chin strap and a big tuft on top. She stared at herself in a full-length mirror and wondered how Scotch transvestites dressed.

The phonograph was playing Vincenzo Bellini's *Il Pirata*, a Sicilian story. It was in the middle of the melting cantilena, "Pietosa al padre," when Amalia brought her into the don's room. Her grandfather smiled at her and bowed with his head but held up a hand to keep her from speaking until the aria was finished. Maerose sat down with her feet held primly together.

The room was a replica of the duke's bedroom

from Corrado Prizzi's boyhood. There was hardly a space on the wall that was not covered with a nineteenth-century painting or aqua-tint in a baroque frame. The furniture was dark, heavy, and overstuffed, and everything in the room except the don had fringes on it.

The aria ended. The don stood and opened his arms to her. She rushed into his embrace — but carefully, because he was so small and fragile.

"My beautiful girl," the don said. "Come, you must sit down and have a cookie, my dear."

They sat side by side with a small tabouret holding a heaping plate of Sicilian sweets and cookies between them.

"How good it is to see you," the don said.

"I wanted you to be the first to have the news, Grandfather. I haven't even told Poppa yet."

"News?" he said delicately.

"I am going to be married to Charley Partanna."

"Oh! What wonderful news." He clasped his hands before his tiny chest and rolled his eyes heavenward. "The two most perfect young people of my life — a marriage!"

"I have come for your blessing."

"You have my blessing a thousand times, if

171

you are sure this is what you want and that there will be a marriage."

"We are sure, Grandfather."

"Then we must have a big party and make the announcement. Because it is for you – my *favo*rite granddaughter – it will be the biggest party our people have seen for months. At the old Palermo Gardens. About four weeks from now?" He held out his hand and she kissed it. She left the room with wet eyes. On the phonograph, the quintet and soon the sextet began to develop with comments from the chorus. It was a beautiful moment, and she had nailed Charley to the stage.

# 24

George F. Mallon had had a hard day of campaigning in the upper Bronx, standing in the freezing rain as his motorcade swept past absolutely nobody, past DeWitt Clinton High School along Mosholu Parkway to the upper Grand Concourse then down to the most miserably attended rally he had ever seen at the Yankee Stadium. The same hardcore congregations of the Electronic Evangelical Church that had been swept up in all five of the boroughs, in New Jersey, and in Connecticut, had been bused there to hear him make the same speech again. There were no television cameras. It had been decided that there would be no radio because they were saving what was left of the appropriation for the last driving week of the campaign after he had arrested Charley Partanna and the real church music would begin to roll out of the mighty organs.

He was weary when he got home to his simple duplex on Fifth Avenue, near the Metropolitan Museum – which, although he had never had time to enter it, underscored his hunger for art and culture.

Luigi, his perfect Sicilian butler, took his coat, scarf, hat, and gloves and handed him a tall whiskey with some water and ice in a large glass. "Mr. Marvin is in the study, sir." Marvin was Mallon's thirty-one-year-old son. Mallon took several sips of his drink before going in to face Marvin because, fact be known, a few hours with Marvin was like several months alone in a spaceship roaming Alpha Centauri. Marvin should have been a clergyman, a spiritual clone of the holy man, the Reverend Jerry Falwell, who had instructed his people thusly: "One day Jesus is going to come and strike down all the Supreme Court rulings in one fell swoop," but Marvin's dad had barred the way. Marvin was his executive assistant, carrying out the innumerable duties of the tabernacle complex construction around the country, while his dad gave everything he had to become the mayor of the City of New York, the second biggest elective job in the United States of America. Mallon finished half the highball standing alone in the foyer, then he squared his shoulders and marched into the study to join Marvin.

Marvin was built more like his mother than like Sean Connery's James Bond. He was short and round. He had butter-colored hair and a mouth full of butter-colored teeth. He sang when he talked and, no matter what he said, he worked laboriously at smiling after he said it, while he was saying it, and before he said it, in the orthodox manner of the Electronic Evangelical Clergy. What *payess* were to orthodox Jews, what a *zucchetto* was to a Catholic cardinal, the shit eater's smile was to the high tech evangelical ministry.

George F. Mallon allowed his son to have access to every level of his business except the money side. There was something in Marvin's manner which hinted that he might have run off with all the money; an illusion, Mallon knew, but Marvin *had* wanted dearly to be one with the Electronic Evangelical Church, whose only sacrament was money.

Mallon sighed. Money was all Marvin would ever run off with. He would be the safest man in the world to leave with a woman. He might attempt to pray over her in a lewd sacerdotal way but he would never run off with her. Marvin was a eunuch, Mallon was sure of that, and the time had come to get him out of town again before the really heavy campaign action started after Partanna's arrest, because Marvin was excited by activity and action and he would only screw up at some crucial moment.

Mallon entered the cathedral-like study with its facing lecterns for joint prayer and Bible study. It wasn't a cozy room because of its six-foot-by-twelve-foot snooker table, its War Room maps from AEF headquarters in Bosnia in World War I that the decorator had off-loaded on the decor, and the enormous carved Florentine desk holding the day's *New York Times* crossword puzzle precisely at its centerpoint. Mallon shook his son's hand in greeting and accepted a kiss on the cheek. He lighted a cigar. Luigi, the perfect butler, slipped another tall drink into his hand.

"Aren't you drinking a bit too much, Dad?" Marvin asked, saying the name as he always pronounced it: Dod.

"No, Marvin."

"Alcohol is a narcotic, Dad."

"Are you keeping busy, Marvin?"

"Yes, Dad."

"The National Electronic Evangelical Convention and Exhibition begins Saturday next in New Orleans, Marvin. I will be otherwise engaged — rather heavily, as you know — so you must represent the firm in our booth and, I hope, on the platform."

"It's all arranged, Dad. I will be the fourth speaker, after Edgar Henshaw Dove. I will leave for New Orleans Sunday morning and I'll be there just in time for the big Monday conferences."

"What shall your text be?"

" 'She brought forth butter in a lordly dish.' Joshua 1:9."

"I would have thought, 'Where your treasure is, there will your heart be also.' Matthew."

Luigi, the perfect butler, tidied up unobtrusively in the room. He refilled Marvin's cup of Ovaltine.

"You will have a selling job to do, Marvin," George F. Mallon said. "You'll need a hard-sell text either from the scriptures or from Will Shakespeare to put across the new Audience-Parishioner's Retirement Plan in your talk. It's such a new wrinkle in church activity and such an opportunity that it will go like hot cakes. It pays a large clergy participation — three percent — for each individual audience-parishioner policy sold, so it should go over sensationally with the conventioneers."

"Dad, let me say this — I think it will be bigger than your concept for the first Christian Resort Complex in America, or even bigger than your new, more aggressive concept for Identity and the Klan." He grinned greasily in his butter-colored way. "I prophesy a thirty-million-dollar gross in the very first year with that one."

"Prophesy, Marvin?"

"As a business forecast, Dad. Not in the biblical or political sense. I'm really going to zing it to them in New Orleans."

# 25

Charley was floating in the middle of a transparent, blue-green sea, taking the sun on Mardell's creamy white belly, her head a few miles to his right and the cliffs of her painted toenails a few miles to his left. Maerose Prizzi was beginning to appear from the other side of Mardell's left breast, the steady, heavy heartbeat making the climb precarious. As Maerose reached the summit she looked around, took out a gun, and shot at Charley. The gun made a terrible noise. It woke him.

The telephone on the night table beside his ear was ringing in the darkness. He picked it up and said hello into it, looking over his shoulder at Mardell, asleep beside him. With her, sleeping pills worked.

"Charley?" It was Pop.

Charley woke up. "What time is it?"

"Ten after six."

"In the morning?"

"The girl with you?"

"Yeah."

"I'll do the talking. Get dressed. Don't pack anything. A car will pick you up downstairs in ten minutes."

"I can't. Something happened here." He whispered into the telephone.

"Charley — I'm talking about that you temporarily got to run for your life."

"What do you mean?"

"Not now. Get moving."

"What about my clothes?"

"You'll get new ones."

"What is this?"

"George F. Mallon."

"Oh."

"We'll talk later. The car will take you to the Miami airport. Go to the first phone booth nearest to the Eastern check-in counter. I have that number. I'll call you there."

"But what about—"

"Leave a note for the girl. Tell her your office called you away on business. Tell her a car will pick her up after she calls the bell captain when she's ready. A woman will be in the car to take her to New York, so she'll have company."

"What woman?"

"Mrs. Bostwick."

"Jesus, Pop, this is more complicated than you think."

"You gotta move, Charley. You'll understand when I talk to you later." Pop hung up.

Mardell stirred dopily. "Whassamatta?"

He leaned over and kissed her bare shoulder. "It's okay. Go back to sleep."

He dressed rapidly, threw some water on his face, and combed his hair. He sat at the small desk in the room. "Dear Mardell," the note said, "I have a business thing that came up. I have to travel. THIS HAS NOTHING TO DO WITH WHAT WE TALKED ABOUT LAST NIGHT." He printed that sentence in fat capital letters and

179

then he underlined it. "When you wake up and are all dressed and packed, call the bell captain and an assistant of my father's will be waiting to take you back to New York. I will talk to you tonight. Everything is fine. No worrying, please. Everything is coming up roses. Love, Charley."

He went to the window and looked out through the heavy curtains to make sure it was as early as Pop said. It was. Everything was coming up poison ivy. He let himself out of the suite on tiptoe and went out to the elevator bank. He pressed the DOWN button. The instantly answering *ping* of the waiting car made him jump. This business of being jammed between two hostile women had him all on edge. He looked down to see if he had remembered to put his socks on.

There had to be a book that would tell him how to handle the situation. He would go to the public library in whatever town he was being sent to. He punched the LOBBY button. When the elevator door opened the Plumber was standing there.

"What's going on?" Charley asked.

"You got me, Charley. I got a limo outside."

The Plumber handed Charley an envelope through the window of the limo. "The ticket," he said. "In the name of Fred J. Fulton."

"Who's that?"

"You."

"To where?"

"Dallas."

Charley put the envelope in his pocket. "What a business," he said bitterly. "See you, Al." The car moved out along Collins Avenue.

As they crossed the Julia Tuttle Causeway for a direct run to the airport, he thought this had to be serious. Pop didn't play games. But what could be as serious as the jam Maerose had put him in with Mardell? "I am Charley's fiancée," she had said — or something like that. How in God's name had she gotten it into her head that they were engaged? He wasn't engaged to anybody, including Mardell. What he and Mae had done on the new bed in his apartment was an absolutely natural thing for people of their age group and health ratings. The Surgeon General of the United States and *Psychology Today* would back him up on that. What they had done on that bed had been nice, it had worked the way both of them had a right to hope it would work, so they had tried it again a couple of times. If every time a young, healthy American male got on a bed with a young, healthy American female they automatically became engaged, there wouldn't be enough engagement rings to go around. Sixty

181

percent of the entire population would be interchangeably engaged to one another. No one could ever get married because they'd be engaged to so many people.

But look what it had done to Mardell. She was nearly totaled, and just at the time when she needed him most this goddam thing had come up to turn him into a fugitive. What would she do when she woke up? How would she ever get herself together again all alone?

There was nothing Mallon could pin on him. Davey Hanly wasn't going to give up a nice steady sixty-thousand-a-year from the pad because Mallon asked him some questions. Anyway, Davey was eight floors below when the accident happened. Mallon could yell all he wanted but he couldn't make anything stick. There was no witness who had seen him zotz Vito. Maybe the crisis was that Pop had a tip-off about Little Jaimito. They probably hadn't even found Jaimito yet and, anyway, there was nothing that could hang it on him, and the cops would be too gratified that somebody did the number on a bunch of guys like that to get in an uproar. Maybe Vincent was setting up a contract in Dallas or somewhere that Pop didn't want to talk over until he knew he had a safe line or until he could send somebody down from New York with what had to be done. But

Pop had said George F. Mallon. How could it be Mallon? If that was it, he was going to have somebody's ass because of all the times for him to have to leave Mardell this was absolutely the worst. She already figured he sold her out. But no matter what Maerose or anybody said, how could she think he sold her out? He brought her to Miami with him, not Maerose, didn't he? It was a no-win situation.

Jesus, next he had to listen to Maerose. Wherever Pop was sending him, she was going to find out where he was and she was going to call him just as if they were engaged and she had the right to call him. It was a toss-up which was worse: Mae or Mardell. How could he tell himself not to lie? When it was all over, what would be the use of lying? If he wanted to get this straightened out, he would have to level with both of them. But if he lied to one he had to lie to both, because he knew in his heart that the one he didn't lie to was the one he wanted to keep. That was instinct, but suppose his instincts were wrong?

It was better to have to hear it the first time from Maerose on the phone than to be in the same room with her while he tried to control his eyes and the sound of his voice. He was going to have to get a book on lying or he was never going to convince anybody. Whatever was going to happen out of all this, it wasn't good for Mardell. This was going to make a lot of trouble for Mardell, and he was glad he'd had that talk with Pop about her because Pop would move in on the situation and ease it up until Charley could get back to New York. Sending Mrs. Bostwick in to ride up with her to New York showed how important Mardell was to him and he was grateful Pop had thought of it. But whatever it was Pop wanted him to do, wherever Pop was sending him, he couldn't stay away more than a couple of days because he had very bad vibes about Mardell and he didn't want anything to happen to her.

It was the usual pandemonium at the airport. Time of day made no difference in airports: it was about half past six on a Friday morning, and it looked like Ghandi's funeral. How could tens of thousands of people even think of going anywhere at this time of day?

He located the phone booth nearest the Eastern counter, sat in it, and closed the door. In the next five minutes two different people came up to it, even at that hour of the morning, looked in, and banged on the door. Charley opened the door with deliberate slowness, thought of Humphrey Bogart, hosed fear all over them, and they went away. The phone rang.

"Pop?"

"Yeah. Did you do the work down there?"

"The work?"

"On Jaimito."

"Yeah."

"Good. Lissena me. You know Mallon who is running for mayor on the Reform ticket?"

"Yeah, yeah," Charley said irritably.

"A week from Sunday, like at dawn, that is according to *his* plan Sunday dawn, he has organized U.S. Marshals and a gang of media to go out to your apartment and take you in, then he is going on television that night so it will be all over the papers – on the Monday eight days before Election Day, and accuse the mayor and the police commissioner of ordering you to do the job on Vito to protect their drug empire."

"*Whaaaat?*"

"Yeah. Can you believe it? And he is gonna try to get a lot more mileage out of it than that. So far, the only name he has is George Fearons, the detective they say did the actual job on Vito. But the day you did the job on Vito, the computer mistakenly gave the cops the name of a cop who retired three years ago and lives in Montreal now. Mallon's people were also all over Willie Daspisa, who says he seen you go into Vito's building on that night. And he has Davey Hanly on the mat for all the good that's gonna do him."

"What kind of a frame-up is this?"

"He has a TV cameraman who went into Vito's apartment right behind the task force sergeant and he says part of Vito was on his back on the floor and the rest of him was all over the walls before the sergeant fired a shot."

"Politics. Boy!"

"But he can't prove nothing — he can't even get started — until he can close in on you, arrest you in front of two hundred media people, and nail you up in front of the cameras. He's started the whole thing so now he has to follow it up wherever he can find you."

"This is the craziest thing I ever heard."

"He wants to nail you, but he don't care about you. He wants to nail the mayor. All you gotta do is lay low until after Election Day."

"Where?"

"I got it all set up."

"What about school? Shit, Pop, I got exams coming up."

"I'll take them a doctor's certificate that you got the flu. I'm your father. What can they say except too bad."

"You got to send the Plumber over there

starting Monday night to get my homework."

"Don't worry about it."

"Jesus, Pop — you don't know what else is going on. I'm in a bind not only with Mardell, but with Mae."

"They'll have to wait, Charley."

"Is Eduardo handling it?"

"Eduardo can't do nothing with this guy — directly. But he can slow him down. Eduardo and the don want you on ice until it's over."

"Jesus, Pop, that's almost ten days away. Mardell'll go outta her mind."

"I'll talk to her."

"Pop. Lissena me. Last night she said to me that Maerose had called her and said that she and me was engaged. I mean — you can't imagine what it was like."

"Engaged? Mae told her that?"

"She's gotta have me mixed up with somebody else."

"Well — whatta you gonna do? Two women. I mean, it hadda come out."

"But Mardell is very shaky, Pop. You don't know. She gets that yesterday from Mae, now she wakes up and I'm gone. What's she supposed to think? That I ran out on her, right? But with her, with Mardell, it's ten times worse than if it happened to somebody else. Like I told you. About the father and having the

187

kid and all that."

"You didn't tell me about that."

"Well, it's very rough."

"Charley, life is life. Things happen. You'll talk to her tonight from Dallas. I am gonna take her to dinner and explain everything."

"*Every*thing?"

"About why you hadda leave Miami this morning. Not the real reason."

"Well – Jesus. What about Maerose?"

"That's easy. I'll talk to her."

"No, no! I mean what about that she thinks she and me are engaged?"

"So it's some whim she has. It ain't official. I mean, it ain't like she announced it to the don or Vincent. She's just trying to steamroller you."

"Pop, listen. I think it would be better if you didn't talk to Maerose. She's very proud. And we can't blame her if she is so in love with me, because she tells *me* we're engaged, it ain't something she wants the family to know."

"I'll dummy up with her."

"Where do I go now?"

"You got a reservation at the Mockingbird Hilton in Dallas, in the name of Frank Arriminata, after that pasta you make with the broccoli so you won't forget it."

"Arriminata. *Arriminarsi* means to move about."

"That's what you'll be doing. I'll call you tomorrow night. Stay over the weekend. See the Cowboys. Go to a movie. Monday they'll be ready for you in New Orleans."

"Gennaro?"

"Yeah. Rent a car in Dallas and drive to Tyler, Texas. Go to the city airport they got. One of Gennaro's planes will take you to New Orleans."

"Why can't Mardell come with me?"

"You know why. Because she makes you more traceable."

"But doing it like this is really gonna wreck her."

"Even if Mallon's people get lucky and they can trace Fred Fulton from Miami to Dallas, which is practically impossible, the trail stops there. At the Dallas airport."

"How is Eduardo gonna handle Mallon?"

"Don't worry. The verce of the people will be heard. The don is giving this his best thinking."

"We now got one more reason for Eduardo to find Willie in the Program."

"After Election Day. When you get back. That's what we're gonna do. No more Mr. Nice Guy." Pop hung up.

# 26

When Mardell opened her eyes up and stretched out her hand across the bed to touch Charley, she woke up with a shock because the other side of the bed was empty. He had to be reading in the other room. Reading? What was there to read?

"Charley!" she yelled.

Then she remembered the woman who called her. She moaned, wondering whether she had overcharacterized the thing. She propped herself up on three pillows and thought the situation through objectively. It clearly had been a mistake to have taken the two aspirins as if they were sleeping pills, as if she were Cleopatra with her asp and she couldn't bear to keep on talking to him. There was no question about it: the thing to have done would have been to just melt into the whole thing as if she couldn't stand the agony it was causing him; holding him and kissing him and telling him that whatever had happened to him back in the past before he had ever set eyes on her was nothing she could possibly have anything to say about – and other nonsense like that.

She got out of bed, lay on the floor, and began to do the Royal Canadian Air Force exercises, remembering that she was missing a sensational shoe sale at Saks in New York. She had to locate a cleaning woman. Cleaning was wonderful exercise, but it kept her in the house and, more and more, Freddie was taking that shuttle flight from Washington to New York. Her mother thought he was behaving very seriously. Mardell *knew* he was behaving seriously. She was determined that he must value the prize (herself) that he would win, but she felt he really had to strive just a little more for it before she lowered her eyes and said yes to hear him say that she had made him the happiest man in the world. But it mustn't all happen too fast. She had to round out this organized crime case history for Hattie Blacker before Mardell La Tour could cease to exist.

She was sure she had gotten herself into some kind of Sicilian blood feud with that intense woman on the phone yesterday. Still, that Charley was a real little devil, having a loving fiancée on the side and carrying on with her like the whole thing was a French farce. She yawned and stretched, wondering whether she should rent a car and go up to Palm Beach to see the Spaldings.

She found Charley's note on his pillow and read it with amusement. He must have known his fiancée was capable of coming down here with a large gun and letting him have it. She tried to imagine what the fiancée could be like: short, with a light mustache. She probably wore little bows on her shoes and had an ankle bracelet.

God knows what time he had gotten up to make his escape. She knew that he knew he didn't intend to see her again because he couldn't stand the heat from the Sicilian fiancée. It had been good fun while it had lasted. She decided to have a pitcher of grapefruit juice for breakfast. It was very filling and wouldn't put one ounce on her.

She began to think of the fun of playing the whole string out with Charley and his fiancée. God, the passions these people could go through; it would be like singing the soprano role in grand opera; being right onstage in the middle of all the noise and the action. Although this looked like a very appropriate and natural time to withdraw discreetly from the adventure, she felt in her bones that she couldn't just disappear in the middle of the second act. She had to wait around and see how the whole thing was going to turn out. She owed it to Charley. He was too sweet for her not to stay around to find out what was going to happen to him.

The phone rang. She picked it up, dropping back into her tremulous character of Mardell La Tour, fighting not to overdo it.

"Charley?"

"Miss La Tour?" It was a soft, low, sympathetic voice.

"Yes?"

"This is Charley's father."

"His father?"

"Charley works for me. A very big opportunity came up. I talked to him this morning but he must have taken it in the other room because he didn't want to wake you up. You are a very important element in Charley's life. You know that, I'm sure."

This was a real pro. This man was smooooth.

"Where is he, Mr. Partanna?"

"I'm in New York. The main thing is — there was no time so early this morning for Charley to wake you up and go over everything with you — but he insisted that I call you at the earliest civilized hour. So here I am."

Mardell had never heard a slicker, trickier voice. She was beginning to realize that this whole thing could have many dimensions. Maybe Charley did have to go away on some awful criminal business.

"My assistant in our Miami office — a very dignified lady — will bring you back to New York, Miss La Tour, a first-class seat and a nice meal — then you and me will have dinner in some nice restaurant tonight and I'll tell you the whole story about what Charley is doing for us. It's a very big deal, a big responsibility. He had to move on it, Miss La Tour."

"Please call me Mardell."

"Mrs. Bostwick will have the tickets. The limousine will take you to the airport. Just tell the bell captain when you are ready. I will call you at five o'clock this afternoon at your place to tell you when we will meet tonight."

"You are *very* kind, Mr. Partanna."

"No, no, Mardell. Please. Not kindness. It is Charley's way."

"How will I know Mrs. Bostwick?"

"Mrs. Bostwick will be carrying two large suitcases and she'll have one of them on the pavement at the door of the limousine." Mrs. Bostwick was the mule who brought the pure to New York twice a week, where the Prizzi lab stepped on it only six times.

# 27

Charley checked into the Mockingbird Hilton in Dallas as Frank Arriminata. The reservation was waiting for him. Along with the room keys, the clerk handed him a large, heavy manila envelope, which had been scotch-taped at every seam. He told the room clerk that his baggage had been lost by the airline and asked where he could buy some clothes and luggage. The room clerk told him to take a cab to the Highland Park shopping center. Charley went into the coffee shop and had a real breakfast. He didn't approve of airline food. He had never heard of anybody ever getting a good Italian meal on any airline, including Alitalia.

After ordering breakfast he opened the manila envelope. It contained a Texas driver's license, a Mobil credit card, an AAA membership card, and an American Express card all in the name of Frank Arriminata. There was a heavy gold signet ring with the initials F.A. carved into it. He slipped the ring on his finger and stuffed the IDs into his wallet — after removing his own, putting the latter into the manila envelope, and addressing the envelope to his father in New York.

At five after ten he went out front, got a cab, and directed the driver to take him to Highland Park village. On the way out he saw that Dallas was the Brooklyn of tomorrow; the same low buildings, plenty of trees and sky; small houses with the occasional high-rise jutting up here and there, just like Bensonhurst. The people who lived here probably thought it was the greatest place in the world only because they lived here. He missed Brooklyn — known to anybody who knew anything about places as the Greatest Place in the World — and not just because he lived there.

He got out of the cab in front of the entrance to Sanger-Harris, a department store, so he went in and started buying. Using the fake credit card, he bought another suit, two shirts, some underwear and socks, a toothbrush, shaving equipment, a suitcase, and two identical cultured pearl necklaces — one for Mae and one for Mardell. He thought about the marvels of progress, how ten years before he would have had to carry a big roll of bills on him if he needed to shop like this. Progress was there to serve.

He walked around the shopping center, had some iced tea, and found a book called *Lying Techniques* whose cover said it had been twenty-two weeks on the bestseller list. He went into the movie house to cool off. He got back to the hotel just after three and went to bed. He woke up at four twenty and called Mardell. It was five twenty in New York.

"Mardell? Charley."

"What can you possibly say to me, Charley?"

"Well — just for beginners — I can say that I love you."

"Ah, Charley."

"The note explained why we didn't go to Marineland."

"I talked to your father in Miami. I just talked to him again about twenty minutes ago."

"We gotta straighten everything out, Mardell."

"Your fiancée called me. I can't stop thinking about that."

"Well, stop thinking about it. She is not my fiancée. Can I help it if a woman walks around saying I'm her fiancé? I'm not engaged to her, and if she calls you again tell her I said that."

"We're going to have dinner tonight."

"Who?"

"Your father and I."

"This thing I'm doing down here — it's going

to tie me up until like the second week of November. Then I'm coming right home."

"I just don't know what to say to you."

"Don't say anything. Just say we'll be together again very soon. Just give me a chance to straighten everything out."

"I have to hang up now, Charley." There was a soft sound, then the phone was dead. He couldn't figure out whether things were better or worse than he thought. He stretched out on the bed and started to study the lying manual, but when he came to a part that said men were better liars than women, he sat up and dumped it in the wastebasket. Why didn't they say that men who lied were better at it than women who lied? Did everybody lie? He had to watch himself.

He turned on the television and then sat in a low chair, staring at the tube but not seeing it. He let its familiar presence comfort him, his mind almost a blank in the American way that had been formed and molded by twenty-two years of television, but beyond its numbing edges he knew he was still in big trouble. He turned the sound off and let the bright, moving colors soothe him. There was a talking toilet seat commercial that was very well done, he thought.

He was to blame. He had let himself get involved with two women at the same time. He had cheated on two great women and now they were all paying for it. He felt such a wave of self-pity that he had to turn off the television and take a cold shower. He dressed in his new clothes and went down to the lobby to find out where there was an Italian restaurant.

They sent him to an Italian-type restaurant on Mockingbird behind the hotel. The pasta was out of a package and had been made with plain white flour. It lay there in lumps. The sauce was like hot ketchup. He ate the bread and the salad.

He passed a half-price bookstore on the way back to the hotel and bought a James Bond paperback; one guy who never had any problems with women. The book would get him through Saturday but he would rather have been doing his homework. In two weeks Roja-Buscando was going to be able to skunk him. She was never absent. She probably went to day high school just so she could walk into the class every night and try to make him look like a bum. When you came right down to it, she was a pretty terrific-looking head even if she was a Puerto Rican. She was like the color of the don's almond cookies, with a great pair of eyes on her, and very smart. He sighed. She was absolutely going to skunk him. She was going straight to the head of the class and there was nothing he could do about it. God damn George F. Mallon!

He left for Tyler in the rented car at seven o'clock Sunday morning, made it across some pretty flat country, and found the Tyler airport. He called the rent-a-car place and told them where to pick up the car. A two-engine Piper was waiting for him and it flew him to New Orleans.

# 28

Later that Sunday morning, two of Gennaro Fustino's people met the light plane with Charley in it, and took him to Gennaro's house in the elegant garden district of New Orleans where he sat down to a family-style lunch with Gennaro, Natale Esposito, and Gennaro's wife, Birdie, who was Don Corrado's little sister. She was a very jolly, fat lady in her early sixties who never actually sat with them but kept bringing more and more food to the table. She was certainly a lot better-looking than her brother, Charley thought, then he had a pang of disloyalty.

The meal started with *chinulille*, small fried ravioli stuffed with a mixture of sweetened and spiced ricotta cheese and egg yolk. Gennaro, a Calabrese who was famous for owning 117 pairs of shoes, piled it on about how Calabrese food was so much better than Sicilian food, to the point where Charley decided he had to be kidding. Charley (and practically everybody else in the world, Charley thought) preferred his ravioli stuffed with salami the Sicilian way, but he didn't say anything. They had *tonno bollito*, boiled fresh tuna with oil, garlic, pickles, and green salad. It was good, but *spada a ghiotta*, a nice swordfish cooked in oil with onions, celery, tomatoes, and olives, was better. Pop had told him that Calabrese people knew absolutely nothing about food. At least the baked layered pastry called *sammartina* was Sicilian, Mrs. Fustino owed her heritage that much. Charley got out an envelope and a pencil and wrote down the recipe as Mrs. Fustino gave it to him with delight and her husband looked on with amused contempt.

After lunch the men went into the parlor. Gennaro was very hospitable. His operation in terms of square miles was the biggest territory in the country and, pound for pound, he made it pay off in big numbers. He was a powerful man and a good friend to the Prizzis as well as a steady franchisee and a relative. He offered Charley one of his houses, well back in the Mississippi state bayou country about seventy miles away, or an apartment out on St. Charles. Charley said he thought it might be better to be right in New Orleans, in a downtown hotel, where he could get messages and send out his laundry.

"The only messages you're gonna get are from me or Angelo, right? And we got a staff of three out in the bayou. You can have the real Cajun cooking or Italian. They don't care."

"I can't get used to the country, Gennaro. It's noisy. The bugs sing, the birds make a racket, and it's hard to figure out where things are coming from when they're coming at you."

"I can set you up with people — a cook, like, and cleaning people out on St. Charles."

"I'd only have to talk to them, Gennaro."

"I know what you mean. Good. I'll put you in a nice, clean hotel in the Quarter. It's noisy, but it's the right kind of noise. You want a little company?"

"Broads?"

"Sure."

"I already got my hands full."

"Angelo said you'll be here a couple of weeks."

"Yeah."

"What name you traveling under?"

"Frank Arriminata. And hey, Gennaro, I wanna thank you for making room for me here."

"You are always welcome in my house, Charley. But you didn't just land here because I like you, you're here for a reason."

"Yeah?"

"You remember George F. Mallon, the reform guy who hustles Jesus wholesale and who is running for mayor of New York?"

"Yeah."

"Angelo sent a man down here Friday, Al Melvini, you know him."

"The Plumber?"

"He gave me the message from your father, then he went back. George F. Mallon's son is coming down here to go to a big church convention next weekend. Don Corrado has some plans for him. Corrado wants to make sure Mallon is knocked out of the race before Election Day. We got the son's hotel here, the New Iberia, and when he checks in he's gonna get room number eight-twenty-seven, which is at the end of a hall, away from traffic. Angelo wants us to give him a little surprise there."

"How does he want him set up?"

"Seed him with a coupla ounces of smack.

Plant a gun on him — we got just the piece for you. We'll provide a stand-up broad and you'll handle all the details."

"When?"

"Next Sunday afternoon. In the meantime enjoy yourself, and if you need anything just call."

# 29

Gennaro got Charley the whole top floor, three rooms, at the New Franciscan Patio Hotel and Restaurant in a safely nonmusical part of the Quarter. Natale said if you were on the wrong street in the Quarter the Dixieland noise could drive you crazy; it never stopped. Gennaro had the telephone company put in a private line in Charley's room so his calls wouldn't have to go through the switchboard.

Every room was furnished in dark, solid mission style. The bedroom didn't have closets but two enormous carved-wood armoires and a canopied four-poster bed which was so high from the floor that it could only be reached by climbing a four-step ladder.

Monday night Charley ate in the hotel restaurant, a real Italian joint with a terrific stuffed artichoke and a sensational veal involtini. Gennaro had to own this place, Charley decided, except that this wasn't any Calabrese cooking, this was Italian-international and it was only one grade under the real thing. He was lucky enough to notice on the menu that the veal came with polenta so he made sure he changed that part to manicotti. Now he knew Gennaro didn't own this restaurant. Polenta was that bland northern Italian food. Jesus, he would bet they didn't even know about garlic, but they knew. He couldn't figure it out.

The place was run by two Italian families, and he got talking to the woman of one of them. She was crazy about the idea of the Crown of Thorns pasta thing he had picked up in New York for next Easter. He asked her where she was from. She said Calabria. He asked her how come the polenta. She said her husband thought polenta was more European-like. She said people who came in from out of state were very respectful about northern Italian cooking. Charley snorted. Marketing, he thought. Whatta you gonna do?

The weather was still nice so he ate in the patio, which had a big tree and good service. He drank a whole half-carafe of wine with the meal. After that he had his meals in his rooms. He didn't feel much like going out and walking around, because on the first night in the place, after he went upstairs following that terrific dinner, Maerose called him from New York. He kept thinking he better be there at night in case she called back again because the woman had flipped her wig.

She started out cordial – "Cholly? Mae."

He leaped out of the chair and took the call standing at attention. "Hey, Mae!" he said.

"How come you didn't call me?"

"Well – maybe Pop told you – this was an emergency trip."

"Oh, yeah. I forgot. Your father told me a beautiful story."

"Whatta you mean?"

"I thought maybe your woman told you that you shoulda made an emergency call to me."

"My woman?"

"Are you going to tell me you didn't take a woman with you from New York to Miami? Because I got it all in front of me – the limousine ticket for the pickup of you and the woman at the Miami airport, the hotel registration – which it was very considerate at least that you didn't check in as mister and missus – so save it, Charley."

"Mae, lissen –"

"I might have been able to take it if you just got hot for some little local broad you happened to run into down there, but you *took* this one with you. You didn't take *me* with you, Charley. Then I have some people check out this woman in New York and the news comes back that you are at her place half the time you are in New York, when you weren't with me you were with her, so don't hand me any shit, Charley." Her voice broke.

"Mae, you been drinking?"

"Aaaaash, whatsa difference."

"You're never yourself when you drink that stuff. Nobody is."

"Listen, Charley—"

"Mae, I gotta see you. It's no good talking like this on the phone. I gotta look at you and you gotta look at me while we say what we gotta say."

"What do we have to say?"

"That's it. I don't want to say it on the phone."

"How else can you say it?"

"I have to stay away until after the election. Then, when I come back, we have to straighten everything out."

"No."

"No what?"

"I am not going to wait around until you get back. I am coming to New Orleans and I'll look in your eyes and tell you what I see."

"Mae! Wait! Check it out with Pop before you make a move. This is a tricky thing, the reason I'm in New Orleans."

"Whatta you think? I just got off the boat? I know why you're in New Orleans. You are in New Orleans because you want to duck me until you think this whole thing has blown over. It ain't going to blow over, Charley. Either it's going to be on or it's off. For good and forever. I'm coming to New Orleans."

"Mae, listen. I got a job your Uncle Gennaro wants me to do. I won't have any time to see you — as much as I want to see you."

"Either this whole thing matters to you or it don't. If you won't come to New York then I'm going there. I'm gonna make you drop the other shoe either on her or on me, Charley. And you know something else?"

"What?"

"I hate big, sloppy broads."

"Who?"

"You know who."

"She may be big, but she ain't sloppy. And I'd say the same for you, Mae, if anybody ever said that about you."

She slammed the phone down on the receiver from somewhere high over her head. He was bewildered. What did he say wrong this time?

# 30

On Saturday afternoon at 4:23 P.M. Keifetz, George F. Mallon's chief investigator, and shadow Minister of Defense in the event that Mallon's destiny would one day call him to the highest office in the land, brought the news that Charles Partanna had disappeared.

"He's not in New York?" Mallon said, dismayed. "He's got to be in New York."

"He left La Guardia on Eastern flight twenty-one a week ago Wednesday for Miami, our investigators say."

"They are saying that *now*? Where have they been?"

"Partanna hasn't been under surveillance, G.F. You ruled that out. Too expensive. This was just a check to have him ready for the big strike tomorrow morning."

"Well – where is he?"

"He left the Miami hotel at about six ten that Friday morning, our people tell me, and a car took him."

"Took him? Took him where?"

"That's the big blank space, Chief. It was so early in the morning they couldn't find a cab to be able to follow him."

"Then, by God, we won't pay them! That is gross negligence. How are we going to roust him out of bed and arrest him at dawn tomorrow morning if we don't know where he is?"

"I have people working on it at the Miami airport, and with the flight attendants."

"What attendants? What flight?"

"Well, that's hard to say, Chief. Miami is an international airport. He could have gone to South America, or Europe, or a couple of dozen cities in this country. But they have pictures of Partanna and if we get very lucky we might run him down."

"He ran, then. Well, great. That's something."

"Pardon?"

"It could be better than nabbing him in New York, TV or no TV."

"Better?"

"He's a fugitive. It's an admission of guilt. We have all night tonight and all day Sunday to fine-tune this thing. Cancel the arrest at Partanna's apartment."

"Yes, sir."

"I'm going on the air with the whole story

at seven o'clock Monday night and accuse him of being the mayor's tool in a capital murder. We'll sensationalize the city with front-page stories. It will rock City Hall back on its heels and right out into oblivion."

"Yes*sir!*"

"Get Marvin in here. I want him to set up mass sermons from every pulpit in Greater New York on Sunday morning deploring the extent of corruption and vice at City Hall and throughout the police department of this city."

"Marvin left this morning to prepare for the New Orleans convention meeting."

"Then put his assistant on it. We've got them at last, Norman. I can't believe that a seasoned hoodlum like Partanna would lose his nerve and run. He's not only made my day – he's made me mayor of this city! Good God – the accidents of history. A man kills two policemen, there is a confrontaton, the mayor appears on the scene to take advantage of a photo opportunity, and the whole thing leads to the election of a new mayor – and who knows, Norman, that new mayor may go onward and upward – perhaps to the highest office in this land, and *then* we'll see if the Commies in our government are going to be able to keep prayer out of the schools."

"God bless you, G.F."

"Tell my chief of staff to notify every leader of the Electronic Evangelical Church from coast to coast so that they can point the finger at the mayor of New York, castigate his police, and warn America. And Norman—"

"Yes, G.F."

"Call my butler, and tell him we have Charles Partanna on the run. It will make him proud to be a righteous Sicilian-American. Tell him I'll be bringing all the news home tonight."

# 31

Pop called him just after eight o'clock Sunday morning.

"How they hanging, Charley?"

"Did you talk to her?"

"Who?"

"Who? Fahcrissakes, Pop—"

"I took her to dinner."

"Then you saw her. How is she? Did she look all right?"

"She looked any better and I'd have to build a museum around her. She is a masterpiece, Charley."

"Did you see Maerose?"

"They didn't neither one of them believe me. And Mae was on the sauce."

"What did you tell them?"

"I told Mae you had a big job in New Orleans and I told the other one the same thing, except it took longer."

"What am I gonna do?"

"You got to give it time. Sooner or later the going is gonna get too tough for somebody."

"Me, you mean. I'm gonna fall apart. Mae called me. She said she's gonna come down here."

"Charley — what can I tell you? What can you do? Nothing. In the meantime, Mallon is getting ready to throw the book at you. He's gonna make his big announcement on all the networks tomorrow night. All bullshit. But very dangerous, Charley. You gotta tuck the son in down there this afternoon."

"Pop, what do I care about that? I'm in deep trouble. What am I gonna do if Maerose shows up here?"

"So you'll come back here. After the media finishes with the story on Mallon's son, it'll be all over and you can come back to New York."

"That would really fix it, if she gets here and I'm gone."

"Well, sooner or later you gotta see her."

"Well, I ain't ready for a meeting with Mae anytime this year, that's for sure."

"I'll call her and tell her nobody wants to upset the don, that she shouldn't go to New Orleans. I'll tell her you're on your way home."

"Call her in the morning when she's sober."

"Charley — one other thing."

"What?"

"The other girl — Mardell—"

"Yeah?"

"She picked up a little pneumonia."

"*Whaaaat?*"

"She's all right! Don't get in an uproar! I got her with a good doctor in a nice hospital and she's gonna be fine."

"What hospital?"

"Santa Grazia."

"In *Brook*lyn?"

"Why not? We know every doctor and nurse in the place."

"What doctor?"

"Cyril Solomon."

"What room?"

"Three-eighteen."

"I'm going back to New York."

"Charley!" Angelo's voice went harsh. "You got a job to do in New Orleans. You think this ain't a serious thing with Mallon? At the very least you could get fifteen to thirty. Now lissena me. The girl is in the best hands and she's getting better. Are you a doctor? I see her every day and we talk aboutchew. There is nothing you can do to help her. You stay where you are. Be a man!" Pop slammed down the phone.

Charley stared at the telephone. He understood what Pop was telling him. What kind of a freaked-out thing was getting pneumonia at a time like this?

He called the long-distance operator. He told her he wanted her to get the number of the Santa Grazia Hospital in Brooklyn, New York, and to put in a person-to-person call to room three-eighteen.

"I am sorry. We cannot place a person-to-person call to a number, only to a name."

"Whoever answers."

In twenty seconds the number was ringing. The hospital answered and the operator asked for room three-eighteen. Some voice answered. The operator put Charley on.

"Miss Mardell La Tour," he said.

"Miss La Tour can't speak on the phone. You shouldn't have called this room."

"Where is she?" Charley's voice panicked.

"She is in an oxygen tent. Who is this?"

"Tell her Charley. Charley Partanna."

"*What*? This is Angie Aragona."

"Angie? Jesus." The nurse. He had once been

215

very close with this woman. She hadn't lived in the neighborhood. Nobody in her family was in the environment so they had been very close, in an intimate way.

"Gee, it's swell talking to you. Like old times."

"How is she?"

"She's gonna be all right. A little congestion, a little fever, but the lungs aren't filling anymore. It's okay. If she's a friend of yours I can tell you she's going to be okay."

"Then why can't I talk to her?"

"She's not that okay. Two or three days. Call back and she'll be able to talk to you."

Charley was dazed. He knew he couldn't override orders from his father and the don, but he also didn't see how he couldn't jump on a plane and go back to New York. But what could he do? He might only agitate her and make everything worse if he forced himself into her room. How could he say what he had to tell her talking to an oxygen tent? He didn't know what to do. He was standing in the middle of the most important thing of his life and he didn't know what to do. He wired her ninety dollars' worth of flowers.

# 32

As Angie Aragona hung up the phone she turned to Mardell, who sat in a big, upholstered armchair and was wrapped in a blanket. Angie looked dazed by the forces of memory. "That was Charley Partanna. How come he calls you?"

"It's a small world," Mardell said.

"I haven't seen him myself for like eight years. Not since I'm married. I know you said you wouldn't take any calls, but if you know Charley and he knows you're here — how come you don't wanna take *his* calls?"

"He hurt my feelings, Angie."

"Charley? How? — if it's not too personal."

"We were — well, we were going together, he was very serious, he said, but — he was engaged to be married to another woman."

"Yeah? Who?"

"A woman named Maerose Prizzi."

*"Prizzi?* Maerose *Prizzi?"*

"Don't tell me you know her, too."

217

"That is very high *fratellanza,* Mardell. That is the very top in the — uh — the honored society."

"The Mafia?"

*"Sssh!"*

"What's wrong?"

"Nobody — the politicians, the media, particularly the — the — *fratellanza* — wants anybody to say that word."

"Why not?"

"It shows a lack of sensitivity toward Italian-Americans."

"Then they should pass a law that would change the name of everybody with an Italian name and a police record."

"To what?"

"Well, to an Eskimo name."

"Wouldn't that show a lack of sensitivity toward Eskimo-Americans?"

"It wouldn't matter. There aren't any Eskimo politicians."

"No wonder you didn't want to talk on the phone with Charley. A woman like that could be dynamite."

"Oh, I'm not *mad* at him. I'm just teaching him a lesson. My general theory is that if he can't get me on the phone, he'll come home sooner."

"But what about — you know who?"

"Who?"

"Miss Prizzi."

"I think that's going to be all right," Mardell said. "She wants to have a meeting."

When Angie left, Mardell settled down to write a letter to her mother.

Dear Mother,

I'm pretty sure now that I'll be home for Christmas and stay on for a while. You and I have to talk about Freddie. He is pressing me very hard and sooner or later I will have to have a respectful answer for him. We are both fairly certain what that answer will be, because I love him and he loves me and you have always told me what should be the proper outcome of that sort of thing. My job in New York is just about over. They want to move me to Nevada but that doesn't appeal to me at all. The "hit person" in New York about whom I wrote to you is still on hand and he's very good company. Hattie Blacker says the material I have dredged up on him is going to be the absolute center of her master's thesis. The surprise of all is that I had a touch of pneumonia. I was playing tennis at the court the Laverys have in their field house at the very elegant place on Sixty-fourth Street, then, all sweat, I went to change and some clown had turned the air-conditioning on. Don't get all upset because it's all over. The father of my Brooklyn friend had me deposited into a hospital at the first sign, and before it could take any hold, it was gone.

There was a knock at the hospital room door.

"Come in," Mardell sang out.

A very tall young man wearing a dark gray vicuña overcoat with a velvet collar came into the room. He smiled at her warmly.

"Hi, Gracie."

"Freddie! What a surprise. How ever did you find me?"

"Edwina told me. How did you ever find this hospital?"

She filled the room with her smile. God, she thought to herself, what a beautiful man.

# 33

On her way back from the office, Maerose stopped off at a florist and sent a small bouquet of gladiola to the woman at the hospital, with her business card enclosed. Directly under her name on the card she wrote: "CP's fiancée."

After she found out about Charley and the woman, she told her father she had to go to Washington on business. She went into the apartment she kept in New York on East Thirty-seventh Street and took her own time about getting drunk. She knew she had to clobber Charley to make sure he knew who was boss and who was going to be boss for the rest of their lives. But she had to move carefully, because if her grandfather found out that Charley was cheating on her with a two-ton showgirl, it was really going to hit the fan. And if her father ever got it into his head that Charley had dishonored her, than it could even be goodbye Charley. Her father was such an animal about honor!

She had to stay cool if she was going to get what she wanted yet protect Charley from her family. The girl she would buy off. She would give her a chance to get back to New York, then she'd sit down with her, give her a check for fifteen hundred dollars, maybe two thousand, and watch her while she changed the locks on her doors. There was no rush. It would all be done in her own sweet time after she had trained Charley, but nothing must stand in the way of putting Charley in her father's job as Boss of the family. With the clout she would have through Charley, she could put the pressure on her Uncle Eduardo, so that when he had enough of it she could take over his operation. Being a woman could be a drag, but she was a Prizzi.

She sipped more champagne and wondered what it was the woman had that she could get out of Charley more than Maerose Prizzi could get out of him. He went to Miami to do the job on somebody, but he took the woman, not her, so in a lot of ways the woman had to have the edge on her with Charley. It couldn't be in bed. The woman was too big and heavy to be able to keep up with Charley in bed. You had to be a tiger in the sheets to stay even with Charley.

She sipped more champagne and began to see it the only way it could look. Charley being who he was, *no*body could have an edge on a Prizzi with Charley. He wouldn't have to realize it, he would *feel* it on all the levels from his feelings about herself, which she was sure were one-hundred-percent-twenty-two-carat-absolutely-the-most, then on the working level with her father, who Charley knew was famous for his vengeance, then — towering above all of them — on the effect it would have on her grandfather if Charley jilted her for another woman. No matter what, Charley couldn't do it. Charley was hers. The woman was only temporary.

She drank some more champagne. But suppose Charley had flipped? Suppose the woman was to him like the woman who is always showing up in the books and in the movies, even in opera? Suppose he had decided that nothing was going to keep him away from this broad? He wasn't afraid of Vincent; he could take Vincent any day. Charley couldn't take Vincent's entire organization any day, but he would have Angelo in there rooting for him. He had respect for her grandfather but that was a ritualistic thing, a formal thing that his feelings for the woman might brush away no matter how much it hurt his own honor or her grandfather's belief in the family. She knew if Charley really decided to go with this woman even his own father couldn't stop him. Charley was the only man she had ever known who worked like some kind of a horse until he decided what was right, then he did what he thought was right whether it was right or not.

He had blown his best friend away because — need against need — his need against the family's need — he had understood in his heart that Vito had to go. If he decided — need against need — the woman's need against her own need — that the woman had to be supported because somehow he got the idea that she, herself, was strong and could go right ahead with her life without him, then he would throw her away and protect the woman. She had been handling the whole thing wrong. She saw that. She had come on accusing him, trying to get the maximum sweat out of the guilt he had to be feeling. But what was guilt to Charley? It wasn't there. It had never been there because he only understood that all he had to do was the right thing, the right thing in his own head, and when he did that there was nothing to feel guilty about.

She drank more champagne. Charley was a contractor, sure. Out of the 1,800 soldiers in her grandfather's family there were about fifteen or twenty who did that kind of work, but with a big difference. She knew some of the other men who did what Charley did, not the big jobs maybe, but that's what they did, they zotzed people for a living. And they were all mostly a bunch of average slobs who did the work for money. And because they did it for money they felt the guilt and the guilt made monsters out of them. Charley was different, he never took a dime for the work. He had his two points in the Prizzi street operation. He had his Swiss bank account, his Panama bank account, and his Nassau bank account. Charley did everything first and foremost for the reasons that the Prizzis were right, so she was going to have to handle Charley differently.

She got out her book and called her Aunt Birdie in New Orleans. What could she have thought she was doing, telling Charley she was going to New Orleans like he was Prince Nowhere at whom she could scream for a little while and then tell him to do whatever she wanted him to do? It was the shock of Charley's taking the woman to Miami, and not taking her instead, that had wrecked her judgment.

"Aunt Birdie? Maerose."

"Hey, what a treat!"

"I wonder if I could come down and see you for a couple of days."

"Lissen — that would be the most terrific thing that could happen to us. How come we rate a treat like this?"

"Charley Partanna is there. We're engaged?" She said it shyly, very ladylike. "I want to surprise him."

"Engaged? You and Charley? I can't believe it. This is tremendous. Does Corrado know?"

"He knows. I have his blessing."

Birdie got serious. "Lissen, don't surprise Charley. Never surprise a man, because they'll surprise you worse every time if you do it. Those things happen. It's lonesome on the road. I ain't saying that Charley is lonesome, but he could be so don't give him no surprises. When you coming?"

"Tomorrow?"

"Take the courier plane. Eastern. Our people ride down on that every day. Somebody will make your reservation out of New York."

"You are some organizer, Aunt Birdie."

"Wait'll you see how I organize a lunch for you and Charley tomorrow. Bring all the news you can lay your hands on."

## 34

On a beautiful Sunday afternoon on Sheep Meadow in Central Park, George F. Mallon offered 43,900 of his most active supporters (a police count) free hot dogs, free beer, an appearance by the governor of California, a rising star, and three nationally televised electronic clergymen, plus a massing of 219 tubas for a concert of patriotic airs. The massed tubas had been brought in from "the first planned Christian family resort in America," the $150-million-dollar complex at My Birthright, USA, a religiously motivated real estate development George Mallon's vision had fostered. What a vision it had been! It had 2,760 employees and a payroll of $30 million in testament to the Power of the Word of the Lord.

The happy crowd had been assembled mainly through the cooperation of participating television ministries in Greater New York, in New Jersey, Connecticut, and Long Island, and by busing in members of Identity, the Posse

Comitatus, the Klan, and the Christian Defense League from the Midwest and the South. All were strong adherents of George F. Mallon's for devout religious reasons — and because he had pointed out to them that if they donated their possessions to any Electronic Church they could avoid taxes and that, in that event, the church would own their weapons so they could not be prosecuted on any charges of illegal possession of firearms. They were all as white as Wayne, the John Wayne who had done so much to build the American fortress-mentality — and who had watered the desert for Christian television worship and the assorted crazies who supported it.

The candidate told the sea of Christian faces before him, and the audience of 138 people who were watching at home on television, "The city is rotten to its core. Gambling, prostitution, narcotics, labor racketeering, extortion, and massive corruption are rampant in our daily lives, conducted in an evil partnership with the Jewish administration of this city — by its elected black officers and the Catholic hoodlum chiefs of organized crime."

He paused dramatically. He spoke slowly and clearly and his voice roared out over the speakers, which had been placed in trees or on poles throughout the crowd and, most particularly, in the seated media section beside the dais. "Tomorrow evening at seven o'clock I will have in my hands the name of the Mafia hit man hired by the mayor of this city to eliminate Vito Daspisa, the gangster who was murdered five weeks ago in a police stakeout in the borough of Brooklyn. This man, whose name I will announce tomorrow evening from the pulpit of the three local television network outlets in this city, is now a fugitive who broke and ran because my investigation had reached the point of bringing him to justice. Brutal killer though he was, this man was only a tool of the mayor of this city and its police department. The mayor of the City of New York ordered the killing of Vito Daspisa. I repeat – the mayor of the City of New York, protecting his narcotics empire, ordered the death of this man. I shall make specific and formal charges on the airwaves tomorrow night, when justice will be done and the voters of this city can make their choice. Until then, God save you from the Commies, the Jews, the blacks, and the Catholics – and God bless you."

He dropped his head to his chest and his arms to his sides. The enormous crowd cheered wildly, and slowly, across the vast meadow, thousands of voices, backed by the massed tubas, began to take up the hymn "Onward

Christian Hustlers." Thousands of people looked around nervously, waiting for the collection to start, but no collection was made. The handouts had explained this anomaly: those who wished points toward their eternal salvation could send their checks directly to My Birthright, USA, the George F. Mallon Meaning.

# 35

Charley was picked up at the New Franciscan Hotel at 4:45 P.M. that Sunday afternoon by Natale Esposito, a small plump man who was sliding down the backside of middle age in a small, middle-aged Dodge. In the backseat of the car was a teenage girl wearing patent-leather Mary Janes and a modified pinafore. She was able to chew gum and make up her mouth at the same time.

They parked in a side street on the far side of Canal away from the Vieux Carré, and went into the New Iberia Hotel through separate entrances – Charley alone, Natale with the girl. Natale was carrying a suitcase. They rode in separate elevators to the eighth floor and met again at the end of a hall outside room eight-twenty-seven. Natale took out a master key and let them into the double bedroom.

Charley found Marvin's empty suitcase in the large closet. As Natale emptied the bureau drawers of shirts, underwear, and socks, Charley packed them into the empty suitcase with the suit and three neckties he found hanging in the closet. The girl unpacked the suitcase they had brought with them, taking out women's lingerie, sweaters, dresses, and accessories in two sizes, and putting them into the bureau drawers or hanging them in the closet. When the packing-unpacking was finished Natale said to the woman, "Get ready."

She took off her jacket and turned to face Natale. He took a firm hold on the top of her blouse and pulled down heavily, ripping the entire front of her blouse in half. She was not wearing a brassiere. For such a young kid, Charley thought, she was certainly stacked.

"Here comes the hard part," Natale said.

"For you, not for me," the girl said.

He hit her a really good shot on the upper left cheekbone, knocking her down. He helped her to her feet and she sat down, messed up the hair on her head, and lighted a cigarette.

"About ten minutes," Natale said, looking at

his watch. "I gotta pee." He left the room. Charley looked out the window.

"You new at this?" the girl asked him.

"Sort of."

"It's not as tough as it looks."

Charley wandered over and stood at the wall beside the door, to be on the offside of the door when it opened.

"You sure are a good soldier," he said to the girl.

"They are paying me for it." She had hard Texas speech.

"I might as well stay in here," Natale said from the john.

They remained where they were, silently and reposefully until there was the scratch of a key at the lock. The door opened. Marvin Mallon, short, fat, came into the room. He stared at the woman in the chair. "My God!" he said. "Excuse me. I must be on the wrong floor."

Charley chopped him with a rabbit punch across the back of his neck. He went down. Charley closed the door. Natale came out of the john holding two tinfoil packets and a revolver. Charley unzipped the man's fly, ripped open his shorts, and exposed his limp genitals. Natale put the tinfoil packets in each breast pocket of the man's suit jacket and slid a revolver into the waistband of his trousers.

"Okay," he said to the girl, whose left eye was swelling and discoloring nicely.

He and Charley left the room with the suitcase packed with Marvin's clothes. The girl gave them about two minutes to get down the hall to the staircase leading to the lower floor, then she screamed. Almost instantly, the house officer, followed by two city police detectives and a news photographer, let himself into the room with a passkey. The girl tried to cover herself with her bare arms. "Thank God, you are here," she said. "That junkie beat me up and tried to force me into unnatural practices."

Charley and Natale went into room six-ten, two floors below and on the other side of the hotel, unpacked the suitcase, hung up the suits, put the shirts and underwear in the bureau drawer, laid out the toilet articles on the washbasin shelf, and rumpled up the bed.

While the police were doing their best to: (a) cover the girl decently, and (b) interrogate her about what had happened, her "mother," Mrs. Elton Toby, returned to the hotel room from a shopping expedition and, on being told by her daughter what had happened, that the man on the floor had let himself into the room with a key and had attacked her, turned on Marvin Mallon with the fury of a tigress and kicked him so hard and so repeatedly before she could be restrained that she fractured three of his ribs.

Charley was back at the New Franciscan at about six thirty. There was a message to call Birdie Fustino, Gennaro's wife, so he called her.

"Mrs. Fustino? Charley Partanna."

"Hey, whatta you? Call me Birdie."

"Sure. Great. Certainly." She was the don's sister, fahcrissake.

"I had a call from my niece tonight. She's coming down tomorrow."

"Your niece?"

"Maerose. Your intended. She's coming down."

"Oh. Great. She's coming down?" Then he heard what she had said. "My in    ˙ ˧᠌?"

"Whassamatta?"

"Who told you that?"

"She did. Who else? I thought maybe you'd like to go out and meet her."

"Well. Sure. You bet."

"She's gonna be staying with us. Here."

"Sure. Absolutely. You got a flight number?"

"A car will pick you up at eleven. He'll have the flight number. She gets in at twelve five, then youse can drive back here and we'll all have lunch."

"That sounds great."

"Hey, you know what I'm gonna make for dessert, because I noticed that you got a real tooth for a dessert?"

"What?"

*"Uccidduzzi* with *'scursunera!* Real Sicilian. Hah? Hey?"

"Terrific. That will be absolutely terrific, Birdie."

# 36

## SON OF N.Y. MAYORAL CANDIDATE ARRESTED ON SERIOUS TEEN AND NARCOTICS CHARGES HERE

Marvin Mallon, age 31, son of George F. Mallon, the Reform Party candidate for mayor of New York, was arrested last night in a room at the New Iberia Hotel and charged with illegal entry, corrupting the morals of a minor, aggravated assault upon a minor, indecent exposure, carrying a deadly weapon, and illegal possession of two ounces of heroin.

Police said he had battered a 15-year-old girl, Laverne Toby, of Palestine, Texas, while attempting to force her to commit unnatural sexual acts.

Mallon alleges that Miss Toby and her mother were in his room at the hotel, but the hotel's records show that he was registered in a single room, two floors below the Toby suite, on the other side of the hotel.

Police believe Mallon to be a drug dealer. The weapon he was carrying is believed to match the ballistic pattern of the weapon used to kill a narcotics wholesaler, Julius "Little Julie" Mingle, in Baton Rouge, last week.

Reached in New York, the suspect's father, who conducted a "Pray-In" in New York's Central Park yesterday with almost 100,000 people attending including national religious leaders, stated that the charges were "impossible and preposterous."

Marvin Mallon, who gave his occupation as "religions contact person," has no police record either in New York or in local or Federal records, it has been ascertained. The arrest is expected to have a strong negative effect on the Mallon candidacy.

The Mallon television broadcast in New York, scheduled for seven P.M. Monday night, was canceled by Mallon Campaign Headquarters. The candidate was unavailable for comment. He was in executive session with his aides, but ultimately it became necessary to sedate him. With eight days to go until Election Day, Mayor Heller offered the candidate the city's entire cooperation in setting up the fullest flow of information between the candidate and the New Orleans Police Department, the media reported; a gracious gesture on his part, in view of the candidate's announced intentions.

Early Monday morning, Charley dialed the Plumber at the Laundry in Brooklyn.

"Al? Tell Pop to call me."

He ordered breakfast. Then Pop's call came in.

"How is she?"

"She's sitting up."

"I thought pneumonia patients had to sit up so their lungs won't get full."

"I mean she is sitting up in a chair. I seen her last night. She asked for you."

"She asked for me?"

"She wanted to know when you was coming back."

"Yeah?"

"That story broke very good here."

"I hope Mallon saw it."

"Yeah."

"It's going to cook Mallon?"

"He's through. And the Reform horseshit is through. We did everybody a terrific favor — the cops, the judges, the politicians, and millions of people who like to place a little bet, have a little fun, or use a little smack. A whole way of life was threatened here, Charley, but you stopped the bastards."

"Then I can come home?"

"Anytime. But my information from Vincent is that Maerose is flying down there today. So if I was you I wouldn't come *right* home."

"I know. Jesus, Pop, what am I suppose to do with her?"

"My figure is that if she's going all the way down there then she wants to make peace witchew because if she wanted to beat on you she'd make you go to her."

"Yeah?"

"That is my best hunch, Charley."

Charley got dressed, then he read the newspaper story again. The car arrived and he went out to the airport to find out if Pop was right.

## 37

Pop let himself into Mardell's room at the hospital and beamed at her. It was a large, private, well-lit room with a lot of flowers in it that had come almost entirely from either Pop or Charley, with a little something from Maerose, and a bouquet from Freddie. Mardell, perhaps more beautiful because she had lost weight, sat under a blanket in the large upholstered chair, looked across the room at him, and smiled back.

"Mr. Partanna."

"You're looking very good. And when you look good, the whole world lights up."

"You are so sweet. The fact that I am better is all your doing."

"It's a good hospital. I knew that before I had them send you here. Friends of mine own it." He put a package near her on the bed. "I brought you some cookies. Or would you rather have rubies?"

"Cookies."

He sat down in a chair facing her, near the

bed. "The room smells great."

"That gigantic pyramid of flowers in the corner is from Charley."

"If he coulda done it he woulda picked every flower himself."

"See that measly bunch of gladiola? They're from Charley's fiancée. I hate gladiola."

"I didn't know he had a fiancée."

"Please, Mr. Partanna, not you, too."

"She probably hadda phone the order in. You know, you say send twenty dollars' worth of flowers to somebody and that's what they send."

"Twenty dollars?"

"Well – ten, anyway."

"More like two."

"It's the thought that counts."

"That's what I mean. Is she really his fiancée, Mr. Partanna?"

"They grew up together. In the same environment."

"That doesn't answer my question."

"I don't think they're engaged."

"Was it one of those arrangements that families decide?"

"Circumstances change things."

"How?"

"Well, for one thing – you came along. You are important to Charley."

Mardell turned her face away from him.

"This is a short life they give us," Pop said. "If we don't decide what we want and try to get it, then time marches on and we're left behind, right?"

"What is she like?"

"She's a good woman. She's smart. And a terrific competitor. I know her from since she's a baby. I work with her father and her grandfather."

"And I'm a stranger."

"What has that got to do with it? I don't count. I just want the best for Charley. The father and the grandfather don't know you're alive. Charley don't really have much to say about it. It's between you and Maerose. Whichever one wants Charley the most is gonna get him."

"Does it come down to that?" she said, looking at the window, into the distance. "I don't think it does. She wants him just as much as I do. All that wanting has no effect on Charley. He has to decide. Charley has just about everything to say about it."

"Listen, you're a fine young woman. No matter how it turns out — and God knows I don't know what that's gonna be — it ain't gonna be the end of the world. We gotta pick ourselves up and get started again and after a while it ain't as important as it used to be."

"She has a grandfather and a father backing her up. What do I have?"

"Sure, Charley knows Maerose all their lives. But you have important things going for you. He loves you."

"Does he love Maerose?"

"Sure. That's the hard part for him – for alla youse."

"When is he coming home?"

"Next Wednesday. You'll be out of here by then."

"I don't know what to do."

"Wait. That's all. Everything will settle itself by the end of next week."

# 38

Monday at twelve minutes before noon, Charley watched Maerose come off the ramp from the plane at Moissant airport. She was wearing a fitted knee-length red wool suit with black fox collar and cuffs and a zip front jacket. She wore spike-heeled Italian winkle-picker shoes with long, pointed toes. He had never seen her look so gorgeous. She was smiling broadly as she rushed up to him and threw her arms around him. "Jeez, Charley," she said, "we gotta catch up."

"You staying at your aunt's?"

"I'll sleep there. I'm staying with you."

"You gotta be the classiest thing ever to come into this airport."

On the eleven-mile ride back into town they held hands but that was all, because the driver was an old friend of Vincent's and he wouldn't stop talking.

"How's your father, Miss Prizzi?"

"He's fine."

"Give him my best. Tell him Gus Fangoso. We go way back."

"He'll be happy to hear from you."

"I'm talking right after the war. Nineteen forty-six — forty-seven."

"I'll tell him."

"He'll know what you mean."

He kept it up for about four miles. Charley said, "Hey, Gus. Stop at that drugstore onna corner up there." Gus stopped the car. "Come in with me a minute," Charley said to him.

They went into the store. Gus was a paunchy man in his late fifties, maybe six years older than Vincent. When they got inside the store Charley laid the fear all over Gus, then he said, "That is my *fidanzata* in the car. I ain't talked to her for three weeks. I am sitting beside her for the first time in almost three weeks and I still can't talk to her because you keep talking to her. Do you understand what I'm saying to you?"

"Sure, Charley. Absolutely."

"Then we'll go back to the car. And you put up the window. *Capeesh?*"

"Sure. I got it. Absolutely, Charley."

They went back to the car. Gus held the door open and Charley got in. Gus went around to the driver's seat. He started the engine then pressed the button that put up the power window between the front and the back seat. They drove into town.

"You must have said the magic words, or something," Maerose said.

Still, there wasn't time even to get started saying anything. To Charley it seemed like right away the limousine was rolling through high gates into the 150-yard-long brick driveway to the front door of the Fustino mansion, which triumphantly combined English, Mediterranean, and American architectural styles. The door was opened by an elderly, uniformed Italian maid whom Maerose embraced, kissed, and called Enriquette and introduced to Charley as Gennaro's cousin. They had a view of seventy-eight feet through airy, high-ceilinged rooms. All of the space was air-conditioned. Tall cabinets filled with Meissen, Sèvres, and English porcelains stood beside tables that had been made for George IV. The house had been built by one of the biggest Pepsi-Cola bottlers in the South about ten years before, yet the effect the designers had achieved was of a great plantation house over a hundred years old.

The November sun was still high in a perfect blue sky. They were led to an enormous patio where a large oval table had been set for lunch. Two Fustino daughters with their husbands and three of the Fustino sons (out of nine), with their wives, were waiting for Maerose as she came into the patio with Charley. While tumultuous greetings went on, Gennaro took Charley off to one side. "That was nice work you done last night, Charley."

Charley nodded, coloring slightly under the praise. "Natale was solid," he said.

"Mallon looks like getting ninety to a hundred and thirty years on all the counts," Gennaro said.

Birdie Fustino was greeting Maerose with hugs and kisses saying, in answer to Mae's ecstatic comment on the house, "We just took it the way we found it. It takes eleven people to run it, four in the garden alone."

It was a warm, affectionate, and happy lunch. Gennaro sat at the head of the table with Maerose at his right. Birdie sat at the other end with Charley at her right, and all the beautiful young siblings and spouses were spaced in chairs between. None of them was in the environment. The husbands were dentists and software designers, restaurant people, and an art gallery owner. They were a great-looking bunch of women, Charley thought, but Maerose was the absolute standout and everyone in the room knew it, particularly Charley. Nobody, not even Mardell, made him as horny as he got from just looking at Mae. Charley was sure that every now and then Gennaro was copping a feel on her knee under the table. Sometimes he was able to catch Maerose's eye, and they grinned at each other.

Things are certainly looking up in this department, Charley told himself. He didn't know anybody, so mostly he kept his mouth shut and pretended to listen to Birdie while he tried to figure out what he was going to say to Mae when they were alone, whenever that was going to be.

He concentrated on what life with her would be forty years ahead if it had happened that they were engaged and that finally they did get married. He would be seventy years old, she would be about sixty-two. They would have grown-up kids, even married kids. He would be a grandfather. The whole point of thinking ahead like that was: would he still remember Mardell? Would he still be worrying about her? Would he be worrying about where Mardell was and what was happening to her? Forty years was a long time, but better if he made it fifty years. He would be eighty. He would have grown-up grandchildren. Jesus, he thought, life is certainly hard to figure.

Gennaro left at two o'clock. The lunch party broke up at about three fifteen. Maerose went upstairs to change. When she came down, she had on a café au lait sheath with a diagonal silver silk fringe spiraling around her long, lithe body. There was a big gold pin on her left shoulder. She looked like the kind of package anybody would like to get. She had a stab of extreme pleasure when she looked at Charley's face as she came down the stairs and a surge of deep-down elation when she looked at the front of his trousers. They got away from Birdie at about a quarter to four. They sat quietly in the car until they had Gus drop them off in the Quarter. They walked a block and a half to the New Franciscan so Gus could tell Birdie that they had gone sightseeing. When the door closed in Charley's apartment they both started to talk at the same time, stopped, and Maerose put her arms around his neck, holding on silently. After a while they kissed.

"What's it gonna be, Charley?"

"Mae – I gotta say it – we ain't engaged. You know that."

"I didn't come all the way down here to have you tell me stuff like that, Charley."

"We gotta get this straightened out. You know that."

"Are you gonna marry that mountain? She isn't even in the environment."

"I ain't gonna marry nobody, Mae."

"Then dump her. We'll start even again."

"The girl has pneumonia in New York. I can't even think about dumping her."

"You gotta dump her or dump me."

"Why? Why can't we just keep on going the way we been going?"

"I can't do a stand like that."

"I go back to New York next Wednesday. Lemme think about it."

"Charley, look – suppose you decide on her? Whatta you gonna do, the business you're in? Does she know the business you're in?"

"No. Anyway, I don't think so."

"So maybe she's not sure you're legitimate. But how is she gonna get it straight in her head about everything you do? She's English, she ain't American. She's never gonna understand what you do."

"She's had a lot of trouble in her life. Jesus, you don't know. I'm like the only rock she can sit on. I don't know, I get the feeling that if I take that away she's gonna drown."

"What about me? You think I can just throw this whole thing off like a bad cold? What about me, Charley?"

"I gotta figure the whole thing out."

"You think because I fight you on this that I am some kind of Charles Atlas of the heart, Charley? You think when everything is down the tube and you have to make your move that, because she's had a lot of trouble in her life and you think I haven't — you can just figure that I'm gonna be all right?"

"That's the only way I got left to think. What am I gonna think — I mean, how am I gonna get this thing straight if that ain't the way I do it?"

"Get it straight the right way! You and me were meant for each other. We live the same way, we think the same way. Maybe part of the reason why I love you is because of the way you are trying to protect this woman, but nothing fits together with you and the woman. We are talking marriage — a lifetime. Things have to fit together, maybe not everything but the main things, the important things." Suddenly, she switched to Sicilian. "We speak the same language, Charley."

He took a deep breath and exhaled slowly. "Yeah. I know. You're right, Mae. But this girl has everything different. Problems, where she is coming from, she could be the thing from outer space. But, like you said, we're talking about a lifetime, so I can't fool around with your life. We have to be sure. Give me two weeks against the lifetime, Mae."

She took him in her arms and pulled him toward the stepladder to the bed.

"That'll never work, Charley. It'll just go on and on and on. I saw the don. I told him — formally, like I sent him an engraved announcement — that you and me are gonna get married."

Charley's legs gave way. He dropped into a chair beside the bed. "You told the don *that*?"

"He wants to set a date. And after I give him a date, he wants to give us a big engagement party and bring in the people from most of the families around the country. I gotta tell him whether it's on or it's off, Charley. That means you gotta tell me."

"A date? Jesus, Mae—"

"A line has to be drawn, Charley. We can't go on and on like this."

Charley thought of his father and his mother. He thought of the don and the family and how he had never lived outside it because, as far as he was concerned, there was nothing outside the family. If he decided that he had to stay with Mardell he would have to leave the family, leave all his people. If only Mardell was the kind of a girl who would take a bundle of cash and forget the whole thing.

"Yeah," he said to Maerose, staring into her eyes. "We gotta set a date."

She kissed him. "It better be all settled in your mind, Charley, because by now the don has told a lot of people. Like my father."

# 39

George F. Mallon knew he had been outgeneraled by God, by fate, or by some rotten sons of bitches at City Hall. He knew who had done this to him and to poor Marvin; the party in power had cold-bloodedly set out to ruin him through his son; his poor ham-fisted, dim-witted, poor relation of a son. He should have sent the boy into the seminary for television training when he had declared for Jesus. He could have had his own television church by now, raking in the bales of money, helping to set the foreign policy of the United States; but he had to insist on trying to turn the boy into a businessman. Somebody had to take over the business. They were only beginning to build television tabernacles.

Mallon boiled with outrage. A conscienceless pack of unscrupulous politicians had been willing to wreck a fine young man's life just to hold on to their rotten, filthy power over the city he had tried so hard to love. What was there to love? New York was, at most, a picture on an airline calendar which stretched for thirty blocks each way on three avenues in Manhattan, and its symbol was an apple, just as the symbol of the fall of Adam and Eve had been an apple.

Those rotten ward heelers must have been into ten times the graft that he and his people had suspected. The stakes must be higher than heaven for a man like His Honor the Mayor to go along with a terrible scheme like this — using his whey-faced, boob-brained son's natural life as if it were some ten-cent chip in an evil gambling game.

George F. Mallon certainly knew about organized crime. He was an American businessman who had been in the construction business all over the country for most of his life. Even though he had been building for the Greater Glory of God and His Nielsen ratings, that fact had not spared him from the inexorable demands of hoodlums. He had paid them off. He had even entertained them from time to time because it had seemed like sound business policy. Some of the most religiously thrilling Christmas cards he had ever received had come from organized criminals, their wives, and their families.

Nonetheless, the main plank in his platform had been to use the powers of his office, if elected, to crush, or otherwise negotiate with, the forces of organized crime in the City of New York. But, despite his long experience with them and his plans for organized criminals, he did not make the connection between the heinous threat to his candidacy and the future of his son with the life and liberty of the underboss of the Prizzi family. George F. Mallon knew it was just rotten politics and rottener politicians who had framed his boy and would continue to threaten his future until the election had passed.

He was sickened by the enormity of knowing that people outside his intimate circle of counselors, aides, and speech-writers had known about his determination to prosecute the hoodlum who had shot the other hoodlum almost in the actual presence of the mayor of New York at Manhattan Beach that fateful night, and most certainly in the presence of and with the full knowledge of high officers of the police department, and it was slowly coming to him that perhaps even the criminal organization of the city had had something to do with Marvin's predicament. He spoke with perplexity to the two campaign aides who were hunkered around his desk.

"I can't believe it," he said, "I simply cannot believe that in this day and age the mayor of the City of New York would stoop so low as to do this thing to my son just to ensure his chances of re-election."

"Well, you better believe it, G.F., because that's what he did."

"You don't think it was the hoodlum element?"

"What could they have to do with the election?"

"Set up a meeting with the mayor for tonight."

"Tomorrow is Election Day, G.F."

"He is holding my son as his hostage! I have to see him."

The meeting was arranged with considerable

difficulty because the mayor, understandably, felt that George F. Mallon had maligned him beyond the call of political campaigning. The meeting was to be held in a room reserved by a Mallon aide at the McBurney Branch of the YMCA on West Twenty-third Street for fifteen minutes between six thirty and six forty-five that evening. The mayor arrived alone, wearing shades. George F. Mallon was waiting when the mayor knocked on the door of the single room. He sat on the bed. The mayor sat on the only chair.

"I'm sorry about your troubles, Mallon," the mayor said. He was a hyperkinetic man who thought of himself as being at the center of a sea of calm.

"Let's not waste this precious time with hypocrisy, Heller. My son is in a Louisiana prison. He could be seventy-three years old before he gets out — at the minimum."

"Whatta you want from me? Maybe you should have gotten him laid before you sent him to New Orleans."

"I will pray for you, Franklin Heller. Now. Let us talk about how you can undo what you have done to my boy."

"Done? What *I* done? Who gave him such an allowance that he could afford two ounces of heroin? Did I tell him to carry a gun?"

"Who planted that dope and that gun on him?" Mallon exclaimed. "Who switched his room at that hotel while he was out at the Evangelical Convention? Who framed him?"

"How do I know? *What?* You mean you think my people set your kid up?"

"Who else?"

"Who else? You're six months in politics and you think this is how people get elected? You should have your mind washed out. I'm twenty-one years in politics. You win some, you lose some, but you don't frame people on narcotics charges and murder charges and rape and indecent exposure charges just to keep a city job. Shame on you, Mallon. And good night, you disgust me." He leaped to his feet.

"Mr. Mayor! Please. Accept my profound apologies. I am — I'm distraught. I have no experience with this kind of thing — politics included — I'm grabbing at straws."

The mayor shrugged. He knew less than Mallon about how it had happened that Marvin Mallon had been arrested in New Orleans. George F. Mallon had told the world that he planned to break his back and throw him out of office by making him an accessory in the zotzing of Vito Daspisa. But he didn't know Vita Daspisa had been zotzed. He thought Vito Daspisa had been shot while resisting arrest.

He had been there himself. He had seen most of it happen with his own eyes, and the rest of it, like everybody else, on a television screen. Mallon was a monster but he had been ruined, and his kid was in trouble.

"All right. Listen to me, Mallon. About what happened to your boy in New Orleans, I don't know whether he is innocent or guilty. But I can tell you two things. First, whatever happened down there cost you the election — although, frankly, you never had any chance to win the election — and two, me and my people had nothing to do with it. What happened to your kid, I mean. Now I gotta run. We got a big rally at the Garden. Tomorrow is Election Day, in case you want to remember." He patted Mallon on the shoulder and left the room.

# 40

Mallon did the straightforward, law-abiding, thing. He retained the most influential law firm in Louisiana for his son's defense, Groot & Talliesen, a member firm of the Barker's Hill Enterprises Group, which was run by Edward

S. Price. Although they put their best people on it, they had to tell him that the case against Marvin was watertight; there wasn't a chance of even getting him off with a suspended sentence; Marvin faced forty years for the possession of narcotics with criminal intent alone, which under federal law had to be served without the possibility of parole, but his attorneys thought they had a chance, at least, to bring the charges down to mere possession, with a sentence of only seven to fifteen years. With the right judge — and money could do a lot in the state political machine — Marvin might get a suspended sentence at least on that charge.

The murder charge was tricky and dangerous, the lawyers said, but it was circumstantial. If they could find an explanation for why Marvin was carrying the weapon that had caused the death of the narcotics wholesaler in Baton Rouge, they could, thanks to Marvin's lack of prior criminal records, feel confident that they'd win a jury over to Marvin's point of view. If not, Marvin would surely be sentenced to a fifteen- to thirty-year prison term.

"Explanation?" George F. Mallon exploded. "It was a plant! The whole goddam thing is a plant deliberately calculated to cost me the election."

"Then there is the aggravated assault and

the attempted rape of a minor, the indecent exposure, and the illegal breaking and entering," the lawyers told him on the roundtable conference call between New York and New Orleans. "Those could bring an aggregate of twenty to thirty years." But the real difficulty, the lawyers felt, beyond the rape and the aggravated assault, were the charges that Marvin had tried to force a fifteen-year-old girl into committing unnatural sex acts, because Marvin had been caught in flagrante delicto on those counts: he had broken into the girl's hotel room and ripped her clothes off, battered her and assaulted her. There were badly damaging pictures of Marvin after he had exposed himself to the teenage girl. The girl and her mother were pressing the police and the media to urge the courts to bring the case to earliest trial. The two arresting officers and the house officer at the hotel would testify as to how Marvin had battered the girl. There was absolutely nothing anyone could do for Marvin about those charges, which could carry a thirty- to fifty-year sentence in Louisiana.

"My God, poor Marvin—"

"He faces a total combined sentence of a possible 150 years in the state's prison — although of course he could be out in sixty-five with good behavior — unless—"

"Unless — what?" Mallon asked.

"There is a — ah — man — here — in New Orleans, that is, who has considerable — ah — community influence and the consensus is that if you could talk to him—"

"Who is he?"

"His name is Gennaro Fustino. He is a — ah — philanthropist."

"You are speaking euphemistically?"

"Yes."

"What can he do?"

"I would say there is no limit to what he *could* do, in this case."

"Like what? How?"

"He might be able to persuade the — ah — girl, Laverne Toby, to withdraw her testimony and — ah — in the case of the narcotics and the — ah — alleged murder weapon which your son was allegedly carrying — well, we would say it would most certainly be worth your talking to him."

"What church group is he with?"

"Why?"

"I'd like to have some pretty formidable introductions arranged. If he can do anything, I want to talk to him under the best possible auspices."

"From his name, I would guess he's a Catholic."

"I can get to the Pope. Check the man out on his religious affiliation, please."

"Well – perhaps this office can – ah – arrange such a meeting."

"Set it up for late Wednesday morning. I'll fly out as soon as this election is definitely settled. Not that it isn't definitely settled right at this moment. I had this city government on the run and now they have broken my back." Mallon slammed the phone down.

# 41

Charley rode back on the plane sitting beside a man who hummed "These Foolish Things" for three hundred miles. It was torture, not because it reminded him of Maerose or Mardell, he didn't need any help with that, but because it was one endless drone.

Charley changed his seat. He looked out the starboard window and began to hum "The Washington Post March" and tried to think. A week after Election Day it was all set up that Laverne Toby and her mother would fade out of the picture, unavailable to testify against

Marvin Mallon, the ballistics report would turn out to be a mistake and, on laboratory examination, the contents of the two tinfoil parcels would turn out to be talcum powder. After Marvin signed a release absolving the hotel of any responsibility for his misadventure, he would be all fixed up. But he, Charley Partanna, would be in exactly the same bind with the same two women in his life.

He was all clear on George F. Mallon, but he was going to have to live like a thief on the lam. If Mae had been shook up enough to hire private detectives to check him and Mardell out at the Miami airport and to pin down that he had stayed over at Mardell's apartment in New York a couple of dozen nights, then she was going to keep the same people on him until after the engagement party, when there wouldn't be anything he could do about it anymore.

But Mardell had had pneumonia. Nobody just turns his back on somebody who has just had pneumonia. If she needed him before, she needed him triple now. Pop would have handled the hospital bill, but who knew how much cash she had on hand? How much food could she have in the house, and how could a woman who had just come out of the hospital be expected to carry heavy groceries home from a supermarket? She wasn't working, and also she was nuts enough to send any extra money she had to her mother in England, so it could be that she didn't even have enough money to buy groceries. He had to see her. He had to talk to her and make sure she was all right. If she was all right, he would be able to cool it because, after almost a three-week break, she might even have gotten used to it.

He could bring her a list of club dates from Pomerantz and make sure that Pomerantz had the loot to take care of her if she wasn't strong enough to work yet. The time had come to lop her off, Charley admitted that, but even Maerose would understand that the only thing he could do was to go and see Mardell so he could tell her all this. But it was risky, so the best thing would be to not even go home to the beach but to lose any possible tail Mae might plant on him at the airport, and to go straight to Mardell's. Not so straight, either. Down the alley behind her house and into the building by the back door.

The cabin attendant brought lunch. "How come airlines never have Italian food?" he asked her.

"You ever eat reheated pasta?" she asked him. "You know what it's like?"

"I can guess, I guess."

"You ever eat canned spaghetti?"

"Canned spag*hetti?*"

"Reheated pasta is worse. I know — my husband is an Italian and he can handle canned spaghetti. But when it comes to reheated pasta he like wants to slash his wrists."

"I'll eat the salad. I hope I can keep it down."

"The bread isn't great, but it isn't bad."

The flight came in at La Guardia. Charley got on the non-public phone on the tarmac outside the airport building and called Arrigo Sviato, who headed up the high tech freight and luggage robbery unit at La Guardia for Religio Vulpigi, Charley's old boss. He told Arrigo he had to get out of the airport without anybody seeing him go. Arrigo asked him for the number on his baggage check, then where he was, and when Charley told him he said to stay right there until they could send a van over for him that would take him right into Brooklyn. "I gotta go into New York, actually," Charley said.

"Why not? The van will bring your bag."

## 42

Mardell dressed carefully. She put on her gold sweater, which she had worn the first time she had lunch with Charley, and made sure that her Cleopatra hair was precisely in place. The outfit had moved Charley to expressions of admiration and she did want to make a good first impression on Miss Prizzi, if only because she wanted Miss Prizzi to be proud of Charley's choice of her as a rival for Miss Prizzi's affections.

Miss Prizzi had telephoned the evening before. She had been very correct, not one bit rude or vulgar. She said she wanted to come by for a chat. A chat? Well! Miss Prizzi had been so correct that Mardell had felt constrained to invite her for tea. Promptly at five the doorbell rang, and it was Miss Prizzi.

Mardell's English speech was entirely in place. "How do you do, Miss Prizzi," she said, extending her hand. She felt that it was impossible to overdo the accent. Maerose took her hand and shook it, silently. They went into the living room, where the tea things had been laid out.

"I didn't know whether you preferred high tea," Mardell said, "so I settled at a medium-high level. Please do sit down here."

Maerose sat contemplating the medium tea, staring hungrily at the small pile of tiny, paper-thin smoked salmon and cucumber and watercress sandwiches. "That looks delicious."

"The tea is vintage Darjeeling, from the highest Himalayan tea gardens. One hopes you like Darjeeling. One was leaning toward Lapsang souchong even though it is smoky and pungent."

Maerose glared at her. "I have looked forward to meeting you."

"I, you, as well." Mardell tried to pattern her performance on her distinct memory of Dame Edith Evans.

"I understand you work at the Casino Latino?"

"Yes."

"My grandfather owns it."

"Well! Your grandfather. There is a really famous man."

"Yeah."

"I have a friend — a Miss Harriet Blacker — who is working for graduate degrees in the behavioral sciences. She would give her *toes* to meet your grandfather."

"He's quite old, my grandfather. And retired. He doesn't see people anymore."

"Pity. How nice of you to come by."

"I am here to talk to you about Charley." Maerose's speech was taking on the slightest of British accents, Mardell noted, feeling that scored points for the La Tour side.

"It would all have been so much more effective if Charley had been here," Mardell said. "While we were both here, that is."

"Charley's in New Orleans."

"Yes, I know."

"Miss La Tour – I do not want you to think I am interfering in your life, but there are things which I had to be sure that you understood completely."

"Tea?"

"Thank you."

Mardell poured the tea. "This tea is better by itself or with a slice of lemon. It is a totally distinctive tea. Lemon?"

"Yeah."

"Salmon?"

"Why not?"

Mardell served her a plate with five half tea sandwiches. "It is just that I don't think the decision is ours to make," she said.

"Decision?"

"About Charley. If one or the other of us left him, he might decide it was the wrong one. You see, I feel he must decide this thing."

"It is out of the question. Our engagement — our intention to marry — is very much a family thing, Miss La Tour. My family have made involved plans over the years, since we were kids, actually, so — well, even if he were to choose you over me — temporarily — it couldn't last." Maerose's voice hardened. "Do you understand what I am telling you?"

"But if he chooses me over you, I would feel there was no need for me to — ah — sacrifice myself. I would feel, in fact, that you did not — ah — deserve Charley. No, Miss Prizzi. Not at all. I am not going to withdraw without hearing a decidedly firm expression. There is no other way. Charley must decide this."

Maeorse sipped her tea delicately. She opened her purse after biting into the second paper-thin smoked salmon sandwich. She removed a checkbook from the purse.

"Since I am going to have you fired from the Latino," she said, discarding stilted speech. "You are gonna need money. How much you think you're gonna need?"

"Money?"

"A straight payoff, baby. I'm gonna give you twenty-five hundred of the easiest dollars you ever made, and you are gonna change the locks on your doors here."

"Suppose I take the money but Charley won't let me go?"

"Look, Mardell — I'll make it an even thirty-five hundred dollars. Also, I'll pay your expenses for like a week in Nassau or someplace like that. Why not go back to England? You stay away for ten days, two weeks. By that time it will all be over."

Mardell smiled a pussycat smile. "I'm so sorry, Miss Prizzi. Can't be done. I'll wait right here and put the question to Charley a few moments after he walks through that door."

# 43

The van dropped him right in front of Mardell's building. In his brooding about the two women, he had forgotten to tell the driver he was going to use the back door. As they stopped in front of the apartment house, Charley felt as if he had just stabbed himself; he could feel the eyes of Mae's agency man clocking him as he went in.

Charley stood outside Mardell's apartment door, took a deep breath, and pushed the doorbell. He heard faint noises of movement inside the apartment so he waited without ringing again. He heard Mardell say, "Who is it?"

"Charley. I'm home."

The chain lock rattled, the three dead bolts snapped, and the door flew open. Mardell stared at him wide-eyed. "What do you want?"

"Jesus, you lost a lotta weight, Mardell." He reached out and pulled her into his arms.

She began to weep. "Buckingham Palace has forgotten me, Charley. She must be in Australia," she sobbed. "I've been so sick."

He eased both of them into the apartment and shut the door.

"Don't cry. It's all right. Everything's gonna be all right."

She turned away from him and tottered down the hall, turning left into the first doorway. He followed her. She got into bed. He covered her and tucked her in. "Pop told me how sick you were," he said.

"I'll be all right," she said, lying on her back with her eyes closed, her arms stretched at her sides, palms upward.

"How come Pop didn't get you a nurse here? You ain't well enough to be all by yourself."

"I didn't want a nurse."

"Why not?"

"Because I wanted you to come here, and when you came I wanted us to be able to talk without a stranger in the place."

He pulled up a chair and sat where he could look closely at her face. "I go away on a weekend business trip to Miami and I'm gone almost three weeks. While I'm gone, you get pneumonia. If somebody said to me that was gonna happen, I woulda said they could send somebody else to Miami."

She didn't answer him. Two large, clear tears appeared at the corners of her closed eyes and ran down the sides of her head.

"I can't tell you how much I thought about you, how much I missed you," he said. He picked up her hand and held it. He kissed it.

"That – your fiancée came here yesterday."

"Who?"

"She said she had just been with you in New Orleans."

Charley blew up. "What the hell is she? My keeper?" he yelled, getting to his feet with his fists clenched and staring down at Mardell, who opened her enormous eyes at him. "She got herself invited to New Orleans by her aunt. The aunt is my boss's sister. I had to go to the lunch and see her."

"Is that where you were? Lunching with her?"

"I didn't wanna see her. And she's putting pressure on you for two weeks — Pop told me about those dried-up flowers she sent to the hospital after she practically handed you pneumonia on a silver platter by bugging you and trying to worry you to death."

"Your father was very kind to me."

"What is she tryna do now? Give you leprosy? Hey, Mardell — no offense."

She began to giggle. She pointed her long, thin arm and a long finger at him as the giggle built into bellowing laughter. She held up both of her arms to him and he went into them. They held each other tightly.

"Now I'm sure my mother was putting me on with that story about my dad being a leper," she gasped.

"You are tremendous, Mardell," he said. "There ain't another woman like you in the whole world. And that's okay with me because, if you gotta know, I love you." He kissed her. Then, recuperation or otherwise, one thing led to another.

After a while, as they rested on a pile of pillows, Mardell said, "I had a lot of time to think about everything, and I decided that I have to accept whatever happens."

"Whatever happens?" Charley said with

alarm. "Whatta you mean?"

"Charley — we haven't known each other very long. A few weeks. She's known you all of your joint lives."

"Know? She knew I was there, I knew she was there. It was strictly zilch. This whole engagement thing is a mockery. I never had nothing to say about it. She said we was engaged, that's all. *I* never said we was engaged."

"She loves you."

"Aaaah!"

"You don't love her?"

He went silent. "I like her. She's okay."

Mardell started to get out of bed. "I'd better think about making us some dinner."

He held her down. "What can I tell you? I don't wanna lie to you. My father proved to me a long time ago that lying makes things worse."

"What are we going to do, Charley?"

"Why are we alive? That's what we gotta ask ourselves."

"Why are we alive then?"

"I read about it in a magazine. I never forgot it because it's logical. We are alive so we can reproduce ourselves. What are we? the magazine asked — and it was written by a famous scientist, I forget his name. We are envelopes for the genes that rule us, control us, and use us until we reproduce, and then they pass themselves along to a new fresh body that we reproduced from ourselves. So when a baby is made, the whole thing makes the genes what they are — immortal."

"That's beautiful, Charley. But what does that have to do with you and Miss Prizzi?"

"The article said the atoms that make us up altogether rule the genes. Who rules the atoms?"

"God?"

"Let's not get too deep on this. Anyway, men look around to spread their seed, to reproduce. They don't have the hard part — having the baby — so their instinct is just to spread the seed."

"So?"

"That's what I mean that I can't lie to you, Mardell. I was following my instinct to reproduce. I was spreading my seed with her."

"That is as neat an explanation for this sort of thing as I have ever heard."

"It's the truth."

"My mother told my father that all a woman really asks is that a man know his own mind, that a woman will accept almost any conditions if she is sure they are what the man believes."

"Yeah?"

"You are sleeping with another woman. I have to accept that because I believe in you."

"I never had such trouble in my life. I can't keep it up. No matter how rough it turns out to be, I gotta make my move, one way or the other — you or her."

# 44

George F. Mallon was deeply impressed by the outside and inside of Gennaro Fustino's New Orleans house. He was taken into Gennaro's office by the elderly woman in a Victorian maid's uniform who answered the front door. It confirmed his hunch that people of real wealth and taste did not have butlers. But even if he fired his butler, where could he get a woman as distinguished as this one to answer the door? The uniform alone bespoke a long tradition.

He was admitted to a large room with fourteen-foot-high tiers of books lining three walls, the fourth being made of glass and having a glass door that led to a patio that could only be described as being the epitome of gracious living. There was something of old Europe about the charm of this place, he thought, although to get a climate like this you'd have to go to North Africa.

A round, quite overweight, sixtyish man came into the room. Aristocratically, he didn't apologize for keeping Mallon waiting. He sat behind the enormous, bare desk and smiled.

"Good afternoon, Mr. Fustino," Mallon said.

The plump man nodded benignly.

"I am sure the mutual friends told you about the reason for this visit?"

Gennaro nodded.

"My son — my only son — is in a great deal of trouble, and I can assure you, Mr. Fustino, that every charge against him is the result of a criminal conspiracy."

"Why not?" Mr. Fustino said. "For the sake of discussion."

"On the surface, my lawyers tell me, the case seems to be hopeless, but, on the other hand, they said if you could be persuaded to take an interest in it, what could seem to be miracles could be performed."

Mr. Fustino shrugged.

"Can you help my son?"

"Those things are very difficult, if they can be done at all. Maybe it's better to find out how the court is gonna handle your son's case before thinking about any appeal?"

"What happened to my boy is a deliberate

consequence of my being one of two candidates for the office of mayor in the City of New York in the elections held this week. My opponent denies it – I have met with him and made the accusation to his face – but who else in this world would do such an infamous thing – and for what reason?"

Mr. Fustino made an abrupt moue as if in sympathy.

"I say to you my son was brutally, criminally, and unjustly framed, Mr. Fustino. I think that is the word. He had his life ahead of him. But now, instead, he faces up to 150 years in prison. He must be freed or spend that life behind bars, and since it has been so expertly arranged through due process that he most certainly will not be freed, then urgent steps must be taken."

"What steps?"

"I – ah – looked you up, Mr. Fustino. I am a man of the world and I did not rely alone on the counsel of my lawyers. I – ah – understand that you are – ah – able to make certain contacts with key elements and—"

"Key elements?"

"The Mob, I think they are called. People who are adept at bribery and coercion, people who think nothing of suborning public officials."

"I don't know what you mean. I don't know any people like that." He winked.

"I see that we understand each other. Very well." He removed a long, brown, oversized legal envelope from his side pocket. He slid it across the desk to Gennaro. "In that envelope you will find one hundred thousand dollars. I am pleading with you to agree to pass that along to the right parties inside the – uh – Mob who will know the who, what, why, when, and where concerning precisely the right people in your state's police and judicial systems who can bring about the early release of my boy."

Gennaro swept the envelope into the top drawer of his desk with a move so fast it was difficult to know that it had really happened except that the envelope was no longer there.

"You mean you want to *bribe* people to persuade them to go lightly with your son?"

"I mean they must be bribed so that they will free my son."

"I am happy to make your acquaintance, Mr. Mallon. May we meet again in the near future."

George F. Mallon held up a hand. "There is one more thing, Mr. Fustino. I have been wondering if – in the course of your contacts in the *milieu* –"

"The what?"

"The underworld — what I referred to as the Mob—"

Gennaro made a gesture to indicate his understanding.

"—if you could find me what is known among those people as a hit person."

"A *hit* person?"

"You know what I mean," Mallon said grimly.

"Why?"

"Because I have been thinking about the trouble my son finds himself in and it all goes back to one man."

"One man?"

"A man we need feel no compunction about rubbing out, as they say in the underworld. He is himself a killer, and because it was my declared intention to unmask him and to prosecute him to the fullest extent of the law, his people caused my son to be framed and brutalized."

"His people?"

"The mayor and others. He is a criminal who is employed by New York mobsters. His name is Charley Partanna."

Gennaro's face remained impassive.

"I want to talk to someone in the New Orleans underworld, far removed from the New York mob, who will take on the assignment of rubbing out Mr. Charley Partanna."

"Charley Partanna."

"That is his name."

"You feel this man costed you the election, Mr. Mallon?"

"Yes. And I would be less than human if I did not admit to a need for vengeance for that, too. As well as what he brought upon my boy."

Gennaro wheeled his swivel chair around so that he could stare out at the patio, his back to Mallon. He rolled his eyes to the heavens.

Mallon said, "Can you arrange such an introduction, Mr. Fustino?"

Gennaro turned his chair around to face Mallon and said, "What is this? Whatta you think I am? How can you ask me such a thing?" He winked again.

"Thank you, Mr. Fustino, and good day to you."

When George F. Mallon was gone, Gennaro took the exposed reel of film out of the 8mm movie camera that had photographed and recorded Mallon and his measured words. Then, picking up the telephone, he asked that his driver, Gus Fangoso, be sent in. He slipped the negative reel into a heavy manila envelope and addressed it. When Gus came in, Gennaro gave him the envelope.

"Take it to Jerry at the lab. Make one copy.

Bring the negative back to me and take the print to Angelo Partanna in New York. Then come back here. I'm gonna need you to drive me out to the track tomorrow."

# 45

The 8mm print went to New York on an afternoon flight that day, and the delivery was made to Angelo Partanna at St. Joseph's Laundry at 4:40 P.M. Angelo had dinner with Rocco Sestero, whose wife was visiting her daughter in Michigan, but he flatly refused to eat at Tucci's. He got home a little after ten and ran the film. He told himself that, if he hadn't been around for all the years he had been around, he couldn't believe it. If they didn't bother to find out what the environment was doing to them, then it had to be that they deserved what they got.

He called Gennaro Fustino.

"Gennaro? Angelo. How they hangin'?"

"You see the movie?"

"My God."

"I sat here staring at this guy. You wouldn't believe it. He was in charge, the big executive."

"Did you put him in touch with the guy he wanted?"

"They have a meet set for tomorrow night."

"Where is the contractor gonna take Charley?"

"Wherever you say."

"Charge him extra for what the contractor's gonna do for him."

"Don't worry."

"Thanks for the help, Gennaro. We owe you one."

"Listen, for favors that pay as good as this one – anytime, Ang."

Angelo called Eduardo Prizzi and made an appointment at Eduardo's office the next morning. "It won't take ten minutes," he said. "But it'll be very productive."

Maerose ran a finger over the heavy engraving on the rich parchment paper and drank in the words that glowed like jewels under her eyes.

Mr. Vincent Prizzi
of
New York City
announces the engagement
of his daughter
Miss Maerose Amalia Prizzi
to

Mr. Charles Amedeo Partanna
son of Mr. Angelo Partanna
of New York City

For the fourth time she read the information that Eduardo's people would give out to the press:

*Mr. Vincent Prizzi has announced the engagement of his daughter, Miss Maerose Amalia Prizzi, to Mr. Charles Amedeo Partanna, both of New York City. Miss Prizzi is a graduate of the Marymount School in New York and Manhattanville College in Purchase, New York. For the past year she has been working as a partner of Price-Hoover Designs, interior decorators. Mr. Partanna was also educated in New York. In Vietnam he served as a Staff Sergeant, Special Forces, where he was decorated with the Bronze Star and the Purple Heart. Since then he has been associated with the St. Joseph's Laundry and Dry Cleaning Service of New York as general manager.*

Maerose then reread the small, oblong card that was an invitation to the reception at old Palermo Gardens. It was the absolute clincher.
She folded one copy of the formal announcement and one copy of the press release and

stuffed them into a heavy cream-colored envelope, then dropped the small card into it. Smiling serenely, she sealed it and addressed it to Miss Mardell La Tour at 148 West Twenty-third Street, New York, NY 10011. She stamped the envelope and put it carefully aside in a small drawer of her desk before beginning to address the other envelopes from the long list at her elbow.

# 46

Natale Esposito went into the Purple Onion, a vegetarian restaurant on the West Esplanade in Metaire, New Orleans Parish, at exactly seven fifteen the following night and joined George F. Mallon, who was seated alone by the far wall beside the men's room door, as prearranged. Natale was wired with a transmitter to send whatever he and Mallon were going to chat about to the recording machine inside the van parked thirty feet down the Esplanade from the restaurant entrance. Natale was dressed for the contractor bit: shades, floppy Capone fedora, and a horseshoe stickpin in his tie, which he had picked up that afternoon in a pawn shop.

"Mr. Mallon?"

Mallon half-rose, slightly flustered at his first meeting with a professional hit person, a figure that loomed so importantly in his country's folklore. Although Natale had never killed anybody in his life, he had hung around with and bossed a lot of guys who had, so he knew how to comport himself with verisimilitude, which, excepting his apparel, did not differ very much from the comportment of a successful chiropractor.

"Ah. Yes," Mallon said. "Are you the – ah–"

"Yeah. Keep your voice down." Natale wasn't being cautious about their being overheard – they were the only diners on that side of the restaurant – but he was afraid of causing an overload on the tape machine.

Natale sat down. He stared at Mallon.

"Are you George F. Mallon?"

"Yes. Were you – did they tell you about the assignment?"

Natale nodded. "Well – yeah. They gimme the general idea. You want somebody taken out, right?"

"What?"

"You want somebody zotzed?"

"Oh. Yes."

"They never talk straight out about business. The man who puts out the contract lays out the hit. They call it insulation. The fewer people know, the better."

Mallon nodded sagely. "Have you — ah — decided on your terms?"

"Sixty thousand. Forty down, twenty when the job is done."

"That's quite a lot of money, Mr. — ah—"

"Call me Tony. What are you talking about, a lot of money? That's my standard money."

"All right. I'll pay it. I hope you know that the man I want — ah — handled — is in New York."

"What's his name?"

"Charles Partanna."

"You want him hit."

"Yes, but your fee will have to be all-in, no expenses. Air ticket, hotel, haircuts, meals, and transfers will all have to be included."

"You drive a hard bargain."

Mallon took a slip of paper out of his side pocket. "This is the man."

"Read it to me. I forgot my glasses."

"Charles Partanna. His business address is the St. Joseph's Laundry and Dry Cleaning Service, in the telephone directory in Brooklyn, New York. His home address is Number Three Manhattan Beach Plaza, Brooklyn. He drives a

Chevy van with midnight black glass all around. The license number is WQH 285."

"You want me to rub him out?"

"Yes."

"You mean you want him dead."

"Yes. Take him for a ride. Blow him away. And just before you do it, I want you to tell him that he is getting it courtesy of Marvin Mallon, son of George F. Mallon."

"Your son is in on this?"

"No, no. But say it just that way. He'll know what you mean."

When Angelo told him at the Laundry the next day, Vincent wanted to know who got Mallon's one hundred and forty thousand dollars.

"Who gets it? Gennaro gets it."

"How come? He should at least split it."

"How come? He gets it because he's got it. Who's gonna take it away from him?"

"I see what you mean," Vincent said.

## 47

Eduardo had a private screening room just off his office in the penthouse of the Barker's Hill Enterprises Group Headquarters. When Angelo Partanna told him the film was your-eyes-only stuff, Eduardo told the office boy who usually ran the machine to go and get a cup of coffee and he asked his personal secretary, Arrigo Garrone, to run it.

He enjoyed the film. They sat together in the screening room discussing it afterward.

"You mean that on top of this crazy movie, Farts Esposito has a tape on which Mallon actually puts out the contract on Charley?" Eduardo said incredulously.

"Absolutely."

"This is unbelievable. The Mallon kid gets released down there this morning. The girl refused to bring charges and she and her mother went back to Texas, et cetera, et cetera," Eduardo marveled.

"He'll think Gennaro spread his money

around and got instant results."

"This guy has to be the first nine-year-old who ever ran for mayor. Did you tell Charley?"

"Charley has his hands full with his engagement party coming up."

"This is terrific work you did here. Leave the movie with me, and when the audio track comes in from Gennaro, send it over, straight to my apartment."

The following Tuesday afternoon, at the cocktail hour, George F. Mallon arrived at Eduardo's mansion apartment and was shown into the intimate study on the third floor, which was the sixty-first floor of the building. Mallon had got off the elevator at the fifty-eighth floor and Eduardo's houseman led him into a second elevator, which took him to the most elegant room Mallon had ever seen.

Flowers, arranged in the nine parts of the Rikka style (Muromachi, fifteenth century) by an ikebana master, dominated the room at center and in its four corners. Covering almost the entire east wall was the James Richard Blake portrait of a perfect gardenia. The furniture was made of gleaming turned silver and glass, with deep-emerald upholstery. The interior window frames were made of silver. The elaborate and wholly compelling rug in front of the large emerald and silver sofa had been woven into an enlarged replica of a sketch made by a ninth-century Chinese emperor while shaving. From somewhere a tape machine was delivering exalting sounds of a great fiddler playing Tchaikovsky before a sonorous orchestra. Reflexively, Mallon glanced at his watch to see whether time had stopped.

Edward Price was seated on the large sofa. He rose to greet his guest. Mallon had heard of Edward Price as a great financier, a patron of the arts, and as a generous contributor to the evangelical church, which was not only Mallon's own passion but his principal source of income. He had no idea why Edward Price had invited him here, but, overcome with curiosity, he had come with some eagerness.

"How good of you to come, Mr. Mallon," Edward Price said. "The Most Reverend John Jackson has often spoken of your abiding interest in the American television church."

"That is very kind, Mr. Price, I am sure. Dr. Francis Winikus of the Southeastern Evangelical Movement, who is such a friend of the White House, has been equally praising of you."

"He's a great man. Please sit down here, Mr. Mallon."

Seating himself, Mallon said, "This is a magnificent room. May I ask who decorated it?"

"A firm called Price-Hoover. Very talented young people."

"It is an extreme pleasure, but also something of a mystery, to be invited here."

"I have something I want to show you."

The two men were seated side by side, facing the Blake painting on the east wall. "Would you like a drink?" Eduardo asked his guest. "An RC Cola? A Dr. Pepper?"

"No, thank you. The fact is, I cannot contain my curiosity."

Eduardo pressed a button on the end table. The Blake portrait of the perfect gardenia lifted itself into the ceiling exposing a motion picture screen. The window curtains drew themselves. The lights were dimmed. A moving picture image of George F. Mallon in fullest Eastmancolor came on the screen and began to talk to them. By the time it was over, Mallon's face had become dead white. His mouth moved but he made no sounds. There was a light foam at the corners of his mouth.

Edward Price said, "And that's not all." He turned on a tape recorder, which was also built into the table at his end of the sofa, and they heard George F. Mallon's voice ordering the murder of Charley Partanna.

"What are you going to do with that?" G.F.

managed to say, although his voice hardly sounded like his own voice.

"Both the film and the audio tape are going into my deepest vault, Mr. Mallon," Eduardo said.

"You are going to blackmail me."

"Not unless that becomes absolutely necessary."

"What are you going to do, Mr. Price?"

Eduardo smiled on him benevolently. "My dear Mr. Mallon," he said. "You have only to do as you are told and this information will never leave my vault. I am going to run you for the United States Senate and — who knows? — perhaps someday for an even higher office."

# 48

Four hundred and nine announcements and invitations went into the mail, to a net of eight hundred and twelve guests. All Prizzis, Sesteros, and Garrones were included down to the ages of eighteen.

Maerose was on the phone constantly with

her Aunt Amalia. Her grandfather insisted on being consulted at almost every turn about the list because, whereas there were people who had to be invited for family and business reasons, there were quite a few other people whom he absolutely couldn't stand, or didn't trust, or had tried to kill, or who had tried to kill him, so the don had to double-check everything.

When the list was finally approved and all the invitations mailed, one hundred and ninety-six tuxedos were sent to the dry cleaners around the country; a total of $476,000 was spent on dresses, furs, and hairdos; eighty-three advance reservations were made for 137 stretch limousines, and travel agents and airlines customer relations people felt a strain.

There weren't going to be enough available suites in the three midtown Prizzi-owned hotels, so twenty-seven of the year-round tenants were given free, premature holidays in the Prizzi hotels in either Miami, Atlantic City, or Las Vegas — the spa of their choice — together with $500 worth of chips. They went out; the guests to the engagement party went in.

Angelo Partanna had agreed to respond to Vincent's announcement from the dais that his daughter was to be married. Don Corrado

Prizzi personally had a meeting with Biagio, the florist who now operated all the way out in Newark. Despite the distance, Maerose's grandfather insisted that Biagio be the one to handle the decorations at the Palermo Gardens.

A courier service was laid on between the Lum Fong Chinese Restaurant on West 127th Street, which the Prizzis operated, and Gennaro Fustino's hotel suite — a gesture of hospitality, because Mr. Fustino enjoyed that cuisine so much. A total of fifty-eight full-sized pizzas were delivered in warming ovens to the various guests. Barbers shaved men stretched out on Chippendale sofas, somber priests heard the ritual confessions of four visiting wives who expiated themselves of the sins of sloth, taking the Lord's name in vain, and thinking bad thoughts, in $600-a-day suites. The weather held; clear, sunny, crisp, and altogether admirable all during the engagement party weekend.

Eight judges and three congressmen, feeling sufficiently anonymous in a crowd of that size, had accepted with pleasure. Two Cabinet members, eleven U.S. senators, and the White House sent their wives or secretaries out into the stores in Washington to select suitable engagement presents. In all, 419 invitees spent $405,289 on congratulatory gifts for the young couple; a future Boss of the Prizzi family was going to marry the granddaughter of Corrado Prizzi.

Lieutenant Davey Hanly and the entire Borough Squad accepted the invitations as tokens of the New York Police Department. The mayor of the City of New York personally provided the motorcycle escort to take the bride-to-be and her father to the reception, and he also pledged to her and to her fiancé a seven-year lease on a six-room apartment in the new luxury Garden Grove apartments, which were rapidly being constructed in an emerging part of the city, even if it wasn't in Brooklyn.

The principal families of the *fratellanza*, from New England, Miami, Chicago, Philadelphia, Los Angeles, Detroit, Cleveland, and New York planned to send not representatives but contingents, including many blood relatives of the Prizzis: Sal Prizzi had married the sister of Augie "Angles" Licamarito, Boss of the Detroit family. Two of the Garrone daughters had married sons of Gennaro Fustino, who was married to Don Corrado's baby sister, while the don's niece was married to Sam Carramazza, son of the head of the Chicago family. Don Corrado was second cousin to Sam Benefice, head of the New England family, and to Carlo "Gastank" Viggone, Boss of the Cleveland combination.

In addition to the more spectacular guests, the third generation of Prizzis, Sesteros, and Garrones, the strictly legitimate members of the family, had to be accommodated because each one of them knew there was no way to get out of attending the engagement part of Maerose Prizzi.

There were so many connections with the Los Angeles outfit that it had been a hard job for Maerose to boil down a final list. To bulk things up further, she had attended Manhattanville with the twin daughters of the Boss of the Seattle family, with whom the Prizzis also maintained a joint military industrial extortion business which involved national politics, and somebody, thank God, had remembered at the last minute.

With a profound sense of ritual, Mae dropped the first invitation into the mailbox herself, addressed to Miss Mardell La Tour. Then she went back into the maelstrom of dressmakers, caterers, car-parkers, musicians, balloon suppliers, memento manufacturers, floral delivery schedules, waiters, table and chair rental companies, and faced a meeting with the three *capiregime,* all cousins, about selecting an honor guard of eight bouncers from the family's 1,800 soldiers to keep order as the hour got late, the wine got flowing, and the men began to get accustomed to the presence of the new ladies.

Mae didn't sleep much. She kept sipping champagne all through the work of planning so she didn't eat much. She wasn't really physically ready for it when, ten days before the engagement party was to happen, the people she had following Charley reported that he had gone directly from his New Orleans plane connection to Miss La Tour's apartment and had been spending every other night there.

That really did it. Maerose's wig slipped. She went into a kind of controlled hysteria which pulled her further and closer to the edge of doing something irreversible.

She couldn't believe the written report that she held in her hands and read over and over. In New Orleans he had looked her in the eye and had renounced this woman. That was how she remembered it. She tried to firm it up in her mind, but now that she thought about it, it was all kind of vague. He had pulled her up that ladder to the bed, held her in his arms, and said — maybe she was kidding herself, she knew she couldn't remember much after they got to the top of that ladder. But he knew the engagement was officially announced, because he knew she had told her grandfather so he should have known that the woman had to

297

be thrown away.

She felt burning contempt for Mardell for pulling that pneumonia shit. She had to have found some quack doctor who had injected her with pneumonia because she knew that a boy scout like Charley couldn't walk out on a sick woman who was playing it so helpless that he probably had to lift her on and off the john like the soprano in Puccini's French opera *La Bohème.* Everybody knew Charley was a goddam dummy where women were concerned and she had been willing to make every allowance for that. But he had *promised* her, he had given her his *oath* that he understood that they were the family and that the woman was an outsider and that he knew that it was all over, that he had to be finished with the woman forever. He was marrying a Prizzi, for Christ's sake. What was this woman — some hick from the English sticks, a nothing who came over here to get her hands on American money.

Her second thoughts were that Charley didn't deserve to live. He had dishonored himself, and by dishonoring her as well he had dishonored the Prizzis. She decided the quickest way to have the job done on Charley was to tell her father how she had pleaded with Charley, shaming herself and her family, in New York and in New Orleans, and how each time he had given his sacred oath that he would never see the woman again, but, as soon as her back was turned, he had gone into the bed of the woman who must, every day of her life, laugh at her and at the honor of the Prizzis. She knew her father. He would put out work on Charley. Charley wouldn't last two days after she finished massaging her father.

But even while she was thinking that way, she knew she couldn't let anybody give it to Charley. If her plan to take over the Prizzi family was going to work, she needed Charley. Charley was her ticket to the whole thing.

How could she make him come to his senses? She could make up her face with ashes and dress in black and go to see her grandfather and tell him what Charley had done to all of them, but that would diminish her to nothing in her grandfather's eyes and she would never ever be able to persuade him to make Eduardo give her the job as his assistant so she could take over Eduardo's operation someday. But what the fuck was the use of taking over Eduardo's operation if she didn't have Charley to protect her off side as Boss of the street operation? Charley had totaled her life in more ways than one.

The terrible blow to her pride she knew she would eventually get over. Why not? The only place women didn't get over the betrayals by men was the opera, but that figured, because they were all so fat that they knew they couldn't get another guy if the tenor dropped off their string.

If she were a man, which she wasn't, she would have had that Mardell La Tour zotzed.

The idea hit her like a bolt of lightning. She could go to Eduardo, throw herself on his mercy, and have him turn Washington upside down until he got Mardell deported back to England. Let's see how she likes Shaftesbury, England, with her great lover three thousand miles away and no chance of getting back to him or him getting to see her because she would get Eduardo to get the State Department to pull his passport.

She broke down in tears. She couldn't go to Eduardo for anything. Eduardo would go to her grandfather about anything as serious as the jilting of a Prizzi, and her grandfather would tell her father, and her goddam barbarian of a father would right away put out a hit on Charley, and that would cause a split between Angelo and the family, her father and her grandfather, and it could break up the whole family and wreck every dream of power she had for the future.

She decided not to believe that agency's

report on Charley. She decided to find out for herself.

# 49

Reviewing her characterization as an English country girl, Mardell rated herself as about a seven out of a possible ten. She didn't think she could have brought it off with someone like Freddie, for example. Freddie had gone to university in England. He knew English people. Her mother, her father, Hattie Blacker, Edwina – all of them – wanted her to marry Freddie and she had always intended to marry Freddie from the moment she had met him in the Kennedy White House five days before that terrible day in Dallas, but she had to finish her work with Charley first.

The plain fact was that, by any definition, a really great performance had to carry the entire audience with it. Still, the characterization had carried Charley along with it, and Miss Prizzi, and Charley's father. They were, after all, her audience, not Freddie. She had enjoyed every moment at Yale, but she had been much more interested in dramatic writing then. The fact was, life must be the true school, she felt. She had been fulfilled by the whole La Tour experience. If everything had been just a routine theatrical performance instead of what she was doing, which was *living* the part, as she was required to do, she knew she could not have placed as much importance upon Charley as she was doing. A little bit of Charley went a long way and, in the passion of her art, she had let him become too important to her. He was really very, very sweet even if he was abominably sincere. Fortunately, she realized that it would soon become difficult for her to let go of him. In the middle of her characterization she would have to tell herself that, after all, he wasn't Freddie. She wondered whether she would have seen Charley in the desperate way she saw him now if her life had been different.

If it had been different, she would never have left the Shaftesbury that she had hardly ever seen. Her imaginary father wouldn't have been a leper. The Queen of England would not have directed radio beams into her mind, a spoof she still couldn't believe that Charley had swallowed. She would have grown up there and married and by now have had children the way she was supposed to live. She wouldn't have left home at fourteen with only her body, to be hired out as a decoration for nightclubs, with an urgent need to put a distance between herself and her mother and the place where she should have belonged.

She knew that, no matter how lucky she might have become, if all the other things had been the way those things were, she couldn't have been given a more suitable, a finer leading man than Charley. He had played his part superbly in a role that called upon him to really love her. There was nothing new about being loved, but there was something awfully sweet about it. It was neither right nor wrong. She may have muddied Charley's fiancée's surety that things were preordained but that was the old *la vie.*

When the announcement of Charley's engagement came in the post, she hid it and the invitation at the bottom of her bureau drawer, under her smalls. She thought of the scene that would take place if she accepted the invitation. Miss Prizzi would stare with horror at her acceptance, but she had sent out the invitation herself so there was nothing she could do about it. What would happen if she arrived at the engagement party and went through the crowd of guests to congratulate the young couple? The woman would attack her, she knew it.

There would be an enormous scene, which she could play to the hilt, but Charley didn't deserve such humiliation. She had to swallow her pride and let the woman score off her.

She got out a calendar and calculated that the date of the engagement party, Thursday, November 27th, was exactly two weeks from the day Charley had told her it would all be settled in two weeks. He wasn't a complicated man. He had always done what he said he was going to do. He had tried to be honest. When he said things would be settled in two weeks, she had to accept that it meant he was acknowledging that he would be formally engaged to be married in two weeks but that he would still consider it to be an open contract; anything could be revoked up until the day he was actually married.

She would accept that. She wouldn't be there to complicate it anyway. The announcement was just a formality which recognized the condition that the woman had said had existed between Charley and her since long before Mardell, herself, had met Charley. The time between the formality and the absolute truth, in Mardell's eyes, a marriage between Charley and the woman, was an extension of her right to hope that, at the bitter end, he might not marry the woman. She thought fleetingly of throwing herself off the World Trade Center, or of casting herself into the polar bear cage at the Central Park zoo, or of asking Mr. Pomerantz to get her a job as a white slave in Rio or Hong Kong, but she thought of the fun in Washington during the Christmas season and of the entire promise of Freddie when she got around to it, so she grinned happily and decided just to send Charley and Miss Prizzi a wedding present instead.

That afternoon, when she was going to rehearsals at a hall on West Forty-sixth Street for her first time as a stripper-chanteuse, working out the new act that Mr. Pomerantz said had cost a lot of money, someone bumped into her on the crowded sidewalk, and in turning her body around to deflect the collision she saw Miss Prizzi about eleven feet behind her. Mardell was so surprised that her jaw dropped. The woman didn't have any shame. Mardell went to her, the crowd needing to work its way around them.

"Are you following me?" she asked with curiosity rather than resentment.

"Are you still seeing Charley?"

"Not here. Not at rehearsals."

"Is he going to pick you up there?"

"No."

"Are you going to see him tonight?"

"Well — it *is* my night. Last night was your night."

"Didn't you get the announcement this morning?"

"Oh, yes."

"Then how can you see him tonight? It's a matter of pride, isn't it?"

"I don't suppose that following people in the hope of discovering something you can use against them is a matter of pride, is it?"

"I have to protect what is mine."

"We can't stand here. Let's have a cup of coffee."

They walked together silently. They found a luncheonette on Eighth Avenue. They sat at the counter.

"Are you sure you want Charley?" Maerose asked.

"I'm just treading water, Miss Prizzi."

"You know how Charley makes a living?"

"There has been too much else to think about."

"He's a hoodlum."

"Other people told me that the first night I met him."

"He's a special kind of a hoodlum, he's—" She wanted to tell the woman that Charley was the family's *vindicatore,* but she couldn't say the words. If she told an outsider about family business and, through Charley, it got back to his father and then her grandfather, she would be punished by her own people. But she had to do it, Charley was the most important part of her future moves. This woman had to be made to give up any claim on him. "He's the avenger for our family. You will have to imagine the meaning of that for yourself."

"Miss Prizzi — you have humiliated me on the telephone. You humiliated me at the hospital with those out*land*ish gladiola. You came to my apartment and humiliated me there. You have been following me in the streets, and now you are willing to pour shame on Charley with lies that only humiliate you. Let me help you. If you can marry him, he is yours. If you can marry him, I will go away. Until then, he is fair game — if you get my meaning. This coffee is giving me indigestion."

# 50

At about a quarter to six, Pop came into Charley's office at the Laundry and offered to drive him to night school.

"Thanks, Pop. I got the van outside."

"It'll be nice to ride together."

"How'll I get home?"

"The Plumber will drive your car to school."

"Well – okay."

They got into Pop's beat-up Buick and drove out Flatbush Avenue toward Midwood.

Pop said, "We gotta talk, Charley."

"A problem?"

"Worse than you think. Mae came to see me last night. She was a little drunk maybe; a little hysterical. I don't know how things can go so far, but she's had people following you. She showed me their reports."

"I know, Pop, she done it in Miami."

"I been around the Prizzis for over forty years. You gotta never forget that she is a Prizzi – maybe the most Prizzi since the don.

She don't give up. She don't accept things the way they are."

"Whatta you want me to do, Pop?"

"Charley – look. I only want the best for you. The last thing I'm gonna do is interfere with your life. I appreciate how you feel about Mardell. I like her, and if everything was normal I would say, if you love her, go marry her if you want."

"Pop, what can I do? She's still weak from the hospital. She wants to make out like she's strong so she tells Pomerantz to set her up with a job. She won't take any money from me. She never would. He books her into Newark. She ain't strong enough for that. I can't just walk out on her. She needs me."

"I am not saying you gotta walk out on her. But you gotta understand that you only got a few more days either way."

Charley expelled all the air in his lungs in a short, hopeless burst.

"I am saying that whatever you want to do now is strictly your business. Now, that is. I mean, right now. It may drive Maerose out of her skull, but it's still a fair competition. But – when that engagement party at the old Palermo Gardens happens – when you stand beside Mae and take the congratulations of the people from the big families and from

Eduardo's contacts while the don and Vincent are looking at you and smiling at you – then the competition is over, Charley. You – and I am talking strictly about the situation you are in – might have it in your head by mistake that Mae doesn't have any real claim on you until after you and her get married. You know better, Charley. When Corrado Prizzi lays out all that money to put all them people to the trouble to come all the way to Brooklyn to celebrate your engagement to his granddaughter, then that is the cutoff date as far as Mardell is concerned."

"Pop, fahcrissake. This is the twentieth century. This is a free country."

"Charley, what are you, an American? You are a Sicilian. You been a Sicilian going back hundreds of years. You know how the Prizzis think because they are double Sicilians, and if you keep up with Mardell after that engagement party – Jesus, Charley, can you imagine the shame on the don and on Vincent – on the whole family – when they have to send back five hundred engagement presents including a six-room apartment from the mayor, who is always playing both sides of the street anyway? I am not gonna speak for the don – you can figure that out for yourself – but Vincent is gonna want to have you whacked, you know that. I am not complaining, but I gotta be in the middle on all this. I mean — whose side am I on? I am on your side against the don and Vincent, so there goes forty years of friendship — and who else do I have? — I'll sit alone in my house until I die."

"That Mae is a hard woman," Charley said. He held his stomach with both hands. "Nobody understands. This ain't something which it is one woman over another woman. I got a lot of respect for Maerose. I have a responsibility to Mardell. But Mae is rich and strong and healthy. Sure she can be hurt, but not the way Mardell can be hurt. I don't know, Pop. I just don't know. I don't know what to do."

"Never mind about strong and healthy. You gotta see it that Mae thinks you are worth fighting for, that you are more important to her than anything else. She is a proud woman. You think it was easy for her to come to me and tell me what she said to me?"

"Mardell is very breakable, Pop. Mae, the don, Vincent — they don't break. They may even have forgotten how to bend. It sounds crazy, but I have the feeling that if I walk out on Mardell—" he shrugged hopelessly. He couldn't finish the sentence.

"What?"

"She could kill herself."

"I don't want to make it sound easy, Charley. But what you gotta do is draw a line down the center of a piece of paper. You write Mardell's name on one side of the line and then you write the Prizzi family, Mae, the don, and me, on the other side, with Vincent taking his chances. You look at it and you see that on the crowded side of the line that it's your whole life — there ain't anything else for you. Whatta you gonna do — move to England? Settle down in her hometown with her family?"

"Did Maerose tell you to talk to me?"

"She talked to me in such a way that she knew I hadda talk to you. You know what she told me she did?"

"What?"

"She's been standing outside Mardell's building for two days. She followed her wherever she went, when she went to buy food or to the bank and when she went to rehearsals. She was waiting for you to go into her house or she wanted to see if Mardell went out to meet you."

"Aaaah, *shit!*"

"Mardell spotted her. They had a meet. You know what — if you wanna show how serious this thing is — what she told Mardell?"

"What?"

"That you were not only a hoodlum but that

you do work for the Prizzis."

"Mae*rose?*"

"So Mardell isn't the only one who is breakable."

# 51

After the invitations had been addressed, Maerose told Vincent that she and Charley had become engaged. He responded like a class-A robot. She knew her grandfather hadn't told her father the news because the don's sense of *omertà* was so strong that it would not allow him to reveal any information, even the state of the weather, unless it had been initiated by him. There was the slimmest chance that Amalia might have called Vincent but, over the years, nobody could predict how Vincent was going to react to anything so they didn't go out of their way to clue him in anymore.

"Poppa?" she said as he was lowering himself into his favorite chair to read the newspaper before she called him for dinner.

"What, fahcrissake?"

"I got news."

He looked at her with alarm touching on panic, certain that she was pregnant. He didn't dare speak, he stared.

"Charley Partanna and I are gonna get married."

"Charley? Whatta you telling me? I never knew you and Charley even talked to each other."

"Oh, we talk, Poppa," she said slyly.

"I gotta know something, Mae."

"What, Poppa?"

"Do you have to get married? You know what I mean."

"We have to get married, but not for the reason you're thinking, Poppa."

He was overjoyed. "Jeez, Mae," he said, "I always worried you was gonna marry somebody outside the environment. Charley! That's – well – I guess that's tremendous. But, Jeez, Mae, I'm gonna miss your little feet around the house."

He kissed her on both cheeks and then returned to the newspaper. "You won't believe what it says here," he said, whacking the paper.

"What?"

"The headline is: ORGANIZED CRIME EXPERT SEES DOWNFALL OF MAFIA. Where do they get these crazy stories?"

"From Eduardo, I guess."

"Listen to this — 'New York State's top expert on organized crime said yesterday that efforts to crack down on the Mafia were making major progress. Within a decade these efforts could transform the underworld organization into something unrecognizable' — blah-blah-blah. 'Aggressive law enforcement using federal antiracketeering laws, along with internal strife and changing membership patterns within the Mafia, are undermining organized crime as never before, said the expert.' What *is* this?"

"It had to be Eduardo who planted it, Poppa. He wins either way. It makes the public think we are finished when we never had it so good, but, if it should happen to come true, it's what Eduardo wants anyway."

"Whatta you mean?"

"Eduardo thinks the family don't need the street operation — your side. He wants everything to be legit all the way."

At dinner, which Maerose had cooked for her father while her seventeen-year-old sister was out romancing sixteen-year-old Patsy Garrone in the balcony of the Brooklyn Paramount, a couple of months after Willie Daspisa had turned to the protection of the Program, Maerose said, out of nowhere, "I bet all the families are laughing at us, Poppa, on account of Willie Daspisa."

"What?" Vincent chewed every mouthful twenty times on his doctor's orders, because that kept him from making a pig of himself at the table and having the extra calories churn up his blood pressure. But what could he do about the cholesterol? On television their safe count had been sixty-one points under his own count.

"Because Willie cost us and we didn't do nothing about it." She watched her father closely.

"We're doin' it, don't worry. Willie ain't gettin' away with nothing."

"Poppa, where is he? All the families know is that he cost us nine hundred thousand dollars' worth – the fines to the bank in Boston, and a hundred and fifty a year to the families of the guys he railroaded. That we *know* is an *infamità.* That we *know* has to be avenged. We also know – our *honor* knows – that Willie Daspisa tried to nail Charley on a crappy political rap over Vito. So where is Willie and when are we gonna pay him off?"

"Mae, how come you're the only woman in the whole family who always wants to talk business?"

"Because I'm a Prizzi, that's why, Poppa."

"It ain't right. It ain't even natural."

"Did the Prizzis lose their clout or their honor, or both?" she asked him relentlessly.

"Take it easy, here. You don't know what you're talkin' about."

"Poppa, you *know* I know what I'm talking about."

"What can I do? Am I Eduardo?"

"Eduardo! You are Vincent Prizzi, the Boss. You are the Man. Eduardo is a fixer. He buys every connection there is with the money you generate, so how come he hasn't told you where you can find Willie?"

"That Eduardo. Jesus! Everything is for show with him. How long is it, Willie went into the Program?"

"Months, Poppa. For months you've been taking the shame of what Willie did to the family."

Vincent pushed the food away. "You ruined my dinner," he said.

"I'm sorry, Poppa. But I made some cannoli just the way you like them, and I got some *conchiglie* to go with."

"I'm gonna talk to the don at the meetin' tomorrow." He gripped his upper lip between his teeth. "Jesus, I shouldn't eat the *conchiglie*, but you make them so good."

317

# 52

The next morning Charley went into Vincent's office at the Laundry to tell him that he was engaged to marry his daughter, closing the door behind him. Vincent stared at him for several beats before he spoke. "You coulda said something, you sneaky fuck."

"Whadda you mean?"

"You know what I mean. You took my little girl away from me, that's what I mean."

Charley thought about how he had been steamrollered by Mae and all the trouble she had caused in his life, but he felt sympathy for her, she was just a woman in love, a woman who couldn't help herself.

"It hadda happen, a beautiful girl like Mae. If it wasn't me, it'd be somebody else."

"But do I have to find out about it from my little girl? Not from you?"

Charley sat down. "It just worked out like that."

"The daughter of my heart, and you come

right in and take her away and you don't say nothing."

"What could I say? She hadda clear it first."

"No. That ain't the way. You go to the father. You show respect. You ask the father if he will bless the union, if he will give his okay for you to ask the daughter to marry."

"Only in the old country."

"Here! Wherever. You coulda knocked me over."

"So I am here to ask for your blessing, Vincent."

"What can I tell you? Does a man give up a treasure?"

"It hadda happen. The time has come for you to get grandchildren."

"Well, it's not like you was an outsider. Angelo's son. The son of my *consigliere*. My father's oldest friend. His son." Tears filled Vincent's eyes. "My life is full, Charley. I give you the daughter of my heart with my blessing."

"Thank you, Vincent."

Vincent lit a large Mexican cigar to cover his mixed feelings and polluted the air of the room with heavy smoke. He decided to change the subject. "How long did it take the cyanide to work on Little Jaimito and his people?" he asked with professional interest.

# 53

At breakfast the next morning, while the don drank his one ounce of olive oil and watched Amalia lay down two hot *focacce* in front of her brother, he smiled his terrible smile and waited for Amalia to finish her ritual.

"How are you feeling, Vincent?" Amalia asked.

"Better. I feel better."

"You look agitated. That's not good for the blood pressure. But I am happy for you about Mae and Charley." She patted his cheek fondly and left them. As soon as she was gone, Vincent laid it on his father.

"It's been months, Poppa, since Willie Daspisa went into the Program and Eduardo comes up with zilch."

"First we'll talk about the betrothal."

"It was good news."

"Did you talk to Charley?"

"Yeah, about that and about Willie Daspisa. Charley has been with almost every family in

320

the country about Willie. He is also hot, and he's got a right to be, about Willie throwing him to Mallon. He's got people on the street from coast to coast lookin' for Willie and he also talked to Eduardo about it twice. Evvey time he talks to him, Eduardo don't say nothing. He stiffs Charley, Charley told me this morning, he changes the subject. Why is Eduardo laying down, Poppa? Willie cost us. Everybody knows Willie cost us. He's gotta pay."

"It must be a misunderstanding, Vincent, my son. I remember Eduardo was upset because Willie's brother got it after Eduardo had wasted a lot of money on arrangements for Willie's brother to be handled, and — the way Eduardo sees it — if Vito had been taken care of in a different way, Eduardo's way, Willie would never have gone in the Program."

"What kind of thinking is that, Poppa? We don't have Eduardo to tell us why he thinks Willie went into the Program."

"You're right, Vincent."

"We gotta have a meeting with Eduardo, Poppa."

Pop and Charley arrived at the don's house together that night at seven o'clock. Vincent came in ten minutes later, then the don and Eduardo came down from upstairs together.

They all sat around the table with the hanging light over it, a light with a large, round shade that had golden fringes on it. There was a big bowl of fruit at the center of the table.

The don said, "I been talking to Eduardo about Willie Daspisa. He wants to tell you about it."

Eduardo said, "I didn't see any reason to rush. Willie will be there, wherever he is."

"You gotta put your arm around a whole new bunch of people in Washington," Vincent complained. "It could take months."

"So the longer we take the more Willie suffers when we give it to him. Every day gives him more of a false sense of security."

"I think we gotta know now where he is," Charley said in an even, ominous voice, which was all the more frightening because he felt it, he didn't even have to think of Bogart when he said it. Even the don was hit by the fear. He blinked.

Eduardo tried to stare Charley down, but he couldn't hold it. "You are at this meeting, Charley," Eduardo said slowly, "only because you were the whole cause of Willie going into the Program."

Charley didn't answer him. He just kept staring at him.

Vincent said, "Whatta you mean, the cause?

Willie went into the Program because he stole money from us and so he could keep doing it to Joey Labriola without anybody saying anything. Charley done Willie a big favor by icing Vito and giving Willie an excuse to go into the Program. Charley actually fixed him up with Joey — and what does Willie give him back? He tried to turn him in to Mallon."

"I don't mean the adverent cause. I mean if Willie's brother were alive today, Willie would still be working for us."

"That's a lotta shit," Charley said.

"Why are we getting ourselves lost in words here?" Pop said. "We are here to get something done about Willie Daspisa."

"Then you want me to go to the Democrats for the information?"

"Eduardo — what's the difference? Republicans or Democrats? You sound like you think we was children," Vincent said. "Call your people in Washington and tell them what you want. Willie Daspisa has been living on velvet long enough."

Eduardo looked at his father. The don nodded benevolently.

"Charley can go out there wherever Willie is right after the engagement party," the don said.

Of the 25,465 lawyers who practiced in Washington, D.C., which came out to one for every twenty-five inhabitants, the law firm sponsored by Barker's Hill Enterprises — Schute, Fink, Blanke and Walker — was the most effective because it had connected lawyers who had the most money behind them to solve their clients' problems.

An Assistant Attorney General of the United States had a purely social lunch at the Metropolitan Club with the firm's senior partner, Basil Schute. The distinguished lawyer explained with profound delicacy why his firm was interested in locating the former Guglielmo Daspisa, who was under the protective cloak of the Witness Protection Program. It could mean an inheritance for Mr. Daspisa, and although the bequest could not be paid out indirectly, if it were possible, in this unusual instance, to divulge Mr. Daspisa's whereabouts — the matter would be wholeheartedly appreciated by his firm's clients.

Later, while they were having coffee and enjoying the AAG's Havana cigars with a Honduran trademark on the box, the AAG earnestly brought up the matter of contributions to the Political Action Committee, which was seeking legislation to aid destitute corporation lawyers. The counselor agreed. "No cause could be nearer to my heart," he said.

"Make the check out to the Needy Attorneys of America PAC," the AAG said. "That will handle it."

When Schute got back to his office, a Justice Department courier delivered an unmarked brown manila envelope containing four-color Polaroids of Willie's and Joey's new faces: full front and profile. They had raised Willie's eyebrows and dyed his hair white, straightened his nose and put a bulb on the end of it, and sagged the right side of his face slightly by lifting the left. They had put a cleft in his chin and given him a crooked set of caps on his upper teeth. The double chin was gone. The eyes were still feral, but they were in a different face.

The more characteristic protective coloration was Joey's. The surgeons had made him a pretty storybook prince; perfect teeth, where before they had looked like a mouthful of Roquefort; wide blue eyes where they had been squinty, small, and brown; perfect nose and cheekbones, which triangulated with his chin in a chatoyant, feminine way. His hair was blond, cut in the Prince Valiant style. It was so long the ends rested on his shoulders.

Willie's new name was Hobart Thurman. He was living and working in Yakima, Washington, which was about ninety miles south-

southeast of Seattle, over the Cascade Mountains, population about 43,000. Yakima was the commercial center of an agricultural region, very big on apples, and it manufactured lumber, flour, and cider. Mr. Thurman lived with his nephew, Chandler Owens. They were partners in an upmarket furniture and decorating business.

Schute slipped the information into another envelope, called for a car to catch the next shuttle, and sent a junior partner to fly the pictures and Willie's new name and address to Edward Price in New York.

"If I didn't know it was them, I wouldn't hardly know who it was," the don said at the meeting with Eduardo, Pop, and Charley. "Look at that Joey Labriola. How can that be? I knew his father and his mother, they lived six miles from Agrigento on the Caltanissetta road." He shook his head in awe. "How could anybody think up names like that?" As he marveled, the phonograph reeled out Zerlina's aria, "Vedrai, carino," from *Don Giovanni*, in the 1939 recording with Ezio Pinza and Richard Tauber that the don planned to play over again as soon as these people left so he could keep a pure lyric line in his head.

"It cost a lot of money to get that information," Eduardo said, "but just the same we have to be sure it's right. We don't want Charley going all the way out to Yakima and doing the job on some guys who always were Hobart Thurman and Chandler Owens just because the Department of Justice wants to even up some old hassle."

"We'll know the minute they see me," Charley said. "They'll pee their pants."

# 54

The distinguished guests from all over America were pouring into the three Prizzi hotels in midtown Manhattan. The Papal Nuncio went to Brooklyn for lunch with Don Corrado directly after his fittings with Ungaro, planning to avoid the party itself if he possibly could. Movie stars, media stars, and television stars were stacked up like cordwood, waiting to heat up the Palermo Gardens. A story would appear in the society pages, but otherwise, in terms of news coverage, the engagement was strictly not a news event. The people who knew who the Prizzis were knew about the engagement, and the rest of the world had only vaguely heard of the Prizzis so they weren't news — or at least they hadn't been news for quite a number of years since the public relations policy of the *fratellanza* had been changed into a policy of nonviolence or, if there had to be violence, then violence that could be pinned on a lot of wild South Americans and blacks.

Maerose Prizzi, the young woman in whose honor the party was to be given, was the niece of the financier, Edward Price, just to place her vaguely, and no one had ever heard of Charles Amedeo Partanna. Hoodlums, if there still were such things as hoodlums, being the human component of such a nonexistent thing as the Mafia, were confined to television fiction or had become a part of American history. The people who owned the great companies or took them over in elaborate hijacking operations, or flipped them, or merged them with one another to hike the price up, were called financiers, not hoodlums. The public was finally getting its nomenclature straight, as it had when narcotics were renamed controlled substances and taxes were called revenue enhancement.

Everything was done on an enormous scale which dwarfed the antics of old-time "gangsters." Everything was done out in the open, by people who were known leaders and whose names turned up regularly on the business pages. The fact that there was a Sicilian-American family that was prominent in an isolated section of faraway Brooklyn, headed by a forgotten old man, could mean nothing to anyone. So what, if the old man's number in the dusty, never-consulted files of the New York Police Department was #E-14481, or if he was #362142A to the FBI, and #247 in the Federal Narcotics Bureau listings. There was nothing to report about the occasion except the joy of a bride-to-be.

Vincent provided a superstretch limousine driven by his own man, Zingo Pappaloush, to pick up Charley at the beach, then to go to Vincent's house in Bensonhurst to take Charley, Maerose, and Vincent to the old Palermo Gardens near the Navy Yard, which was set among the borders of Brooklyn Heights, Fort Greene, and Williamsburg. The Palermo Gardens had been the hallowed grove for every important Prizzi, Partanna, Sestero, or Garrone celebration for the past fifty years. The building was thirty-seven years old when Corrado Prizzi bought it, and he had used it constantly, organizing dances, observances, and assemblies for the immigrant Sicilian people who had rallied around him in the new world, establishing him as their leader in the right way, not with force, or certainly not entirely with force.

The city had tried to condemn the building twice in the past nine years, but each time Don Corrado had told Eduardo to get the ruling changed. It was now nominally owned by the Blessed Decima Manovale Order, a nonprofit organization of religious ascetics who had taken vows of poverty and who also held a voting trust of oil shares for the don.

Charley, riding from the beach to his fiancée's house in Bensonhurst, couldn't shake the depression he had fallen into. He had seen Mardell for the last time the night before; for the last time in their lives, and he hadn't had the guts to say goodbye to her. He tried. At the time he was trying he reminded himself that he was at least trying, but he never made it. Neither one of them could have stood it if he told her. He would never have gotten away. They would have had to either elope or negotiate a suicide pact or something. It was like when you hit a ball against a wall which faces a wall, after a couple of strong bounces the bounce goes out of it and it can't make it back to the other wall again. He couldn't say the same things all over again. They had both heard the same song too often, so he hadn't said anything; he hadn't even said goodbye.

He couldn't let it lie there like that. He could write her a letter. She liked Pop. He could ask Pop to go to see her and deliver the letter. She was so touchy about money that it wasn't even remotely possible to leave her a big check when he slipped out of her apartment this morning. He hadn't even set up something with a bank to send her enough money every month that it wouldn't somehow make her ashamed – because she was a little off her head where it came to money – but still enough so he would know that she was going to be able to keep eating and paying the rent. He was going to have to get Eduardo to have his lawyers set up a fake inheritance from some phoney relatives in England. That was the only way he could think of to get her to take money.

He knew her. When she figured it all out, or when he figured out some way he could tell her what happened, she would probably never call Marty Pomerantz again or pay any attention to Marty's calls to her because he had set it up and she wouldn't want to have anything to do with him. Aaaaah, shit! He remembered that Vito used to say he didn't have women to bring him trouble. Charley didn't even understand that anymore. If you wanted to be around somebody there had to be trouble, because each side thought they knew better than the other one about what was the best thing for the other one. Jesus, that had certainly happened to him, two women — terrific women — had fallen so head-over-heels in love with him that they had lost all control. That was life. That was nature in the raw. He just had to learn to live with it.

If only Maerose could have been satisfied with being with him three nights a week and every other Saturday. They could have gotten married and he could have gone along with Mardell. His body would have gotten used to it eventually. After a year or two of a steady routine like that, he wouldn't have to rest up in the daytime anymore. It would have been like the boy who had lifted the tiny calf every day until he was a man and the calf was a three-thousand-pound bull; it could be done. Both women would be happy and there wouldn't have to be all this sweat. But no. Maerose had to have it her way.

The motorcycle cops of the escort were talking together on the street in front of Vincent's house when Charley got out of the stretch car and went up the walk to the house. They were waiting for him. The front door opened and they were all dressed to go. Maerose was dressed more beautifully than even she had ever been dressed in her life, or maybe it was because he had never seen her wearing this kind of a long dress with all the bare everywhere and the hair like a helmet. Charley kissed Mae on the cheek. She stayed hanging there after he finished, like she was waiting for something more. They went out to the car. Both men were wearing tuxedos like a couple of waiters. Vincent burped twice getting into the car, so loud that Zingo looked around, alarmed, and put up the glass division in the car.

Maerose sat between the two men inside the enormous tonneau and listened to Charley's silence, interpreting it as indifference. It was the biggest night in their lives so far and she was getting no vibes from Charley, just cold waves. The way he was acting she knew she had won, she knew he was finished with the woman, his father must have finally got him straight. But she also knew she had won nothing. This wasn't Charley, not the Charley she wanted in her work.

There was plenty of time to think. Her contingency plan was flexible.

Nobody was talking. Her father had turned on the television and was watching a show called *Everybody's Health*, about arteriosclerosis. He resented having to get all dressed up like this and to go to a place full of noisy people just so they could all be told what they already knew. He brooded over where they were going to put all those goddam presents.

Maerose stared at her dreams: having Charley, running the legit operation, dominating the family across the board, from the street side to the board rooms — with Charley at her side. But if she could not swing Charley over to her side — willingly and joyously — then she could also have overrated her ability to take over the Prizzi family. The one thing naturally followed the other. The first thing was the absolute measure of the second, so what was the use? If she went along with what had been set up for tonight she wouldn't have any of that, because none of it was ever going to work, and nothing could be clearer than that. So, she explained to herself, because of what she did have, what she would always have — she was a Prizzi — she was going to have to make herself get him off the hook by sliding into the contingency plan.

She had really known all along in her heart of hearts that it was going to happen, she reminded herself. The two-ton showgirl had been too cool. She had been so sure of herself that she had to be sure of Charley. And he had never acted like a man who had been caught having a little poontang on the side. Charley was as serious about the woman as he couldn't get himself to be serious about her. She had to face it. She had to throw it all away and get him off the hook in such a way that neither he nor anybody else would ever know she had done it. What the hell. She had her business and Brooklyn was going downhill anyhow. She wanted to cry, but her father was sitting beside her and he would only yell at her until he got a reason why she was crying, and Charley would only want to shoot himself, so she didn't cry. The car pulled up in front of her family's favorite dump for celebrating the great occasions, so she was going to have to make it a great occasion.

The preternaturally long car arrived at the entrance to Palermo Gardens yard by yard. Zingo Pappaloush seemed to get there some time before the passengers. They all got out.

"Wait here," Vincent said to Zingo, and Zingo knew that the cops knew he would be allowed to move the car a few feet beyond the entrance and be parked there so that it would be ready when Vincent decided to go home.

The rest of the night was a blur to everyone. To Charley, to the don, to Amalia, to every one of the guests, and most of all to Maerose and to Vincent, who were to be ten years getting over it, if Vincent ever really got over it. The terrible night itself was less of a blur to Maerose while it was happening. If a climax is defined as a moment in a play at which a crisis reaches its highest intensity and is resolved, this became the climax of her life and, under the definition of Freytag's Pyramid, her catastrophe.

The enormous room was arranged so that all the guests were seated at large, round tables. The table of honor, where Maerose and Charley sat with the don, Amalia, Vincent, Father Passanante, the priest who would marry the young couple, Pop, and Eduardo, with an aristocratic young woman called Baby who had attended Foxcroft and Bennington, was at the center of the room, at the edge of the relatively large dance floor. Over all of it, banquet room and dance floor, hung three large chandeliers from which were festooned crepe paper ribbons of red, white, and blue from one side of the room and red, white, and green from the other. Balloons bobbed against the ceiling in a dozen colors, rising in the warmed air. There was a raised stage with two alternating orchestras: the four-piece band of white-haired musicians who were the traditional fixtures at all Prizzi affairs, and a modern, eleven-piece group that provided music of more current interest (up to 1955). Along two of the walls there were long, two-tiered tables holding heaped platters of salads, antipasti, cold cuts, and sandwiches, mountains of tiny macaroni and farfalline, piles of salciccia, and banks of pastries and ice cream. On the third wall there was a bar where the extra men congregated. There were six bottles of two colors of wine on each table. At the tables on either side of the table of honor sat the representatives of the families, and equally nearby, if one row removed from the dance floor, were the statesmen, conglomerate heads, and prelates. All the men except the prelates wore tuxedos. The women were dressed merely spectacularly. The clergy, who with two exceptions were parish priests, wore either scarlet or purple soutanes. On each wall – north, south, east, and west – hung enormous sepia portraits: Arturu Toscanini, Pope Pius XII, Enrico Caruso, and Richard M. Nixon in heavy gold frames. Nixon was the chief executive of the country, but the don had admired him closely through his exciting tenure as congressman, senator, and vice president.

Maerose began the evening by clamoring so loudly for champagne that Vincent felt she was making it necessary for him to order at least a token glass of champagne for everyone in the room, which he resented bitterly, and which necessitated hurried telephone calls followed by the rushed dispatching of large trucks from warehouses. Mae refused food. She was getting drunk. Charley kept asking her if she wouldn't like to eat something and then telling her to take it easy with the champagne. She said, "You want me to sit at this table or you want me to roam around and make myself a couple of new friends?"

During the one dance with Charley, she began by mussing the hair of the other women dancers and occasionally goosing the men.

"Mae, fahcrissake! Whatta you doing?" Charley said, locking in a fixed smile.

"Whatta you mean? I'm celebrating. We're gonna get married, remember?"

"Your father is turning purple."

"Charley, what are you — a party pooper?"

After that she refused to leave her chair, urging everybody to drink up, and carrying on shouted conversations with people on the dance floor. "Hey, Rosalia! Look out! Your ass is gonna fall off," and other lighthearted sallies.

The don stared at her, unbelieving. He turned the stare into outrage and beamed it on Vincent. It was 9:40 P.M. when Mae finished her bottle of champagne and made her three big moves.

Move one: Charley was on the dance floor with Julia Fustino, Gennaro's daughter-in-law who had helped to entertain Charley and Mae in New Orleans. Julia had won the Harvest Moon Ball in the lindy class the year before she was married. She was a terrific dancer and that inflamed Maerose, who began to behave like a jealous woman. She kept calling out to Charley from her table, "How come you don't dance with the old bags, Charley? How come you go straight for the gorgeous women?" Or (very loudly), "Hey, Charley – come on! This is your engagement party, not an orgy." And, "Come on, Charley. Drag her into a phone booth and get it over with, why doncha?"

Gradually other conversations at tables near the dance floor stopped altogether as the guests watched Maerose and little else.

Move two: Charley and Julia were dancing a sedate fox-trot when Mae lurched out of her chair and grabbed Julia's arm, pulling her away from Charley. "I saw that, you son of a bitch," she yelled, and whacked Charley across the chops. There was one great gasp from a few hundred throats and no gasps were greater or more horrified than the gasps from the center table directly on the dance floor.

Move three: Maerose pushed Charley away and half-staggered to the bar, where a line of young men had been drinking and watching the dancing; she grabbed a tall, dark one, and pulled him on the dance floor where she went into as lascivious a dance as either Vincent or his father, who took a large gross income out of pornography, had ever seen. Vincent was trying on a case of apoplexy. The don looked as if he were going to turn her into stone. Only Father Passanante at the main table seemed to be enjoying watching the dance. After one turn around the dance floor that, as the Plumber said later, could have got her pregnant, Charley came forward from having returned Julia Fustino to her table, Mae threw her arms around the young man, socked her hips violently into his hips, and kissed him passionately. Vincent rushed out on the floor, got there ahead of Charley, and pried the two of them apart.

He grabbed her arm and began to pull her toward the door and said, "We're going home."

She jerked her arm loose. "Go home, Poppa," she said. "It's past your bedtime." She grabbed the young man's arm and pulled him away. She yelled at everyone, "In your hat and over your ears," and sprinted out of the Palermo Gardens, pulling the young man along behind her. They disappeared from the room. Nobody knew what to say. Then, all of a sudden, everyone knew what to say all at the same time.

Hitting the outside pavement running, dragging the man, Mae yelled, "Zingo!"

The driver broke away from a knot of drivers. "Yes, Miss?"

"Get me out of here. Where's the car?"

Zingo ran to the limousine and backed it up in front of the two people. Mae got into the car and pulled the man in behind her.

As the limousine pulled away, Charley and Vincent came running out of the building.

"What the hell is this?" Vincent said. "Did somebody put something in her drink?"

"Holy shit," Charley said. He wasn't sure what had happened, but he knew Mae had made her move and that he didn't want it that way. She had gotten him off the hook but she had fallen in the soup. It was bad enough the way it had been, but who needed this? He couldn't figure out what to do except to let her sober up then to take her out to Vegas and marry her and stay away until the whole thing blew over.

She hadn't been any drunker than Father Passanante, who didn't drink. She had set the whole thing up because she thought he wanted to get off the hook but that he didn't know how to do it. He knew one thing: it was never going to blow over with Vincent. As far as Vincent was concerned, she had dishonored him in front of the most important people on the planet. She was dead where Vincent was concerned.

She had fixed everybody – herself, sure – but him, too. If she was dead with Vincent, he, himself, was dead with her. She was his. She still knew that as much as he knew that. But she had run away from him. She was gone.

"I am ashamed in front of you, Charley," Vincent was saying. "She has spit on all of us." Vincent was so shaken that he was speaking in Sicilian. "She ain't my daughter no more."

"Come on, Vincent. It's cold. We gotta go inside."

"How we gonna face all them people?"

"We're Prizzis, Vincent. That's enough for them. We found out all about that tonight."

When they got back to the table, Pop wasn't there. They took their seats. Charley began a conversation about the Mets with Baby. Eduardo talked about the stock market to Father Passanante. Amalia wept quietly. Vincent took three pills. Don Corrado remembered, aloud and in close detail, some wild boar he had eaten, years before, on a trip with his wife after Vincent was grown up, on a grand tour of Italy, in a restaurant in Rome. It was called *cinghiale in agrodolce*, the latter being a sweet-and-sour sauce, and it could not in any way compare with the young lamb they had there. The boar was cooked with vinegar, anchovies, and flavored with rosemary, garlic, and sage, and his wife had said it wasn't worth it to ask for the recipe, but she said that when they got back to New York she was going to see about getting some real baby lamb. The don wasn't talking to anyone in particular. He could have been talking to his dead wife. He was just talking.

Pop returned to the table at ten fifty.

"She went to the airport," he said. "She caught a plane for Mexico City with the man."

The don turned politely to Vincent. "Get her back," he snarled, then smiled terribly. "Mexico is no place for a young, single woman."

"I had a talk with the airline's night manager," Pop said. "They issued Mae entry cards. She asked them to make a hotel reservation for her and they set her up at the Molina on Avenida Juárez."

"Get on the phone, Vincent," the don said.

# 55

The party broke up early. The people at the main table sat where they were as if everything were normal. After the Fustinos came over and said good night to everybody at eleven o'clock, Eduardo and Baby left. The don, who usually left all parties at half past ten, was still in his seat at the table at a quarter to twelve, after the last guests had come to them to say good night. No one mentioned Maerose. No one was solicitous of Charley. When the hall was empty except for the cleaning people, the don got to his feet. "I wanna talk to you tomorrow, Charley," he said. "Come to my house at five o'clock."

They all went outside. The don, Amalia, and Father Passanante got into the don's limousine. Zingo, parked again after his trip to the airport, backed the stretch up for Vincent. Charley and Pop drove south toward Bensonhurst in Pop's battered Chevy.

"Well," Pop said, "she solved the problem."

"Yeah."

"She's a great woman."

"Yeah."

"The fact is — I'm proud of alla youse. Class told. Everybody did what they was supposed to do. Mardell laid back. You accepted the facts of life. And Mae worked it so everybody has an out."

"What happens to her now?"

"She knew what it was gonna be. She jumped out of a plane without a parachute, that's all. What the hell, Charley, Mae didn't belong in Brooklyn — she's a modern woman. She belongs to the world out there."

Pop dropped Charley off at the beach. Charley was just about inside his apartment when the phone rang. It was Vincent.

"Charley — what was that all about? I don't wanna talk about her. I'm not gonna say her name after this. But I need a reason or I'm gonna — well, I need a reason."

"I don't know if I know, Vincent. I ain't figured it out yet."

"Did you have a fight or something?"

"No."

"Then — what? Is she crazy?"

"I gotta think about it."

"Who was that guy?"

"I never seen him before."

"You're a big fuckin' help, you know that,

Charley? You was suppose to marry her. So whatta you know about her — nothing."

"That's right. You're her father and you don't know nothing, either. I thought I knew her, but I had it all wrong. I didn't know nothing about her."

"She didn't care about honor. She lost her faith."

"Maybe you'll find out about that someday and maybe you won't," Charley said, and he hung up.

Charley changed into street clothes, then he got into the van and drove to New York and was able to find a parking spot in front of Mardell's apartment house. He rang Mardell's doorbell. There were many sounds accompanying the unslotting of locks and door chains. She pulled him into the apartment as if assassins were running up the stairs after him, shut the door, and relocked it rapidly.

"Wasn't tonight the — the party?" she asked him, wide-eyed.

"How'd you know that?"

"Somebody sent me an invitation."

"Yeah?" He was astonished.

She nodded solemnly.

He shook his head in puzzlement. "I'm knocked out, baby. I gotta go to bed." He walked ahead of her along the hall and turned left into the bedroom.

"Are you going to stay here tonight?"

He peeled off his shirt. "We'll talk tomorrow."

"I have a nine o'clock rehearsal. I open tomorrow night in Newark."

"Okay. I'll pick you up after the show." He got into bed and went to sleep.

When he woke up, Mardell had left to go to the rehearsal. He got dressed and made himself some breakfast, then he called the Laundry and said he was going to be out of the office until two o'clock to let Vincent plan his own day around him and not be there when he went in. They had brought Louis Palo in from Vegas to set up the moves on Willie and Joey, so he called Louis at the hotel and went over to see him. Two broads were just getting out of Louis' room when he got there. One was Chinese. The other one could have been from outer space. Louis was a big ladies' man, maybe even a little degenerate.

Charley laid out how he wanted everything to work. "You know where the big library is at Forty-second Street and Fifth Avenue?"

"I'll find it."

"They got telephone books on all the cities.

Go in there and look up real estate agents in the Yakima telephone book."

"Yakima?"

"It's a city in the State of Washington. Write down the names. Then, when you get to Yakima, call one of the agents — case him first, maybe, to make sure he's the biggest one — then tell him you want to rent a three-bedroom house somewhere not in town but just outta town. Okay?"

"Yeah."

"After you got it rented, then you go and see Willie at his furniture company and tell him you want him to tell you what you need for furniture and decoration. The decoration part brings Joey in. Then, while they're working all that out, you call me at the Olympic Hotel in Seattle, and I come out and do the job on them. You got it?"

"Are you gonna bring the tools?" Louis asked.

"Except one. Pick up a good hatchet at the local hardware store and leave it in the cellar at the rented house."

"A hatchet?"

"The don promised the thumbs to Willie's wife."

At four fifteen he got into the van and drove

out to the don's with a feeling of dread about what the family was going to do to Maerose. He had to back her play. He had to show that he didn't know any more than anybody else about why she did what she did, because that was why she had done it, to convince everybody that she had sacked him, to show everybody that she didn't want him anymore. If he began to chop away at why he thought she did it, she would be even deeper in the shit than she was now. She had set the whole thing up right down to the last detail of importing that young guy from somewhere to be her stage prop. She had put on a tremendous performance and he wasn't going to take anything away from her with anybody.

Amalia took him upstairs to the don's room. The house itself was overheated, but as he entered the don's room it was even warmer. The don was seated in his usual chair listening to the music. It sounded to Charley like his father's favorite, the *Simon Boccanegra* by Verdi. The don was playing Fiesco's noble, restrained cry of grief, "Il lacerato spirito."

"Charley. Good," the don said. "Siddown. Will you have a glass of grappa? A cigar?" The don spoke in the Agrigento dialect. Amalia left the room, closing the door.

"No, *padrino*. Thank you."

"It was a bad night, Charley."

"Yes."

"But she did the right thing — wouldn't you say that?"

"The right thing?"

"She was unhappy because she knew you were unhappy. She wanted to end that. She went too far, but she wanted to end that."

Charley looked into Don Corrado's tiny, cold eyes, but he didn't answer the don's statement. "What will happen to her?"

"Her father must be considered. He was wronged in front of all of those people. The family was wronged. He will bring her back here, then he will banish her from the family. You are a part of the family, Charley."

"How do you mean, *padrino*?"

"It is finished, you and Maerose. What is over must never start again. She will be taken care of, but she will be banished from Brooklyn. What I am asking you to understand is that she will be banished from the family — and you are a part of the family. She is banished from you. It was her choice. She banished herself from you."

"I understand, *padrino*."

"Have a cookie, Charley. Let Amalia get you a nice cup of coffee. Tell me about how you are going to handle Willie Daspisa."

## 56

Charley got to the theatre in Newark at the end of the last performance. It was a tryout engagement for the new routine that had been worked up for Mardell: a flashy, complicated thing that had cost Charley $2,300. The two guys who had routined the act were there with Marty Pomerantz, but Charley sat by himself so he could form his own opinion.

The first half of the act was a refined strip-tease with some very basic bumps and grinds. When she had made the point and had gone off to heavy mitting, she came out again and stood between two pianos that had been painted black, keyboards and all. The two men playing the pianos were covered with black velvet, faces and bodies, except their calcimined white hands. The stage was dark except for three white spots – on Mardell and on the piano players' hands. As they accompanied Mardell's singing, the hands were reflected in an arrangement of vertical mirrors and the effect was of their hands moving up and down her body as she sang "That Old Feeling." It was the second time she had tried it out before an audience and, as far as Charley was concerned, it worked.

He sat out front until she went off, then he worked his way backstage, meeting an excited Marty Pomerantz at the stage door. "We can go anywhere with this," Marty said excitedly. "A Broadway show, into clubs, or take it on tour and then clean up in Vegas. This is a big act, Charley."

"I was thinking maybe it would be better without the strip."

"Without the strip? With that body?"

"Just keep her in town and get the money, Marty," Charley grinned.

It took almost an hour to get her away from the people. The two guys had a flock of notes and they went over them with Mardell and Marty while Charley sat in a chair and waited.

For a change, Mardell was hungry, so he packed her into the van and took her to La Costa on Twenty-second Street, near her apartment, and watched her eat a steak while he had some minestrone, gnawed on a roll, and sipped some red wine.

"That is one terrific gimmick, that act," he said. *"Gimmick?"*

"Hey, the rest was great, too. I mean, how could anybody know you could sing that good?"

"I like to sing. What did Mr. Pomerantz say?"

"He said he can book you anywhere — a Broadway musical, the big clubs — anywhere."

"God! I can't believe it."

"You're gonna be a big star, Mardell."

She smiled, chewing the steak pensively.

"Lissen — I gotta tell you something, but don't get your balls in an uproar. I gotta go outta town."

Mardell dropped her fork. "Out of town?"

"Seattle."

She touched her face in about five places with both hands. "How long will you be gone?"

"It depends."

"On what?"

"On how it goes."

She slumped in her chair. Her face got haggard. "You shouldn't have come back after that party, Charley."

"Hey, Mardell! Come on!"

"I made my peace when you went away the day of the party. I knew I'd never see you again. Then you just come back as if nothing had happened. You don't belong to me anymore, but you came back long enough to see that everything went all right on my tryout night so you can tell yourself I'll be all right and you and she can go on with your life."

He grabbed her hand across the table. "That isn't gonna happen, me and Maerose. It's finished."

"Finished?"

"Lissen – I gotta make this trip. It's a very important trip for me. I'll be gone two days, tops, and that includes the traveling time."

She stared at him spookily. She was breathing as if all the air was being pumped out of the room.

If he could have watched the whole thing as if he were all-knowing and on the outside of both of them, he would have been knocked out by her performance, because Charley had a real appreciation for good acting; he certainly had seen enough television in his time. But doing that was impossible. He saw it all the way he saw it, the way she had conditioned him to see it, so he thought, Hang around with a nut and you'll go nuts, but he held her hand and looked right into her eyes.

"Lissena me, Mardell," he said, "if I could take you with me on this trip, I would absolutely take you. But I can't and you can't go anyway. You're gonna get a Broadway show with this act. Just hang in with me. I'll be back here in maybe a day and a half. I'm gonna call you and talk to you at your place or at your dressing room at the theatre every morning and every night. You want somebody to ride home with you after the show, I'll send two guys."

"Will you stay with me tonight, Charley?"

"What else? I won't only be witchew tonight, and when I'm away, but" — he took a deep breath and made the biggest decision of his life — "when I get back we're gonna get married. That's the way it's gotta be."

"Married? What about—?"

"That's all over. We called it off."

Mardell let the tears fall. She forgot the makeup and wept with joy. She saw it as a genuine tribute to Mardell La Tour, fictional character. She was living a character which was now hers, completely and utterly. It belonged to her. Hattie Blacker would absolutely get an A+ on her thesis.

## 57

There was a heavy rapping on the bedroom door of the suite. It was five after eleven in the morning. Maerose yelled, "Who is it?" A muffled voice through the door said it was the assistant manager. She yelled, "Go to the other door." She put her evening wrap over her slip, crossed the living room from the bedroom, and opened the door. It was the assistant manager, but he was standing beside Al Melvini and Phil Vitimizzare.

"What is this?" she asked them.

They pushed into the room and closed the door behind them. "Get the hell out of here," she said. "Get these hoodlums out of my room," she told the assistant manager.

The Plumber said, "Where's the guy, Miss Prizzi?"

The young man came out of the bedroom, tying the belt of the terry-cloth robe the hotel had provided. He walked into the room. "What's going on?" he said.

"You son of a bitch!" Phil Vittimizzare said, grabbing both his arms and holding them behind his back. The Plumber stepped in front of him and punched him heavily in the stomach, not once but three times. The young man's breakfast came up all over the carpet.

"Al, for Christ's sake!" Maerose yelled, trying to hold his arm. He shook her off and slugged the young man in the face. The body slumped. Phil held him up. The Plumber hit him heavily in the face three more times, marking him good, messing him up. Phil let the body fall to the floor, and the two men, still wearing their hats, kicked his ribs in on both sides of his body. The assistant manager watched them, appalled.

The Plumber turned away from the work. "Get dressed, Miss Prizzi," he said. "We got a plane to catch to New York."

"Drop dead, Al," she said.

"You get dressed or we dress you. It don't matter to us."

She went to the small desk in the room and wrote a check. She gave the check to the assistant manager. "Listen. This check is made out to him and he better get it, you understand? I want the hotel to guarantee all expenses for him with the doctor and the hospital, then you send the bill to me. The address is on the check. You follow me? You understand?"

The assistant manager looked at the Plumber. The Plumber nodded.

"If he doesn't get the best attention from you and a doctor and the hospital, and if he doesn't get this check, then I am going to make an affidavit about what happened here this morning and I am going to hire a press agent in New York to get the story into the papers all over the United States, you understand what I'm telling you?"

The assistant manager rolled his eyes to look

at the Plumber. "Do what the lady tells you," the Plumber said, "or I'm gonna flush you down the terlet."

She rode back to New York in row A of first class. The Plumber and Phillie rode in row B. She refused to eat or drink. The two men ate for six. When the plane got to Idlewild a car was waiting. It was six o'clock in the evening. The car drove them to Vincent's house in Bensonhurst. Vincent greeted them at the door. The two men left her there.

She sat in the living room of her father's house. He didn't speak to her. He stared at her like she was garbage, until she wanted to yell at him.

"You put shame on your family in front of everybody who is anybody in this country," he said to her. "You showed the whole world what you care about the Prizzi family. You never had the faith in this family. You were allowed to marry the son of your grandfather's oldest friend but you decided to be a *passeggiatrice* instead. Thank God, your mother can never know what you done. She is safe from you with the angels. Lissena me! I am never gonna talk to you again. Angelo Partanna says he forgives you, but Charley can't ever forgive you, you took his manhood from him in front of all the people in this country. You can make believe to yourself that you still belong to this family, you can make believe you are still my daughter, but you are not. You are not in the Prizzi family. You are not my daughter. I will never speak your name, and I am going to see to it that you stay an old maid for the rest of your life."

Pop was waiting for her in the old Chevy when she came out of the house with one suitcase. He smiled at her and told her to get into the car.

They drove north, toward the Brooklyn Bridge. "The don wants me to tell you the new rules," he said. "But first I want to tell you that I understand you, what you done. It took more guts than I got."

"I don't know what you're talking about, Angelo. What are the new rules?"

"You gotta stay outta Brooklyn. You can't come over here to see anybody in the family. You can't come to weddings, funerals, christenings. You can't see nobody in Brooklyn."

"What the hell. I need a change anyway."

"Your Aunt Amalia wants you to call her anytime, anywhere. At the don's house. She don't care."

Mae began to cry quietly.

"The same goes for me. You need anything.

You wanna find out something. You need company, you call me. I'll be there. I'll go wherever you are and we'll have a nice meal."

"Charley?"

"Charley is like Brooklyn. It's all over, Mae."

"That's the way I wanted it."

"We'll let some time go by. Amalia and me will work on the don and Vincent. Gradually, we can get some changes made. Gradually, you can come back for the weddings and the funerals."

"You're my friend, Angelo."

"It's just gonna take a little time. Give it time. There ain't nothing that can't be changed by time."

# 58

Louis flew out to New York one week ahead, to Seattle and then to Yakima. Before he went he was summoned to Brooklyn and received by the don himself, who told him how much he appreciated what he would be doing and promised him that, when Willie and Joey had been straightened out, he was going to make Louis assistant casino manager at the big Prizzi hotel in Vegas. Louis was knocked out by the don. The don had been a legend to him all his life and now there he was, seeing everything was done right.

Louis checked into a hotel in Yakima, took off his shoes because his feet were killing him, and called the number of one of the real estate agents he had looked up in New York. He made an appointment for the agent to pick him up at nine o'clock the next morning to show him three-bedroom houses on the outskirts of town. Then, to relax a little, he called a woman he knew in Vegas and talked dirty on the telephone.

The next morning, after a solid breakfast, he met the real estate man in the lobby and began the circuit to check out houses. He decided the fourth house they saw was right for him. It was a little inconvenient for town, maybe even a little isolated, but it had an indefinable charm, Louis said. "Indefinable charm?" the real estate man repeated. "I've got to remember that."

They went back to the agent's office where Louis signed a three-year lease in the name of Arthur Ventura and gave the man a check for three months' rent. He asked the agent if the town had a furniture dealer, and if there was an interior decorator. The agent said that, as a

matter of fact, a new outfit which sold furniture and did decorating had just opened a
couple of months ago. He didn't know anything
about their work, but the name was Hobart
Thurman, who was a fellow member of the
Optimists, and the company name was Quality
Custom Furniture and Decor. He gave Louis
the telephone number.

"Maybe you could call them for me," Louis
said.

"Sure thing." The agent dialed the number.

"Bart Thurman, please," he said. Louis
blinked. Bart? he thought. Could it be Willie?

"Bart, this is Ev Wisler. At Wisler's Realty?
Sure. You bet. Bart, I've got a potential customer here for you, sitting right in front of me,
just took a three-year lease on an unfurnished
house off the Selah road, and he'd like to come
over and talk to you about fixing it up. Sure
thing. His name is Mr. Arthur Ventura. I'll
send him right over."

Louis didn't see Joe Labriola on the first visit.
Willie took him around the showroom and sat
him down in front of some big furniture catalog.

"What kind of furniture was you looking for,
Mr. Ventura?" Willie said.

"I'm not sure. I am thinking that I might

362

look for an interior decorator in Seattle and have him look the place over and tell me."

"Hey — you don't needa go to Seattle for that," Willie said. "We got a staff decorator right here in the premises. Absolutely top talent. He's New York-trained. I mean, really up there with the top talent." He drew a line across his forehead.

"Well—"

"Listen. You, me, and the decorator will go out to your place, he'll look it over, then in two days he'll come up with a list of ideas and some sketches so you'll see how good he is and you can save yourself maybe three months moving into your place."

"That's fine."

"I can tell you he is an absolutely terrific decorator."

"My wife and kids are in Memphis — I just got transferred — and the sooner I can get them out here the better."

"Yeah? What line are you in?"

"It's strictly confidential, but my company is going to open a factory here. We make bed linen — sheets and spreads and pillowcases. We can't get started till I get settled."

"A lotta your people will be renting here?"

"Oh, yes. At least the four on the executive staff."

"Are we gonna do a job on your house!"

"Great."

"We can go out there right now if you want," Willie said.

"Tomorrow morning would be better." They shook hands and Louis went back to the hotel.

Willie got Joey on the phone, told him the big chance had come — that they had a big, new rush job. Except for selling some Barca Lounger chairs, painting some walls and a dining room suite, Louis was the only decorating action Joey had seen since they opened.

Joey came on very restrained, but he couldn't hold himself down. He wore a trench coat draped over his shoulders and over a white silk Hamlet blouse. He wasn't wearing any makeup, but he looked as if he should. His voice had changed as though the Witness Protection Program had also given him a whole new set of vocal chords, Louis told Charley on the phone from a telephone booth two towns away that night, because he couldn't have sounded like that when he was working in Brooklyn.

They went out and looked at the house. Joey dictated pages of notes to Willie. They went back to town, and Willie told Louis that he'd be calling him as soon as they had everything together. Louis told them he was dying to see what they'd come up with, but the final presentation would have to be made to his boss who would be flying in from Milwaukee.

# 59

Charley flew from New York to Seattle two days after Louis left, intending to check into the Olympic Hotel in Seattle to wait for Louis' call. He had a once-removed sentimental attachment to the Olympic. Many years before he'd had a friend who was an old press agent for the Ringling Brothers Circus who said he had left his last erection in a bureau drawer at the Olympic and, although he had gone back three days later to reclaim it, it had never shown up again anywhere.

The flight got in on time. It was a beautiful day filled with the special air that is carefully guarded by the Northwest. Charley was second in line to get off the plane. He was eager to get the work done and get back to Mardell, while he wondered simultaneously what was happening with Maerose. He felt safer for her since his talk with the don, because it had to be that the don had talked to Vincent so that, when they brought her back from Mexico, Vincent wouldn't beat her up.

He was concentrating on trying to imagine the chaos and misunderstanding the coming announcement of his marrying Mardell was going to cause in Brooklyn – not to mention possible violence when Vincent heard it. After thinking about it, he ruled out violence. The way Maerose had set the whole thing up, he was the injured party; no matter what he did he had a right to do it because he had been wronged. He was a couple of thousand miles away, hovering somewhere near Maerose, trying to think how he could somehow soften the blow on her already broken head when she heard the news about him and Mardell. She had to expect it. Mae had done what she did because she had figured the whole thing out long before he had. She had decided that he wanted to marry Mardell. He hadn't said otherwise because he *had* wanted to marry Mardell, but he also wanted to marry Maerose. If only everything had gone along the right way, the way it had been until he went to Miami and she had to call him there. Mae had it figured, but she had it figured wrong. She wanted to keep Vincent and his vengeance away from Charley and to keep Charley from losing her grandfather's respect. And she certainly knew about Mardell. Every time, as soon as he thought like that, he knew it was all impossible. She had wrecked her life. She was an outcast from the family. It was going to be like living in darkness inside the freezer compartment of a refrigerator, and he was going to be building his own life with Mardell on a foundation of Mae's pain. She had thrown everything away to prove what she didn't have to prove: that she was a Prizzi and that she was going to decide for herself what was going to happen to her and not be swept along and finally discarded because Charley had decided that he had to hold somebody up who was weaker than she was.

The passenger tunnel for off-loading the passengers from the plane into the Seattle airport wasn't working, so they had to roll up one of those old-fashioned boarding staircases that politicians always come down, never wearing a hat even in a blizzard, waving at the TV cameramen.

Preoccupied with the past, favoring the bad leg he had got out of the war, Charley tripped on the sill as he came out of the plane, tried to get his balance, got his foot jammed in a tight place and, while the upper part of him fell down the stairs, he broke his right leg between the ankle and the knee. Then, suddenly freed, he was taken by his weight and gravity down the whole cascade of steps, headfirst. He landed on his face on the tarmac, breaking his nose and picking up two big shiners. Just to make the weight as a hospital statistic, he suffered a line fracture of the skull and a concussion of the brain.

They had to let him lie there until the ambulance came, because his leg was twisted into such a grotesque shape and he was bleeding from the ears. The stewardess would not let anyone move him. The sixty-seven other passengers coming down the stairway from the plane had to step over him. Some noticed him as they stepped over him; they had to hear him because he was making a lot of different kinds of noises even though he wasn't conscious. Most of them didn't look down, either because they were in a hurry or because they didn't want to hold up the line. Three people just didn't see him at all.

When the ambulance got there, they loaded him on a gurney and lifted him into the ambulance where they doped him lightly for the ride to the hospital. While they were getting him ready for the emergency room, a nurse went through his pockets and his wallet and came out with Pop as next of kin. The hospital called Pop. Pop spoke to them in a voice that left no doubt: they were to do nothing until the best of the specialists got there.

When Pop hung up he called Lazzaro Fissa, Boss of the Seattle family, told him what had happened to Charley, and asked him to get the best bone man in the area to look at Charley's head, his nose, and his leg. In ten minutes Fissa had Dr. Abraham Weiler, the best orthopedic surgeon in the Northwest, in a limousine on its way to the hospital.

After a delay of four hours during which Weiler stared at X rays and plotted his procedure, they finally put a helmet cast on Charley's head, operated on his leg and put it into traction, and reset his nose. All the soft flesh around his eyes had turned dark purple. The eyes were closed tight on either side of the huge dressing, which covered the upper part of his face and the back of his head, handling the broken nose, his fractured skull, and his concussed brain.

Dr. Weiler talked to Pop on the telephone after the operation and told him Charley was going to be okay. He gave him a lot of medical bullshit which Pop didn't listen to because he didn't understand it.

Pop called Louis Palo in Yakima and told him to go into Seattle and look out for Charley.

After that was done, he told the don and Vincent, in that order, but he forgot about Mardell. The shock of what Maerose had done still filled his mind. The party had been held to announce Charley's engagement to Maerose, so he figured that Charley had worked out some kind of a solution with Mardell. She had ceased to exist for Pop. She lived in a different kind of world anyway.

It was eight days before Charley could put together the facts that Louis was in the room and that Louis could call Mardell. Time had just telescoped into itself. He'd hear Louis' voice, then the night nurse would be there and Louis would be gone. At the tenth day, although Charley couldn't see through his two swollen eyes, he was able to realize that he didn't know where his wallet was, and that's where Mardell's number was because he hardly ever called her, he just went there. He yelled for the nurse and when she came in he demanded to know where his wallet was. She told him to calm down, his wallet was in the hospital safe. He told her to go get it. She said they wouldn't release the wallet without Charley's signature. Charley wasn't able to see well enough to sign until the twelfth day, and by that time he was in despair. In the vision that his intense confinement had brought to him, he knew what had happened on West Twenty-third Street in New York. He knew Mardell had killed herself. On the twelfth day, although his leg was still in traction, he didn't need Louis to make the call. He called Mardell himself.

He couldn't reach her at the apartment and he couldn't reach her at the nightclub that Marty Pomerantz had booked her into. Those calls covered a time span of five hours, so he really sweated it out. Fuzzily, he decided if she was still alive she must have closed in Newark, but after two more tries he was able to get someone on the backstage phone who told him that Mardell was supposed to be there but that she hadn't come in.

Charley had Louis look up a number for Marty Pomerantz. When he got the call through, Marty said she was on her way to play a club date in Boston.

"Cut the shit," Charley said. "They told me in Newark she was still booked there. How can she play Boston?"

"Who'd you talk to in Newark?"

"How do I know?"

"What do they know? I got her booking slip right in fronna me."

"Boston?" Charley said hoarsely. "Boston is outta town."

"It's a weekend date and it pays two grand."

"Is this a weekend?" Charley asked Louis. Palo nodded.

"Listen, Marty," Charley said into the phone. "I'm gonna give you a telephone number in Seattle. You have her call that number, and if I don't hear from her by nine o'clock tomorrow morning, then you are out of business."

"Charley — what's the matter? Tell me what's the matter."

"I'm worried that she coulda killed herself, Marty. It was in the cards. That was the way she was."

Marty saw he had done everything he could do to protect Mardell if she had done the human thing and had backslid. "Charley?" he said tentatively.

"Yeah."

"She ain't in Boston. She's here, in New York — at the apartment."

"What the hell is going on here, Marty?"

"She's drunk. She locked herself in and she won't answer the phone or the doorbell."

"Then why the fuck did you tell me she was in Boston?"

"Because she's such a nice kid. Anybody can tell she's crazy about you, and I didn't wanna make trouble for her."

"*Drunk?*" Charley was appalled. He couldn't

stand drunks. "She don't hardly drink!"

"Well – I dunno. The only time I got her onna phone three days ago, lemme tell you, she was *drunk*. She kept calling me Charley. I couldn't convince her. It ain't my fault. I can't even get her to answer the door."

"Ah, shit, Marty. I don't wanna give you a hard time."

"Please. Whatta you want me to do?"

"Look, Marty – I broke my leg getting off the plane in Seattle. I got two plaster casts on my head. I'm on a bed, in a cast with a pulley. So can you check her personally twice a day for me? Just for a coupla days till I can get outta here? But don't tell her about my leg or my head – just tell her to call me at the number I'm gonna give you."

"What happened to your head?"

"I broke it when I fell down the stairs from the plane."

"That could be a serious thing."

*"Mardell* is the serious thing. Mardell!"

"Suppose she won't answer?"

"Hang on." He covered the mouthpiece and looked over at Louis. "Suppose she won't answer?"

"Give the super a hunnert bucks," Louis said.

"Give the super a hunnert bucks," Charley

said into the phone. "Then go in. If she passed out, get her to a hospital and let them dry her out." He gave Marty his hospital number.

Charley hung up. Louis took the phone off Charley's stomach and put it on the night table. Charley rang the call bell. The nurse was one of those handsome black women who won't take lip or a compliment.

"Listen, Clarice," Charley said, "can you get Abe in here?"

"Dr. Weiler?"

"Yeah."

"What for?"

"A friend of mine is in trouble in New York. I gotta help."

"Okay." She left the room.

Dr. Weiler was a short guy with a gray mustache, a three-hundred-thousand-dollar-a-year practice, a problem with casino gambling, and a long white coat.

"Look, Abe," Charley said. "I got trouble in New York. If I broke my leg on a ski lift in Sun Valley you could fix me up with one of them metal rockers on the bottom of the cast so I could walk."

"What good would a metal rocker be on your head? You have a fracture and a concussion up there, Mr. Partanna."

"I gotta get outta here."

"The concussion is the tricky part. Let me talk to your doctor."

"Abe — listen. You gotta convince him. I'll take my chances."

"The new electric wheelchairs are nice."

"I'll sign a release."

"Bet your ass."

"Can you put leeches on my eyes or something."

"So you'll wear shades."

"When can I leave?"

"Tomorrow morning?"

As soon as Dr. Weiler left, Louis got up and closed the door. He came back to the bed and sat down. "You want me to handle Willie and Joey?"

Charley shook his head. "I got a lot of time tied up in them guys. I gotta do it."

"Like tomorrow night?"

"I don't wanna come all the way out here again. It made too much trouble. Yeah. Set them up for tomorrow night."

Louis left that afternoon for Yakima. He called Charley at the hospital at ten o'clock the next morning and told him the address of the rented house. "I got a driver from the Fissas to pick you up at the hospital at noon, Charley. He'll get you to the house by the back roads, then I'll bring Willie and Joey out there at six tonight."

The driver brought him a piece. They fitted the wheelchair in sideways, directly behind the driver's seat. Charley sat on the back seat with his bad leg propped up in front. He had a nice view of a lot of trees and land as they went over the mountains. The car rolled him into the driveway of the rented house at five o'clock. Charley told him to park in the woods somewhere and then come back to pick him and Louis up at six forty-five.

He was tired of looking for Willie. He couldn't even remember Joey. The whole edge had come off it, but the work had to be done; nobody who screws the Prizzis can expect to get away with it. Charley sat in the wheelchair in the kitchen of the house and waited, blaming Mardell for taking the whole edge off the end of a hunt that had lasted months for two guys who deserved to get what they were going to get.

He wondered what Mardell had looked like when she was a little kid. He started to feel contempt for her mother, but he remembered what her father must have been like to make the mother like that. He thought about Maerose. He wondered where she was and how she was hacking it. As long as she stayed away from the booze. They had to make sure she stayed away from the booze. Then he really remembered how and where she was and he didn't worry about her and booze anymore, he worried about her getting away from Vincent. Anyway, why blame anybody except myself, he brooded. If I had taken lessons on how to get off an airplane I wouldn't have tripped and I would have been back in New York in two days and Mardell wouldn't have got drunk and I would have had pleasure in putting Willie and Joey away — but that now had become just another job. At five thirty he heard Louis come in with them. Louis walked them around the front rooms, telling them how the landlord was going to move the furniture out when they decided which furniture was going to be moved in, and Charley could hear Joey saying what would look nice.

When Louis got them back in the main room, Charley rolled himself in on the wheelchair.

Willie looked across the room at Charley, grabbed the back of a sofa for support, and vomited. A deep, dark stain appeared at the front of Joey's beige trousers as he sank slowly into a chair. Joey's jaw was on his chest, his shirt was open to his knees with gold chains around his neck and gold bracelets. Charley didn't greet them.

Louis got them to their feet and guided them patiently along the hall to the back stairs, which led down to the cellar. Charley followed until he saw where they were going. "No good, Louis," he said. "The wheelchair is no good on stairs."

"Stairs?" Willie said blankly.

"Take them out to the garage. Bring a coupla kitchen chairs."

They went out through the kitchen door, Willie and Joey each carrying a kitchen chair. "Hey, wait," Charley said. "There ain't no telephone in the garage. We'll have to talk here."

"Talk?" Joey said.

Louis told them to sit down. Charley faced them, about eleven feet away. Louis stood out of the line of the droplight, against the wall.

"Lemme explain something," Charley said reasonably. "I been tryna find you for months but I didn't care if it took ten years. Where'd you get the idea that you could get away with it?"

Both men were very pale. Willie had the shakes, so he folded his hands under his arms and leaned forward on them. Joey started to cry. He leaned over into his hands making high, sobbing sounds. Willie took a deep breath and said, real hard, to Charley. "Whatta you tryna do, Charley? The guvvamint will break your back if you lay a glove on us."

"The guvvamint gave you to us."

Willie thought about that as Charley said, "I

am here to try to make you understand what you done to your own people, the people who gave you your place in the world."

"Joey and me hadda get away, Charley. We couldn't live the way we hadda live. Not in the environment. So when you gave it to Vito, we saw our chance an' we took it."

"You made a lotta trouble, Willie. You almost fucked me up with that Mallon. You cost the Prizzis a lotta money."

"There was nothin' else we could do."

Louis watched Willie and Joey brighten up because Charley was so conciliatory. They didn't seem to have any idea that they were dead.

"Whatta you want from us?" Willie said, hard again. "You didn't look for us for months to give us this Dutch-uncle shit."

"I want you to make some phone calls. I want you to say you're sorry for what you done."

Joey's sobs had calmed down. Willie put his hand between Joey's shoulder blades and patted him steadily. "Who do I call?" Willie said.

"Joey, too." Charley rolled the chair to the wall phone, taking a piece of paper out of his pocket. He dialed a number, then talked into the phone in Sicilian. "Don Gennaro? This is Charley Partanna. I am sitting here with Willie Daspisa and Joey Labriola. They wanna talk to you. Just a minute."

He waved Willie to the phone. "Gennaro Fustino."

"What do I say?" Willie asked.

"Tell him you done wrong to the Prizzis and you deserve to pay."

Willie took the phone. He delivered the message mechanically. Charley gave the phone to Joey. Joey said his piece calmly, no wailing. Charley made four calls to four dons. Willie and Joey said the same thing to each of them. When it was over they were looking much better.

"Now we call Don Corrado," Charley said. He dialed the number. *"Padrino?* This is Charley. I have Willie Daspisa and Joey Labriola here." Willie reached forward to take the phone, but Charley, listening to what the don was saying, held up his hand. He hung up the phone and smiled at Willie and Joey. "He forgives you," he said.

Willie and Joey embraced each other. Joey kissed Willie. Willie kept nodding his head and patting Joey between the shoulder blades.

"But he wants your thumbs," Charley said.

They broke away from each other and whirled around on him.

"Did you expect it wouldn't cost you nothing?" Charley said.

"Our *thumbs?*" Joey was like a dumb ox.

Charley shot them both, at their middles, near where the main trunk of the aorta drops from the heart to the abdomen. They fell face-up, unconscious. Louis walked to the hall, and his steps could be heard hurrying down the cellar stairs. He came back carrying a hatchet.

"Take their thumbs," Charley said. "I can't get out of this goddam chair without falling on my ass."

Louis knelt beside Willie, who was staring up at him. He held one of Willie's spread-eagled arms to the floor and chopped off his right thumb.

"Other side," Charley said.

Methodically, Louis took all four thumbs and wrapped them in newspaper. The shock of the chops had brought Willie and Joey wide awake, Louis realized.

Charley leaned over and spoke to them.

"The don wants me to tell you that the left thumbs will go to your wife, Willie. Rosa gets both thumbs and she will be avenged. The Brooklyn cops will get your right thumbs, and our man will see that a sheet with your prints goes to all the newspapers. You will be more famous than you were at the trial where you ratted on the Prizzis. Famous!"

He shot them both through the head, Joey

first. Willie tried to scream as Charley bent over the wheelchair to do it, but he had no sound left in him that could come out. Charley and Louis left them there. The car came on the dot of six forty-five and they drove to the Seattle airport.

# 60

Flying to New York, Charley hardly knew that it was himself sitting in the airplane. His wheelchair had been folded and stored. He had been lifted into a well reclined first-class seat in the front row. His plastered leg was sticking out into the aisle, his nose was held in place with sticking plasters, and he wore a tight skullcap of plaster around his head. He had borrowed a two-ounce tinfoil smack container from the Seattle people to carry the four thumbs in and they were well sealed and secure in the pocket of his overcoat hanging in the forward locker.

Everything that was new and unknown in his life was spinning out in front of him. He wondered if Pop could fix it so that the mayor's engagement present to him and Maerose could be quietly transferred just to him. The Garden Grove apartments weren't in Brooklyn and it was a gorgeous layout, anybody could tell from the flyer the mayor had sent in lieu of a wrapped present, and he and Mardell had to have a classy place to start their married life, a place which wouldn't be too close to the Prizzis.

He had to straighten Mardell out on this booze thing. She had to swear off it. He knew he could lay his hands on two solid magazine articles by doctors that showed what booze could do to vitamin deficiency. He didn't need any outside evidence to show what it did to the head.

The main thing was that they had to get married so she would understand that nothing could ever shake them up again the way she had let herself get shaken up. Jesus, wait until she saw the plaster helmet he was wearing under his hat plus the wheelchair and the nose, and she would see how crazy she had been to think he had run out on her.

After he found her and got her started on drying out, he would have to call Eduardo and have him line up a judge to handle the wedding, call Pop to be his witness, then go someplace and get married. It put him through a wringer just thinking about it, but he had to do it. She needed him. It had all worked out, just the way Pop said it would. Maerose had run away. He wouldn't ever understand where she'd found the moxie to do it. It was all settled. Everything was the way Maerose wanted it, but he knew in his heart that if the engagement party had gone through the way everybody expected it to happen, then the whole thing would have worked out to be exactly the opposite. He would have married Maerose. He might have had a few bad weeks, but he would have gotten over Mardell. It would have all been settled. But Maerose had run away from him. He still felt her somewhere near around him, like in the air or something, but what the hell, she had solved everything. She had cut loose because that was the only way she could tell him that he didn't have to go through with marrying her. He had certainly made a production out of not being engaged to her, but what else could he do? He was lucky, he supposed. He never'd had to choose between Mae and Mardell. Thank God. It had all worked itself out, just the way Pop said. But, for a guy in his business, he had certainly missed grabbing the brass ring. He could have been married to a Prizzi. He could have been a key part of the inner Prizzi family. His kids could have been Prizzis with all the clout that brought with it. Instead, although he kidded himself about having made the right choice, about marrying the woman who needed him most, when he got off the plane and looked at Marty Pomerantz he knew what he was going to hear. His heart froze in midbeat as the realization came over him. Mardell had loved him so much but she had decided that she had lost him because she got nothing but silence for twelve days, three lifetimes with Mardell's kind of dependency and loneliness, and she had killed herself.

He brought both hands up and covered his face. He tried not to make any sounds.

"Are you all right, Mr. Marino?" the stewardess asked.

The flight got into La Guardia at 7:10 A.M. Marty Pomerantz was waiting for him. He hadn't told Pop he was coming in. This was about Mardell, not business.

Charley and his wheelchair were lowered to the tarmac and then he was rolled into the airport building.

Marty was just standing there, looking like an undertaker. Charley got the message. Marty didn't have to talk. Mardell had killed herself. It was all over. She was gone and nothing could bring her back. She had decided that he had deserted her and that he was never coming back, so she'd killed herself.

"Okay, Marty," he said in a choked voice. "Give it to me straight."

"Jesus, Charley, they really wrecked you. I had no idea."

"Never mind that, fahcrissake — what about Mardell? Did you give the super the hunnert bucks?"

"Yeah."

"And you found her lying there?"

"She wasn't there, Charley. All that time we were breaking our hearts about her she wasn't even in the apartment."

"What?" He couldn't believe he was hearing what Marty was saying.

"I found a letter on the kitchen table. It's addressed to you." Marty slid an envelope out of the side pocket of his overcoat and handed it to Charley. Charley looked down at it dumbly. He had never felt such a vast sense of absolute relief. She was alive somewhere. He didn't know where but she was okay. He felt like some kind of a conservationist who has just saved something of value from some kind of toxic waste. He hadn't saved her. But she was saved. She was okay. And he knew that inside that letter was a message from her that lifted him right off the hook. He had done right with Mardell and now she was going to do right with him. She had lifted him right off the hook. Both of the greatest women in his life had lifted him right off the hook. He knew it. The letter was going to be a Dear John, and it would be all fixed up. Everything had worked itself out. He was absolutely in the clear. There was no possibility anymore that he was going to break the hearts of two women.

He stuffed the letter into his coat pocket. He stared at Marty. Marty looked like he expected to be clipped because he brought the bad news. Charley reached over and patted Marty on the sleeve to let him know that it was okay, that he didn't blame anybody. He grinned at Marty dopily. He wheeled the chair out toward the cab rank, humming "These Foolish Things." Marty came after him saying, "I got a limo for you, Charley."

The limo took Charley out to the beach. The driver manhandled Charley and the wheelchair out of the car. Charley gave him twenty dollars and then rolled the chair into the elevator and rode up to his floor. He let himself into the apartment and, keeping on his overcoat, wool cap, and scarf, he rolled the chair out on the terrace, working hard to relax before opening Mardell's letter.

"Dearest Charley," the letter said, "I am going to try to be very direct because you don't deserve less than that." (Her pen had paused in flight. She knew she wasn't going to be at all direct with him, she was going to have to tell him perfectly awful lies but that was the only way to make absolutely everyone in the whole set piece happy again.) "I met a marvelous man while I was in the hospital, a world-famous Brazilian psychiatrist who became interested in the radio beams that, you will remember, have been coming to me from Buckingham Palace. We fell in love, really in love. By the time you get this — if indeed you do come back to the apartment — I will have been married on the high seas on my way to Brazil. We will live in São Paulo, high on a mountaintop, surrounded by brilliantly colored parrots. I will never forget you. Mardell"

Just like Pop said, everything had come up roses.

He sat on the terrace in the early morning December cold until it was sometime in the afternoon when he rolled himself into bed, humming "These Foolish Things" like an electric cello.

# 61

Eleven chairs were ranged in a semicircle across the stage of the small auditorium, which was used mostly for club meetings at the Luis Muñoz-Marín Junior High School. There was a student in every chair. Señora Roja-Buscando, the class valedictorian, sat at the center. Charley, wearing a pressed dark-blue suit, a white shirt, and a solid dark-blue tie, sat third from the end on stage right, between Miss Edith Molina, a former correspondent of *The Brooklyn Eagle*, and the Russian woman from Brighton Beach named Luba, whose last name he had never been able to remember but which rhymed with the name of a player who was with the St. Louis team.

In the front row of the auditorium, in seats that had been reserved by Eduardo through the Board of Education, sat Corrado Prizzi, Amalia, Vincent, Pop, Eduardo, and a young woman named Baby. The don was wide awake until the actual ceremonies started, to be specific until Mr. Matson walked onto the stage with a cardboard box filled with rolled-up certified diplomas bearing the seal of the City of New York and tied with a pale-blue ribbon, each one individually inscribed with india ink in Mr. Matson's beautiful handwriting in the names of the graduates who were seated on the stage.

Mr. Matson made a short speech of welcome to the sixty-seven people in the audience, then he called out the name of each student on the platform to come forward to receive his or her diploma. When he called out Charley's name he was mindful of the unusual status of the special guests in row one and, advised by his district superintendent, he gave Charley's accomplishments as he called out his name: "Charles Partanna, male recipient of the greatest number of Gold Stars in his class, secretary-treasurer of his class, and a dedicated student." Charley came forward as the audience applauded politely and the front row applauded heavily, he bowed to Mr. Matson, accepted the diploma, and returned to his chair.

After the diplomas had been distributed, Mr. Matson introduced Evelyn Roja-Buscando, the class valedictorian. The señora walked to the lectern holding a thick sheaf of papers in her hand, clearing her throat. She was dressed in a pale-cerise hugger of Orlon that made a soft, rounded shelf of her bosom, which was utterly without the support of a bra, with a two-inch-thick gold ruffle around the bottom of the skirt and across the yoke neck. She wore heavy gold plastic earrings and her hair had been pulled up into a high peruke at the back. Jesus, Charley thought, where has this one been in all the years we been going to school together? He realized they had a lot in common. They were not only both high school grads, they were classmates. She was a gorgeous woman — how come he had never noticed that? She wasn't in the environment so he'd have to get to know her better.

The señora cleared her throat and began to read from the pile of paper.

Oh, boy, Charley thought, we'll be lucky if we get outta here by tomorrow morning.

THORNDIKE PRESS HOPES you have enjoyed this Large Print book. All our Large Print titles are designed for the easiest reading, and all our books are made to last. Other Thorndike Press Large Print books are available at your library, through selected bookstores, or directly from the publisher. For more information about current and upcoming titles, please call us, toll free, at 1-800-223-6121, or mail your name and address to:

THORNDIKE PRESS
P. O. BOX 159
THORNDIKE, MAINE 04986

There is no obligation, of course.